MW00768731

Incredible Us

Me, You, and Us Series: Book 3

by
Deanndra Hall

Incredible Us
Me, You, and Us Series: Book 3

Celtic Muse Publishing, LLC
P.O. Box 3722
Paducah, KY 42002-3722

Copyright © 2015 Deanndra Hall
ISBN-13: 978-0692483657
ISBN-10: 0692483659
Print Edition

All rights reserved. Except as permitted under the U.S. Copyright Act of 1976, no part of this publication may be reproduced, distributed, or transmitted in any form or by any means, or stored in a database or retrieval system, without the prior written permission of the author.

This book is a work of fiction.

Names of characters, places, and events are the construction of the author, except those locations that are well-known and of general knowledge, and all are used fictitiously. Any resemblance to persons living or dead is coincidental, and great care was taken to design places, locations, or businesses that fit into the regional landscape without actual identification; as such, resemblance to actual places, locations, or businesses is coincidental. Any mention of a branded item, artistic work, or well-known business establishment, is used for authenticity in the work of fiction and was chosen by the author because of personal preference, its high quality, or the authenticity it lends to the work of fiction; the author has received no remuneration, either monetary or in-kind, for use of said product names, artistic work, or business establishments, and mention is not intended as advertising, nor does it constitute an endorsement. The author is solely responsible for content.

Formatting by BB eBooks
Editing by Heidi Ryan
Cover design by Novel Graphic Designs, used by permission of the artist

Disclaimer:

Material in this work of fiction is of a graphic sexual nature and is not intended for audiences under 18 years of age.

Dedication

To Lindsey Armstrong:

You never fail to cheer me up when I need it most.
Thanks for being a friend, a reader, a promoter,
and just an all-around great person.

A word from the author . . .

This book was never supposed to happen.

I didn't intend for this to be a series, and when it became one, I knew Dave would have a book. I didn't know what would happen to him, but I was sure it would be spectacular. I never would've guessed that it would be such a bumpy ride, but it was and it is. And even though bumpy and spectacular describe this book, so does precious. I grew to love Dave even more than before as I wrote this book, and I admired Olivia as she grew into the woman she was meant to be.

So here's the final installment in this series. And thanks to Sir, who's kept me going all along. I couldn't do this without you, baby.

Love and happy reading,
Deanndra

You can find me here:
www.deanndrahall.com
Substance B
DeanndraHall@gmail.com
facebook.com/deanndra.hall
tsu.co/DeanndraHall
pinterest.com/deanndrahall
@DeanndraHall
P.O. Box 3722, Paducah, KY 42002-3722

More titles from this author:

Love Under Construction Series

The Groundbreaking (Prequel)

The Groundbreaking is a preview of the main characters contained in all of the Love Under Construction Series books. Not intended as a work of erotic fiction, it is simply a way for the reader to get to know and love each character by discovering their backgrounds.

Laying a Foundation (Book 1) COMBO VOLUME includes The Groundbreaking (Prequel)

Sometimes death robs us of the life we thought we'd have; sometimes a relationship that just won't die can be almost as bad. And sometimes the universe aligns to take care of everything. When you've spent years alone, regardless the circumstances, getting back out there can be hard. But when you've finally opened up to love and it looks like you might lose it all, can love be enough to see you through?

Tearing Down Walls (Book 2)

Secrets – they can do more damage than the truth. Secrets have kept two people from realizing their full potential, but even worse, have kept them from forming lasting relationships and finding the love and acceptance they both desperately need. Can they finally let go of those secrets in time to find love – and maybe even to stay alive?

Renovating a Heart (Book 3)

Can a person's past really be so bad that they can never recover from it? Sometimes it seems that way. One man hides the truth of a horrific loss in his teen years; one woman hides the truth of a broken, scarred life that took a wrong turn in her teens. Can they be honest with each other, or even with themselves, about their feelings? And will they be able to go that distance before one of them is lost forever?

Planning an Addition (Book 4)

When you think you're set for life and that life gets yanked out from under you, starting over is hard. One woman who's starting over finds herself in love with two men who've started over too, and she's forced to choose. Or is she? And when one of them is threatened by their past, everyone has choices to make. Can they make the right ones in time to save a life?

The Harper's Cove Series

Beginning with the flagship volume, *Karen and Brett at 326 Harper's Cove*, find out exactly what the neighbors of Harper's Cove are up to when they go inside and close their doors. According the Gloria, the drunken busybody of the cove, they're all up to something perverse, and she's determined to find out their secrets. As she sneaks, peeks, pokes, and prods, her long-suffering husband, Russell, begs her to leave all of their nice neighbors alone. But could Gloria be right?

The Harper's Cove series books are fast, fun, nasty little reads priced just right to provide a quick, naughty romp. See if each of the couples of Harper's Cove shock you just enough to find out what the neighbors at the next address will do!

Karen and Brett at 326 Harper's Cove (Book 1)

Gloria wants more than anything to be invited to one of Karen and Brett Reynolds' parties, and she's very vocal about it. Karen and Brett, however, know full well that if Gloria were ever invited to one of their parties, she would be in a hurry to leave, and in an even bigger hurry to let everyone know they're the scourge of the neighborhood. Every Saturday night, Karen and Brett keep their secrets – all twelve of them.

Becca and Greg at 314 Harper's Cove (Book 2)

Even though they're quiet and stay to themselves, Becca and Greg Henderson seem pretty nice and average. They don't go out much or have many people over, except for that one couple who are probably relatives. But when that half-sister of Becca's moves in, it all seems a little fishy; she gets around pretty well for a person recovering from cancer. And where was Becca going all decked out in that weird outfit? The Henderson are tight-lipped, but Gloria hopes she can eventually get to the bottom of things. If she does, she'll get the biggest surprise of her life.

Donna and Connor at 228 Harper's Cove (Book 3)

Those nice people at 228, the Millicans? They're religious counselors, trying to help lovely couples who are having marital problems. Problem is, they're not counseling; training, maybe, but not counseling. But no matter what Donna says, Gloria still thinks the truck that delivered large crates to the Millicans' house in the wee hours of the morning two weeks after they'd moved in was pretty suspicious. Donna says it was exercise equipment that the moving company had lost, but Gloria's not so sure. Could it be that they're not as they appear?

Savannah and Martin at 219 Harper's Cove (Book 4)

Savannah and Martin McIntosh are new to the neighborhood, but that doesn't stop Gloria from trying her best to find out what they do on the second and fourth Friday nights of the month. Savannah insists they play cards, but Gloria's pretty sure it's more than that, considering the men she sees leaving the house in the wee hours of Saturday morning. But when she decides to get a little "up close and personal," she may get more than she bargained for.

And we're just getting started!

The Me, You, and Us Series

Adventurous Me (Book 1)

Boring, tiresome, predictable . . . all words Trish Stinson's soon-to-be ex-husband uses as excuses for why he's leaving after almost 30 years of marriage. But Trish's efforts to find adventure and prove him wrong land her in the lap of a man who leads her to an adventure she could've never predicted. And when that adventure throws her into a situation with a man who can't stand her, she's forced to decide between honor and her life.

Unforgettable You (Book 2)

Reeling from a relationship that didn't happen, Steffen Cothran stumbles upon a woman who may be the answer to his prayers, but Sheila Brewster has problems he couldn't have anticipated. They work hard to forge a relationship, only to have it destroyed by someone from Steffen's past – the one person he'd forgotten about. As Sheila, hurt and angry, walks out of his life, Steffen eventually gives up on love until that fateful night when curiosity takes him somewhere he never thought he'd be to see something he never dreamed he'd see.

The Celtic Fan (independent novel)

Journalist Steve Riley sets out to do the seemingly impossible: Find Nick Roberts, author of the bestselling book The Celtic Fan. When his traveling buddies lose interest, Steve continues on to a stolen address and finds someone who couldn't possibly be Roberts. As time goes by, Steve has to decide if he wants to break the story of a lifetime and break someone's heart, or give in to the feelings that promise him the love of a lifetime. Set in the beautiful Smoky Mountains of North Carolina, The Celtic Fan is both Steve's journey and excerpts from the original book written by Roberts about a young, wounded, WWII veteran and the forbidden love he finds.

My Last Dom (independent novel)

Kimberly Hendricks doesn't want a man. She wants pain. But the Dominant who's intent on stealing her heart has other plans. Jasper "Jaz" Givens manages to reach into Kimmie's darkness and take away her pain. And when Kimmie discovers what she thinks is a horrific plot against her, the ghosts of her past take over. Problem is, by the time she chases them away, it might be too late.

Support your Indie authors!

Independent (Indie) authors are not a new phenomenon, but they are a hard-working one. As Indie authors, we write our books, have trouble finding anyone to beta read them for us, seldom have money to hire an editor, struggle with our cover art, find it nearly impossible to get a reviewer to even glance at our books, and do all of our own publicity, promotion, and marketing. This is not something that we do until we find someone to offer us a contract – this is a conscious decision we've made to do for ourselves that which we'd have to do regardless (especially promotion, which publishers rarely do any-way). We do it so big publishing doesn't take our money and give us nothing in return. We do it because we do not want to give up rights to something on which we've worked so hard. And we do it because we want to offer you a convenient, quality product for an excellent price.

Indie authors try to bring their readers something fresh, fun, and different. Please help your Indie authors:

- Buy our books! That makes it possible for us to continue to produce them;
- If you like them, please go back to the retailer from which you bought them and review them for us. That helps us more than you could know;
- If you like them, please tell your friends, relatives,

nail tech, lawn care guy, anyone you can find, about our books. Recommend them, please;

- If you're in a book circle, always contact an Indie author to see if you can get free or discounted books to use in your circle. Many would love to help you out;

- If you see our books being pirated, please let us know. We worked weekends, holidays, and through vacations (if we even get one) to put these books out, so please report it if you see them being stolen.

More than anything else, we hope you enjoy our books and, if you do, please contact us in whatever manner we've provided as it suits you. Visit our blogs and websites, friend our Facebook sites, and follow us on Twitter. We'd love to get to know you!

Chapter One

"Damn it!" It's the third time this month that a bulb's been out over one of the performance alcoves. Replacing them is a pain in the ass. It entails dragging out the ladder, climbing as high as I can, praying I don't fall because this ladder really isn't tall enough to use for the job, then putting the thing away, only to have to do it again in a week or so. I suppose I could leave them until two or three were out, then replace them all at the same time, but I just can't. I have too much pride in the club's appearance.

This place is my second home. Ever since Brian stepped away from it, I've had free rein over everything that takes place here. He trusts me to run it for him, and I do a good job. Bliss is the nicest club of its kind within a two hundred mile radius, and business is good.

Actually, my house is more like my second home. I'm never there and when I am, I'm either asleep or trying to be. Sometimes I do a little laundry, but most of the time I'm here at the club. After all, we've got a washer and dryer here, so it's easier to just do my own while I'm here. Besides, I'm comfortable here. The club members are more like family to me, and I enjoy spending time around them.

It's a Tuesday night and it's pretty quiet. I look up to see Steffen and Sheila Cothran coming through the door. She plops a box down in front of me and grins. "What?"

"I baked this for you." She opens the box with a flourish and pulls out the most lopsided cake I've ever seen in my life. "Well? What do you think?"

I'm just about to laugh when I catch glimpse of Steffen's face and realize that would be a huge mistake. "I think I want a bite right now!"

"Liar." She starts to laugh. "I'm not sure what happened, but I tried the batter, so I'm assuming the cake itself is pretty good. Well, look at this!" Sheila's still laughing when she turns toward the door. Steffen and I both do the same to see my son and his wife, Clint and Trish Winstead, walking in.

"Hey, old man!" Clint hugs me, and I hug him back. I don't care what his birth certificate says – he's my son.

"Good lord! What's the occasion? Why are all four of you here?"

They stare at me like I've lost my mind. Finally, Clint says, "Dad? It's your birthday."

I start to blurt out, *No, it's not*, when I catch a glimpse of the calendar and, by damn, it *is* my birthday. Who knew? Um, apparently all of them. "Well, would you look at that! Everybody remembered my birthday except me!"

"How old are you? Ninety-two?" Steffen laughs.

"No. Sixty-five, thank you," I snarl back.

"Yeah, but that body is still forty. You need to find its owner and get yours back. It's unnatural," Clint snickers.

"Hey, it's pretty damn good, as I recall," Trish grins and winks at me.

"I'll agree with that!" Sheila adds.

Steffen's the one snarling this time when he says, "I don't like this. I feel like I'm getting ganged up on by the 'I've slept with Dave Adams' club over here."

The girls are standing to either side of me, and I put an arm around each. "So, the guys here want to celebrate my birthday. Would you two like to celebrate it together? With me? The three of us?"

Sheila looks at Trish in shock. "Well, I've never had sex with another woman, but if I were going to, it would be with you."

"Same here."

"Whoa, wait!" Clint looks more than a little shocked, and Steffen's starting to tense, I can tell. "We didn't bring our wives in here as your birthday gifts!"

Steffen echoes Clint with, "Yeah. I don't mind sharing when it's appropriate, but . . ."

"What's appropriate, Steffen?" Sheila asks in her usual confrontational tone. Now Trish has stopped and she's waiting and staring too.

"Well, I dunno, but I don't think . . ."

"You know, I think it's time we did a little exploration, don't you?" Trish grins.

Sheila hops down off the bar stool. "Let's do that!" She takes Trish by the hand and kisses her, and I feel myself get hard almost instantly. Doesn't help that Clint and Steffen are practically drooling. When the ladies' lips part, they both take me by the hand and pull me down the hall to one of the private rooms. As we leave the big common room, I hear one of the guys whisper, "Fuck. I really, really want to watch that."

"Well, come on! What are you waiting for?" I call back to them. I can hear them hustling to follow, and I almost laugh. They just can't help themselves. When I walk through the doorway of the private room, the girls are already undressing. Sheila makes the first move and grabs Trish to kiss her, and it's a party. It's a big, deep, wide kiss that makes *my* toes curl. Damn. Their hands are wandering all over each other's bodies. Sheila's stops to tweak Trish's nipple; Trish's hand makes it all the way down Sheila's body and strokes down to her slit, and I hear both of them moan.

There's only one thing I can think to say: "Well, happy birthday to me."

"You joining in or not?" Trish calls over to me.

I glance at Clint and Steffen. Steffen's eyebrows arch in resignation and Clint groans, "Go for it. They're all yours."

As I stand there and watch the two of them, I think back to the first time I ever saw Trish, drunk in that bar, that sleazy guy hitting on her. And I remember Sheila from then too; she looked like a disapproving nun getting ready to rap somebody on the knuckles. Boy, they've both come a long way. I've been with both of these women, but as I watch them, I realize that I can't do it. If it were Steffen or Clint's idea, that would be different, but it was the girls' idea, and that's not right. My son and his best friend acquiesced to me. Maybe because it's my birthday? Or because I'm old? I have no idea, but I'm not going to do this and damage those relationships. I watch their faces relax when I laugh out, "No. We're just pulling your chain."

"Thank god. I thought I was going to have to have her twat fumigated." I'd like to think Steffen is joking, but I'm pretty sure he isn't.

"Nope. I'm enjoying the show just watching the two of you panic. Ladies," I smile toward the girls, "let's try this cake."

We all get a huge surprise: The cake is awesome. It tastes like a cross between peanut butter and butter-scotch, and I wind up eating two pieces and contemplating a third. I finally shoot Clint and Steffen a look. "Well, what do you have to say for this cake?"

"I'd say we need to do this again sometime," Steffen murmurs as he watches.

"Yeah. I'm with you," Clint echoes.

We sit and laugh and talk until it's time for them to get the kids into bed and the sitter's probably about to stage an uprising. They're all at Steffen and Sheila's. When they all walk through the door, I bet it'll suck to be them. They'll be putting the place back together for the next year.

"See you later, birthday boy!" Steffen calls out as he and Sheila head out the door. Trish gives me a kiss on the cheek and follows them.

I take a good look at Clint. Yes, there are little laugh lines at the corners of his eyes, and a little tiny bit of gray at his temples, but he's still the seven-year-old boy I remember from all those years back. He just smiles at me, then wraps his arms around me and hugs me tight. "Thanks, old man. Thanks for being a great dad and teaching me how to be one."

I whisper back, "Thanks for hanging in there and still being here, son. I love you."

"I know. I love you too. And I'm glad I hung in there. I'm glad she hung in there too. Look at what I've got now." His eyes are glistening with tears of joy, and I know the life he has now is one he never thought he'd have. We've all been through a lot, but Clint's been through more than anyone should have to be. Now that's all over and he's exactly where he needs to be. It's amazing and encouraging. I watch him stroll toward Trish, and I smile as she meets him and circles an arm around his waist, then continue on out the door. They look so blissful together.

What a poignant, permeating reminder that I'm alone.

<hr>

"Hey, I'm cooking dinner. Want to come over?"

"Sure! Need me to bring anything?" I wish I could see Marta's face when I say that; she knows if I bring something, it'll be beer.

"Condoms. We've got everything else. So stay later too, if you want. We'd love to play."

In the background I hear a voice yell, "Hi, Dave! Come over and fuck us!" I can't help but laugh.

"Tell the slut back there in the background that I'll gladly come over and fuck her. And you too. On my way in twenty."

We hang up and I sit and chuckle. Most people would be appalled if they could see what takes place between us. It's like a big nasty free-for-all when we're together. I loved Marta, still do, and I don't think I'll ever get over her leaving me for Angela, but I've come to terms with it. And I enjoy playing with both of them. Angela's a spectacular fuck, and Marta is, well, Marta. She's just about as free with her body as anyone I've ever seen.

And now I'm getting hard just thinking about what I'm going to walk into. And for the record, just opening the door and walking in is the way I've always dealt with the two of them. They don't seem to mind; in fact, I think they expect it. I may have wound up alone because of their relationship, but by god, if they expect me to come over and service them whenever they want, they should have to bend to my will. They're in the kitchen cooking up a storm and I just growl, "Okay, if you're both not naked in about two minutes, I'm turning around and leaving."

You've never seen two women shuck clothes as fast in your life. I'd say it was forty-five seconds. Marta's built more like an eighteen-year-old girl than she is a fifty-seven-year-old woman, willowy, slightly-built, with a gently sloping backside and small but firm tits. Angela's just the opposite – she's busty, lusty, and ample. Marta's sandy-blond, blue-eyed countenance is such a contrast to Angela's dark skin, dark eyes, and dark hair, that it's a joy to be with them together, but that's the difference in a German woman and an island girl. Of course, I pick up their clothes for them, take them to the laundry room at the back, and come back. They're both cooking up a storm, radio going, asses swaying to the beat, and I walk up behind Marta, wrap my arms around her, and cup her breasts. "Don't accidentally toast your dangly bits, girl."

She busts out laughing. "Yeah, that would be tragic! But mine would have farther to go than hers," she giggles as she points to Angela. "So baby, if you have to take something out of the oven, let me do it, okay?"

"Yes, sweetheart," Angela purrs.

"No, I'll do it," I offer.

Angela gives me a wink. "And we'll let you."

"What's for dinner?"

Marta sighs. "Oh, just homemade chicken pot pie." That's my absolute favorite, and she knows it. "And we've got green beans and roasted cauliflower. Oh, and those flaky biscuits that you like."

"Beer?"

"Yup. I've got Stella." Oh my god, she obviously wants something. I don't know what, but it must be big.

Once dinner's finished and the kitchen cleaned up, I look around for Angela, but she's nowhere to be found. Then I hear the laundry room door and look up in time to see her come strolling into the living room with a cake. And it's beautiful. Plus it's got to have sixty-five candles on it, because it looks like we need to call the fire department. I manage to stammer out, "That's gorgeous!"

She grins until her eyes crinkle shut. "I'm glad you like it. And I hope you like the cake too."

"You're a naughty girl. I should spank you." No, I'm not a spanko, but she loves it and I'm generally happy to oblige.

"I hope you will, but let's eat cake first." She runs to the kitchen to get plates and forks, and I look at Marta.

She offers me an explanation. "She's been taking cake decorating classes."

"Well, she's obviously learning something, because that thing's awesome." And it is. It's frosted with chocolate icing, and it's got these beautiful, swirl designs piped all over it in white frosting. If the cake inside is chocolate too, I think I'll die. "Is the cake . . ."

"Chocolate? Yeah, of course. I told her that's what you'd want."

"Oh, god, Marta, thanks so much." This is one of those times when I wish we were still married. "I really appreciate it." I lean over and kiss her, and she kisses me back with gusto.

"Would you two cut it out already? Here – have some cake," Angela growls playfully at us as she hands us plates. "Happy birthday, Dave. We love you. I hope you know that."

"I love you girls too."

Marta laughs out loud. "I love it when you call us 'girls!' You're the only person who still does that!"

"Well, you are girls to me. My girls." I take a bite. "Oh my god, Angela, this is delicious. It's just, oh, wow, unbelievable," I mumble around cake as I continue to eat.

"I'm glad you like it." I could swear she's actually blushing.

"I do. I really do."

"Then you're taking the rest of it home. I don't want it here to tempt me," Marta orders. When Angela starts to protest, she barks out, "Yes. That's how it is. Don't buck me on this."

"Yes, ma'am," Angela pouts. You can guess who the dominant member of this household is, even though it didn't start out that way. "Can I just keep one piece?"

Marta drops a kiss on Angela's forehead. "Of course, baby. You worked hard on that."

"Thank you." Angela is beaming.

"You're welcome. Now let's give Dave his birthday present." Marta stands and takes my hand to pull me up onto my feet. "Come on, birthday boy."

Oh, I can tell already – this is going to be good.

"Everything off. And put on this robe. We'll be right back." Marta hands me the robe as I stand beside the bed, and they both disappear into the bathroom. Then they turn on the water, and I'm hoping they're planning what I think they're planning.

And I'm right. In a matter of minutes, they're both back and Angela winks at me. "Come on, birthday boy. Let's get slicked up." I'm hoping she's already slicked up. Then I realize Marta's not behind me.

"Hey! Aren't you coming?"

She shakes her head. "Nope. I've got something to do out here. You two go on."

Don't have to tell me twice.

The bathroom is awash in fragrance, and it's strong on cinnamon and cloves. The lights are off and there are candles everywhere, and the big bathtub is full of bubbles. Angela steps in, then reaches for me. Once we're both settled into the hot, fragrant water, she turns to face me and sits on my lap, her bronze legs wrapped around my ass. The hot, open-mouthed kiss she gives me sets my blood ablaze, and I can feel myself hardening. No doubt she notices it too, because her next little job is to take my cock in her hand and grind against it in the water, moaning and twitching the whole time. Catching one of her hard, thick, cherry-red nipples in my teeth, I give it a nip before starting to suck in earnest, and she increases her grinding. "Want to come, baby?" I whisper to her through those long, dark locks.

"Yes, please, sir," she groans.

"Turn around." She turns around in the water and I make her sit on my abs, my cock sticking up between her legs. "Use one hand to stroke me and the other to play with your nipples." Instantly, she starts to work me and her buds, and my hands trail down her belly, down under the water, and down to her slit. My nimble fingers find her nub and trail little circles around and around it, and her hips buck upward to meet my hand. Even under the water, I can tell how slick she is, how totally aroused and overheated, and I want to watch her come unglued under my touch. That hand around my dick is working it like a pro, and I can feel myself tensing. "Oh, god, I think I'm getting ready to come."

She barks out, "No! Keep stroking me, but you can't come. We've got a surprise for you."

"Oh, so I'm getting you off, but I can't get off?" That doesn't seem quite fair.

"Yes. That's exactly, oh, god, oh, oh, OH, OHHHHHHHHHH . . ." she cries out, and I just keep torturing her. If I'm not allowed to come, I might as well have *some* fun, right? I finally stop and let her catch her breath.

That's about the time that Marta appears in the doorway. "You didn't let him come, did you?" she asks Angela.

"No, ma'am. I did not. I made him stop."

"Good." There's a smile on Marta's face, but it's not mischievous or wicked. It's very, very calm and peaceful, and I'm curious as to what she's got up her sleeve. "Come on. Angela, help me dry him off." She grabs a large, fluffy bath towel and tosses it to Angela, then takes up another one herself.

"That's okay. I can dry myself off." I try to take the towel out of her hand, but she snatches it back.

"No. It's your birthday and . . ."

"Well, technically, yesterday was my birthday," I grin.

"Yeah, but it's your birthday *celebration*," she says with great emphasis, "and we want to do something special for you."

"Well, okay, I'll let you!" I chuckle. When they finish,

they help me back into the robe and lead me out into the bedroom, and I get really excited.

Because there, in the middle of the bedroom, is a massage table. I'm not sure what's going to happen, but I'm pretty sure it's going to be awesome. "Climb on up, sweetie, face down, please," Marta directs, and I make myself comfortable. I expect her to pull a sheet up over me, but she doesn't. Instead, I can feel the drip of massage oil on my back and, before I know it, she's kneading my muscles in ways no one's kneaded them in years. All I can do is groan with joy. I think this is the best birthday present I've ever gotten.

And before I can think, Angela's joined her. As Marta works the muscles in my shoulders, upper back, neck, and arms, Angela massages my lower back, hips, ass, and legs. Her touch is completely different from Marta's; Marta has a firm but gentle touch. Angela's touch is much more aggressive, and she has to use more oil to keep down the friction on my skin. But the combination is heady, and I enjoy every contact, every stroke, and every whisper between the two of them. "Such hard shoulders. Look at these muscles. Oh, Angela, I can't wait until we're done and he can fuck us both."

"Yeah, I know, ma'am. I was working his cock in the tub. My oh my, it was rock-hard. It was all I could do to not mount it and ride."

"Mmmmm. That would be fun." Marta stops and asks, "Hey, babe, you enjoying this?"

"Oh god yeah," is all I can get out.

"Good. Time to roll over."

I roll to my back on the narrow table and she pours oil down the center of my chest. Just watching that is hot enough, but to watch their hands work my skin . . . oh man. I'm so fucking hard that I'm aching. "You know, that's one of the things I always enjoyed about being with you."

I don't know what Marta means. "What's that?"

"Looking up at all these hard muscles while you fucked me. I loved that – always did. Your body is incredible."

"Thanks." They both keep going as I get harder and harder. It's a given that they're watching my cock, watching it pulse and throb.

In a few minutes, Angela looks down in my face. "Relaxed?"

"Oh yeah." Then I snicker, "Well, most of me anyway."

Marta jumps in. "Good. Come over here to the bed." So this is when I'm supposed to fuck them. I need to. Everything below my waist is aching with need, and I'm pretty sure my balls have gone from blue to purple. But she surprises me. "Hands and knees." I'm not liking this much. "Come on, Dave, really. We're not going to hurt you." Complying goes against everything I feel, but I do it anyway. And I get a surprise.

Marta positions herself behind me, and Angela to the side. I hear snapping sounds, like bottle lids, and then Marta says, "Okay, just relax. I told you, I'm not going to hurt you." I feel her rimming my asshole, and I start to tense. "No, don't tense up. You're going to love this, but make it easy on us, okay?"

"I'm trying," I pant out.

"I know. I can tell. It's okay." I feel her finger advancing into my back channel, and I'm trying not to lock up. "There. I'm in. You in place, babe?"

"Yes, ma'am," Angela reports back. She reaches up and under my body and takes my cock in both hands, which I find very weird.

"Good. Babe," she whispers as she leans forward, "you're going to come like you've never come before. I hope you're ready."

Now I know what she's planning to do. "Ready. Absolutely, positively ready." Oh, boy, am I ever.

She starts to manipulate her finger until she's found my prostate, and then she begins to massage it. At the same time, Angela starts to stroke me. Well, not stroke me. How can I describe it? She starts at the base of my dick and strokes down and off the tip while, at the same time, the other hand goes behind it and does the same. Left, right, left, right – I feel like I'm being milked. And really, I am, in more ways than one.

But I have to say, I was not prepared for how it all feels. There's a building pressure and I can barely contain myself. I want this to last forever, but I'm guessing at best I've got five minutes. That's a long way from forever. Be that as it may, I'm so hard that I'm almost whining in pain, and Angela's hands are magical, absolutely magical. It's emphasized by the exquisite torture of having my prostate stroked by Marta's long, strong finger, and the pressure is becoming unbearable, so much so, in fact, that I'm having trouble staying still. She strokes my ass and whispers, "Damn, Dave Adams, you're just as fine as you were when we first met, know that? You're just fucking gorgeous."

Okay, that does it – it's pretty much over. In about ten seconds, I empty out, and I do mean empty. There's got to be a quart on the bed, not kidding. I think there's some there that I've been saving up since nineteen seventy-nine. If I were to lie down right now, I'd probably slip off into the floor. I hear Angela say, "Holy fuck, Dave! It's a wonder you don't have fifty kids."

"Um, I've had that done to me before, but that's never happened before. I don't know . . ."

Before I can finish the sentence, her lips are on me and I'm so wrapped up in her tongue that I can't breathe. I feel Marta making her way up my body, and then they're both kissing me and kissing each other. Somebody mounts me; somebody drops their slit to my mouth. I don't know who, and I don't care. I'm just lost in all the sensations.

Fuck the club. *This* is bliss. These two know exactly what they're doing and in just a few minutes I've got two women screaming in ecstasy under my attentions. Yeah. I've still got it.

Marta was the one riding my cock, so when she's done, I just crawl up to Angela and slip inside her. Marta crawls up beside me and starts kissing me while I fuck Angela with a vengeance. Oh, god, happy birthday to me. Yeah. Hot, tight – I'm the only man she's ever been with – and I've already come once so I've got a good twenty to thirty minutes to just enjoy myself. When she gets started, she really gets started. She starts to come, and then she comes again, and again, and again. Plus she's begging for it, which is a huge rod-stiffener, if you didn't already guess. Any man loves having a woman beg him to fuck her, and this girl's huge tits and plump, satiny ass are all I need to make my joy complete. I manage to huff out, "Oh, god, girl, I wanna fuck you 'til I'm unconscious."

"You fuck me however you want, big boy. Whatever you need. Give it to me, Dave! I want that big cock of yours pounding into my pussy." Angela is coming un-hinged as I stroke into her, and Marta sucks and fondles those big, dark, pebbled nipples. As she does, she leans to me again and locks her hot, soft lips to mine. In a voice hoarse from ecstatic screaming, I hear Angela whisper, "Oh, god, Dave, baby, you're dead-ending up in me like a jackhammer."

I manage to scream, "Oh, motherfucker! Holy fuck-ing shit! Fuck, fuck, fuck!" And that's it for me. I yank out of Angela just in time to spray ropes of steaming, white jizz all over her belly and mound, and I've never seen anything so beautiful in my life. Without a word, Marta leans over her and starts to lap it up with that long, rosy tongue of hers, and I think I've died and gone to heaven.

Unintentionally, I drop to my side on the bed and lie there, gasping for breath, my heart hammering so hard in my chest that I'm pretty sure it can be heard across town. Marta curls up against me on one side and Angela on the other, lying safe and warm in my arms, and I kiss each of them on the forehead. Then Marta says something that surprises me.

"We're going to miss you when you finally find someone."

Even in my orgasm-induced stupor, my eyes go wide, my eyebrows shoot up, and I just blurt out, "What in the hell made you say something like that?"

I can feel her shrug. "I dunno. It just came to me. You will, you know. Find someone, I mean."

"Nope. Not likely." What on earth makes her think that?

"You will." Now Angela echoes Marta's words. "The way you just fucked me? Some sub is going to come into that club one night, you're going to fuck her, and she's going to attach herself to you like a sticky ball to Velcro. And you'll be out of circulation quicker than you can say 'condom.'"

"Oh, come on. You can't be serious."

"I am! Have you looked at yourself in the mirror lately, David Nathaniel Adams? It's like you're caught in a time warp. Sure, your hair is whiter, but god, that body doesn't look . . ."

"I know. Clint said it's unnatural," I laugh.

Marta kisses my nipple. "I don't know about that. It looks just about as natural as anything I've ever seen. Beautifully, magnificently natural."

Wow. This is turning out to be the most wonderful birthday ever!

"What happened to you? You're almost glowing. Are you pregnant?" Ben the Beer-Bringer's trying to be a smartass, and I know it.

"No. I just got spectacularly laid last night, that's all."

He laughs. "Happy birthday bang, huh?"

"You know it. Big, happy, awesome bang. Double bang. Man, I hurt all over. It's been a long time since I've gotten and given a fucking that was that aggressive."

Now Ben really laughs at me. "Getting too old?"

"Fuck you!" I throw a towel at him and he ducks and laughs again.

Now he's really laughing at me, and he's not laughing with me when he says, "You'd better find somebody before you're too old to cut the mustard!"

"I already said fuck you or I'd say fuck you," I play-snarl. Once he's finished with the beer delivery, I look around.

How pathetic. I live in a damn BDSM club. Why does everyone keep telling me, "When you find someone, when you find someone, when you find someone . . .?" Not gonna happen.

Then Melina walks in. God, that woman's something. "Hey, darlin', what brings you here?"

She grins. "Got anybody you think would like to be in a film?"

"Can old guys do that?"

She gives me the once-over. "That old guy standing in front of me right now? Hell yeah. I'll do him on camera anytime."

Oh, god, I want to do that. But Clint would kill me. I

can hear him now: "Dad, what the hell are you thinking? Porn? Really?" And he'd be right. But it would be so much fun, I think. At least with Melina it would. "So, is this a bondage film, or punishment, or what?"

"Whatever it turns out to be. But you know me – I like it rough." She licks her lips and all I can think about is undressing her with my teeth. Yum. Yes. I do know what she means. I've topped her about, hell, I don't know, eighty times? I remember watching her as I fucked her one night, watching the way she was taking it and playing into it. I wondered if she'd ever make this leap, and she did. She loves it, being in front of the camera, showing off her body, performing any and every sexual act she can think of. It just comes naturally to her. There was one night when she put a pair of clover clamps on herself and walked around out in the commons area. Any time a guy grabbed them and pulled the chain to him, she'd drop to her knees and suck him off right there. Porn is just second nature for her.

"Yes. I remember that you like it rough. Would you like it rough right now?" I just have to ask.

To my surprise, she says, "With you? Right now? Hell yeah, Amazing Adams. Let's get it on." And she drops her clothes right there. I mean, it's just a tiny little slip of a dress, but she's naked underneath, and now she's naked all over. By the time she makes the ten steps toward me, my cock is already popping my zipper. There's no foreplay; there's no warm-up. There's no fondling or kissing or any of that stuff. She just looks me right in the eye, throws one leg up and over my hip, and thrusts her pelvis toward me. That's all it takes. I slide in like a saber into its sheath, and in ten seconds we're fucking like rabbits.

I'm pretty sure I get more pussy than any other guy my age that I've ever known or heard of. Except maybe Hugh Hefner, even though I kinda think I probably get more action than he does. And, by damn, it's fun. My finger finds her control button and I pinch hard to initiate liftoff. And away she goes. When she does, she takes me with her, and we fly into our climaxes simultaneously. She takes my breath away, and apparently I do the same for her. "Damn, Dave, you fuck like a twenty year old."

"And when was the last time you fucked a twenty year old?" I laugh as I grip her waist, and I plant a kiss on her nose.

"Um, last week." Why did I even bother asking that question? I could've guessed the answer. I'm trying to tuck myself back into my jeans, but she says, "Here. Let me do that. I'll clean you up good." Her next move is to drop to her knees.

Oh. My. God. "Girl, did you go to college to learn to do that? Because if you didn't graduate from BJU, you should have. You should get an honorary hummer doctorate. Fuck, girl." I didn't think I could get that hard again that fast, but apparently she knows the secret of the powerful erection. No little blue pills needed. To say she makes short work of me is an understatement. I don't think I've ever lost control that fast before, but I do – I really do. When she finishes licking up everything she might've missed the first time, she tucks my limp dick back into my jeans and zips me up carefully. Then she stands and cups my chin in her soft palm.

"Dave, if I were the marrying kind, I'd be all over you like lube on a strap-on, but you know that's never going to happen. I like fucking around way too much." Melina laughs about it, but I know she means every word she just said.

"I know, baby. You don't need to be tied down. Do your thing. Thanks for the fun and go have a good time." As she turns to leave, I swat her on the ass and she laughs again.

"Save that for next time. And get some good rope!"

"You got it!" I call out to her as she walks out the door. Wow. What a way to start the day. Well, yeah, it's four forty-five in the afternoon, but it's the start of the day at Bliss. And I have a feeling it's going to be a good one.

Chapter Two

"**D**o that one more time and you'll never be allowed through our doors again. Got that?" I've got the asshole by the back of the neck and I've shoved his face into the surface of the bar. There are at least fifteen of the regulars standing around to offer me backup.

"Hey, man! I was just checking out the merchandise!"

I grind the cocksucker's face into the bar a little harder and he whines, but I've got a point to make. "She's not 'merchandise.' She's someone's sub, and you didn't have permission to touch her. Didn't you see the collar she's wearing?"

"Yeah, but a lot of the Doms around here like to share."

"That's *their* call, not yours. You apologize to the lady and let me know you've learned something."

When I remove my hand from the back of his neck, he straightens and wipes his mouth. Yeah, there's some blood oozing from the split in his lip. He could've gotten a whole lot worse. He was messing with Bruce's sub,

Valerie, and Bruce wouldn't take too kindly to that. If the Vietnam veteran had gotten to him before I did, he might be in a body bag now. I hear him mumble something. "I'm sorry. What did you say?"

He starts out with a whisper that goes into a crescendo when he says, "I said, I saw her fuck three dudes last week. She's not much of a lady." Before I can say or do anything, he takes a swing at me.

Wrong move, asshole.

I catch his fist, flip his arm backward, and hear the "pop" as it dislocates. As he howls in pain, I hook a foot behind his knees, pull one out from under him, and he lands on his back on the floor with a "BANG!" And I'm pretty damn pissed. "Your membership is permanently revoked. If you ever show up here again, I can't guarantee your safety. And if I run into you in public, god help you."

"You ain't gonna do shit, old man," he growls up at me.

That's when Andrew and Barry, two long-time members, step up. Barry glares down at him and says, "Adams can kick your ass faster than you can spit. And if he doesn't finish you off, there's a line forming to take a turn. Wanna see what he can do?"

The little cocksucker gets up and wanders away. "I'll go back to the fucking Catacombs. I don't have to put up with that shit." Hearing him say Catacombs makes my skin crawl, knowing what happened to Sheila there. If that's where he originally came from, he needs to take his ass back there. I don't want him anywhere near the subs at Bliss.

There's a slap on my back and I hear Andrew say, "Good work. For a guy who's a hundred and eighteen, you still pack a pretty good wallop."

I turn and try to give him a hard look, but I wind up laughing my ass off, and pretty much everybody else does too. Bruce has come out of the locker room, and I glance over to see Valerie still looking like she's going to cry, maybe even a little scared of what's going to happen when Bruce finds out, so I head that way. "Hey, man, we need to talk."

"What the hell was that all about?" Before I answer that question, I turn to Valerie.

"You okay, darlin'?"

She nods quietly, eyes appropriately averted. "Yes, Sir. I am, Sir."

I want to hug her, but she's not mine to hug, so I turn back to Bruce. "Let me tell you what happened, and I want to let you know up front, Valerie had nothing to do with this. We all saw it, and the guy manhandled her. She didn't invite it in any way. He just caught her as she walked by."

There's a look on his face that means death to someone, I'm sure. "Caught her? Caught her how?"

Valerie turns away before I say, "Grabbed one of her nipple rings as she walked by and pulled her over to him. She didn't have many options; it was go or have it ripped out, and I know you wouldn't have wanted that."

"Oh, god, no. Val? Come here, baby." She's crying as she turns back around to face him, and he reaches for her and hugs her close. "Oh, baby, it's okay. You didn't do anything wrong. You all right?" When she nods, he looks up at me from under his brows. "Where's the cocksucker?"

"Gone. Never coming back. He's not welcome here, and if he comes back, he's dead meat. I thought Andrew and Barry were going to take his head off for the way he was talking to me."

"You should've seen Master Dave, Sir. He was awesome. He popped that guy's arm out of place and knocked him to the floor. I was safe the whole time, Sir. None of the other Doms were going to let him hurt me."

"I know, babe. Let's just go home so you can calm down. It'll be okay." As he leads her back toward the dressing room, he turns and mouths a silent *Thank you* to me. I just nod and smile.

What a frickin' crazy day. All the glasses are clean and put away, and the place is quiet, with just a few stragglers left. The door opens and in walks Clint – in a suit. "What the hell? Look at you! Where in the world have *you* been?"

He sits down at the bar. "I had a meeting with a client downtown. They wanted to take me to dinner. Oh my god, what a boring evening talking about metal coat hangers. They make coat hangers. I can't imagine how mind-numbing those jobs must be. Did you know that there are at least eight alloy finishes for coat hangers?"

"Why, no, I did not. Never needed that info, so I never bothered to check it out. Perhaps I should," I grin with deadpan sarcasm. He makes a disgusted face at me.

"But what are you doing here? Where's Trish?"

"Home. With the kids. She wanted me to stop by: Have you found an earring?"

Riffling through the lost and found box, I pull out two. "One of these?"

"Yep. That one," he says and points at a pink crystal drop with a little pearl above the crystal.

"Good. Doesn't look cheap."

"Actually, it was. It just came from a department store around here somewhere. But they're pretty and she likes them, and this was the last place she wore them."

"Beer?"

"Sure." He reaches for it when I've gotten it drawn and I draw myself one so I can join him. I can't help but notice his wedding band as it glitters in the low light. "So, anything exciting happen tonight?"

"Yeah. Melina came by and fucked me before we opened."

"Oh, that's nice. She still doing porn shoots?"

"Yeah. Came in here looking for some members to join her in one or two, but nobody was here yet and she couldn't talk me into it."

Clint shakes his head. "And please don't let her, okay? Please?"

I have to laugh at the look of distress on his face. "No! I won't, I promise. And then I had to bounce an asshole who came over here from The Catacombs." With the word out into the air, I see Clint shiver all over.

"What was that about?"

"Grabbed Valerie's nipple ring as she went past.

Good thing I caught him before Bruce did or . . ."

"He'd be dead. Yeah, he would be. Bruce would snap his neck and not think twice."

I nod. "Yeah. My fear exactly. I don't want Bruce going to jail because somebody else is being an asshole."

We stand in amicable silence for a few minutes as he finishes his beer. "I'd better get home. My clan will be looking for me. Thanks for the beer."

I give him a smile. "Thanks for drinking one with me."

Before he makes it through the door, he comes back to the bar and stands for a second before he says, "I feel guilty."

I'm sure my face registers the shock. "About what?"

"About going home to what I have and leaving you here alone. About you going home alone."

"I don't have to be alone. I could get any of two dozen women in this place to go home with me. You know that."

"You know I don't mean having a sub stay the night with you. Dave, would you please . . ."

I shake my head. "Cut it out. Your mom started in on me about it too. Not happening. Go home. Love ya. Night." I point at the door and he turns and walks out, shoulders drooping and hands stuffed into his front pants pockets.

I get everything put away and grab the bag of garbage that's been sitting under the bar for most of the night. At the back door, I just walk out like I always do. And I get a huge surprise.

There's a young woman cowering there. I've seen her, well, I think it was her, along with about three or four others, seen them running from the dumpster and out into the secondary alley between the buildings. They always do that when they see me come out the door.

But tonight is different. Trapped between the dumpster and me, she really has nowhere to go. Anywhere she turns, I'm right there. And she looks absolutely terrified. As I move toward her, she seems to shrink, and I hear her muttering, "I'm invisible. I'm invisible. I'm invisible."

Towering over her, I peer down through her long bangs and matted hair until I can see into her eyes, big hazel eyes that seem lost. Something in her face, something in those eyes, tells me she doesn't belong here like this. She's shaking like a leaf, her gaze darting around in search of an escape route, and I decide I'll try to make some kind of connection. I don't know why. It just seems like the right thing to do.

"What's your name?"

She just stares at me. For a minute I wonder if she can hear, but when she turns away, I ask again, "Hey, what's your name?"

In a voice so soft and tremulous that I can barely hear her, she whispers, "Olivia."

I squat down on my heels so I can look into her face. "That's a beautiful name. Would you like to come inside, Olivia? I don't have much in here, but I think there are some potato chips in my desk, and we've got plenty of things to drink." I wait, but she just sits, so I stand and motion toward the building. "So come on. Let's find you something, okay?" She stares for a couple more minutes, then stands. I try to let her go in front of me, but she trails behind.

Once we're inside, I can really smell her, and in seconds I'm enveloped in the stench. God, it's horrible. There's no telling when she last had a shower. I go through the desk and pull out a half-eaten bag of chips. Handing them to her, I wait, but she doesn't reach out, so I place them gently on the desk. "What do you like to drink? I've got all kinds of things, sodas, beer, orange juice. I think I may even have a little lemonade out there at the bar. What'll it be?" She shakes her head. "You can have anything you like. What do you want?"

No sound comes out when she mouths *water*. Her face says she's terrified out of her mind.

"Sure?" She nods. "Okay, one ice water coming right up." I head out to the bar, grab a glass, fill it half full of ice, and run filtered water into it. When I go back, she's still sitting in the same spot, and the potato chips are still lying there, untouched. "Don't you want the chips?" She shrugs. "I like them pretty well. You can have the rest. I don't need them anyway!" I laugh, slapping my stomach.

She opens her mouth and asks quietly, "What do you want?"

It takes me a second or two to figure out what she means. "I don't want anything, honey. What I really want is to see you eat something, that's all." She shakes her head. "Really. Just eat them. Please?"

"I can't take things I don't pay for. That's stealing." She says it like it's a final edict and there's no arguing.

"Okay, well, do you have some money?" I know she doesn't by the looks of her. If she had any, somebody stole it long ago. Sure enough, she shakes her head. "Then you can't pay me because you don't have any money. Problem solved."

What happens next will forever be etched in my mind. She stands and turns away from me. I watch as she slowly pulls off her jacket, then pulls her top off over her head. I'm terrified that I know where this is going, and I'm not wrong. She drops the oversized sweat pants she's wearing, and between them and the top, I find she's wearing nothing underneath them. She steps out of them, walks slowly to the desk, and puts her hands on the surface, then spreads her legs apart and waits. My heart very nearly stops. It's not just what she's doing. It's the sight before me.

Her body is covered in bruises, scratches, cuts, and scars. And there are fresh burn marks on her back and buttocks, something round and most likely a cigarette. Here and there are patches of dried blood, but some of the marks appear fresh. It's easily the most horrifying thing I've ever seen, simply horrifying. There are rope marks on her wrists and ankles, and some kind of ligature mark around her neck. Totally at a loss, I don't know what to do, and I stand there, stupefied and motionless, frozen in fear and disgust, trying to put rational words together.

When I finally collect myself, I walk out of the room and go straight to the lady's locker room. Trish's locker is there, but her padlock is on it. And that's when I lose it. I pull out my phone, gasping for breath, and dial Clint's number. He answers on the second ring. "Hey! What's up?"

"Clint, where's Trish?"

"What's wrong? She's right here. Dave, what's going on?"

"I need to borrow her. Please, god, bring her down here to the club as fast as you can. Please?"

"Okay, now you're scaring me. What's wrong?"

I bellow into the phone, "Please, Clint, JUST DO IT!" And I hang up. I can't talk anymore because I'm too busy trying hard not to break down and sob. I look toward the door – I've got to go back down there. What the hell do I do? What do I say to her? I run out to the common room, grab the largest towel I can find, and head back toward my office. She's still standing there, spread eagle, head down, hands on the desk, waiting for me to do whatever it is that so many others have obviously done to her.

She's been trading her body for food. I'm just your average middle-class white guy and I know homeless people exist, have even had some contact with a few, but not like this. This is something I really don't have the expertise, nerve, or stomach to handle. I walk up behind her and drape the towel, more like a bath sheet, over her back, then try to help her stand. She shakes my hands off. "No! I'm hungry! Just do it, please? Just hurry? I'll be still, I promise."

My heart is so broken for her that I don't think I can even swallow. I try my best to hide my emotion when I speak, but I know she can hear it. "No, honey. It's not like that here. I want you to wrap this towel around you and sit down and eat these chips, you hear me? I don't want that from you. I just want you to eat, that's all. Please? Please sit down?"

I can feel her relax a little, and she lets me help her straighten up. I wrap the towel around her from the back, my stomach rolling from the stench of body odor, stale sweat, urine, feces, and general filth coming off her almost-naked body. Once she's holding the ends of the towel clutched tightly to her chest, I pull out the chair and motion to it. She finally shuffles over and sits down. I move the chips over in front of her, scoot the glass of water over to join them, and tell her again, "Please, Olivia. Just eat the chips. And then I'll help you a little more, okay? But eat first." When I finally see her reach out a tentative hand, I say, "That's a good girl. Go ahead. I'll be right back."

I can't get to the reception area fast enough. I manage to make it through the inner door and I'm on my hands and knees, wailing. I'm still in full-blown meltdown mode when I hear the front door open and Clint's voice rings out. "What the hell . . ."

All I can manage to get out is, "Oh, god. Oh my god. Oh my god. Oh, Clint, oh my god."

"What? What the hell? Are you okay?" I shake my head.

I hear the door open again and Trish's voice says, "Sweet mother of god! What's going on?"

"I need your help." I manage to sit up on my heels

and wipe my face with my hands. When I finally get a look at both of them, I realize they're terrified. "I'm okay, I'm okay, I swear. But I need your help, please! Please, Trish."

"You know I'll do whatever you need me to. What? What do you need?"

"Come with me." I start off back into the common area and wind past the bar and down the hallway, both of them trailing me. I stop right outside my office door and put my finger to my lips, then whisper, "She needs a shower. Some clothes. I'd like to get her some medical attention, but I think we'll have to take it slow. But please, try to act as normal as possible and help me out here, please?" They both look at me like I've lost my mind, and I step into the room with them right behind me.

The chip bag is empty, and half of the water is gone. When Olivia looks up and sees the three of us standing there, she skitters out of the chair and down into the corner by my bookcase. There's a whine that comes from her throat, something almost animal-like, and the fear in her eyes takes my breath away. I hear Trish fail in her silence when she whispers softly, "Oh my god."

Thankfully, that's when the Dom in Clint rises up and he takes over. He leans into Trish's ear and whispers, "See if you can get her into the shower. You've got stuff in your locker, right?" Trish nods. "Okay. Clothes? Got any in there?"

"Um, maybe. I'll have to look."

"If you don't, get a look at her while she's readying

for the shower. See if you can guess a size and I'll go buy her something real quick."

"Yes, Sir." Trish walks timidly toward Olivia and squats in front of her. "Hi. My name's Trish. What's your name?"

She whispers back, "Olivia. Olivia Warren."

"What a lovely name! Okay, Olivia, I have some shampoo and soap and things like that in my locker. Would you like to shower?"

Olivia leans conspiratorially toward Trish and whispers, "Will you stand guard?"

Trish is fighting tears when I get a look into her eyes. "Yes, I promise I will. Besides, neither of these guys will hurt you. That one is Dave, my father-in-law," she says, pointing at me. "And the other one is my husband, Clint. He's a very good guy. No one is going to hurt you. Will you let me hold your hand?"

Olivia nods and we watch as she slowly rises from the floor and then, clutching the towel to her front, she reaches for Trish's hand. The instant she clasps it, I feel a flood of relief wash over me. Watching as they leave the room and head toward the locker room, I can't take it anymore. I collapse in one of the chairs in front of the desk.

Clint takes the other one and reaches a hand to my shoulder. "You okay?"

"No."

"What the hell happened?"

"I found her out by the dumpster, looking for food. I brought her in, offered her those chips and some water.

And . . . and . . ." I don't think I can force out the words.

"What?"

A big shuddering sigh escapes my lips. "She pulled off her clothes and assumed an anal-entrance position at the desk." Clint's eyes go wide. "And she's covered in scars, bruises, cuts, scratches, dried blood, and burn marks. Burn marks," I repeat, trying to forget the sight. "Fresh burn marks. And ligature marks – wrist, ankles, and throat."

"Dear god." Clint shakes his head slowly. "I don't want to even think about what she's been through. Has she been hanging around out back very long?"

"I've been seeing her for a couple of weeks on and off. This was the first time I've opened the door and she's been close enough that she couldn't run. Son, she was terrified of me. I can't turn her back outside. I don't know for sure what to do, but I can't just pitch her back out the door."

"I think you should call the police. Maybe they can get her into a homeless shelter somewhere."

I nod. "Yeah. Maybe that would be a good idea." Phone in hand, I dial nine-one-one and wait.

A female voice answers, "Nine-one-one. What is your emergency?"

"Yes, it's not really an emergency, but I do need an officer."

"What's going on, sir?"

"I have a young homeless woman here who needs some assistance."

"Give me your location, sir, and I'll send a cruiser."

As soon as she has the club's address, we end the call and I sit there not knowing quite what to say or do.

Trish appears in the doorway. "She needs some ladies sweats, extra-small, top and bottom. I'd say a thirty-two B bra and panties in an extra-small. Maybe some size seven tennis shoes and some plain white socks. Dave, do you still keep a supply of that lice stuff?"

"Yeah. Bad?"

"No head lice that I can see, but she's got a raging set of crabs. I need a razor for her and shave cream if you've got it. And you're going to lose a towel. I hope that's okay."

I hand her the lice stuff, a razor, and a can of half-full shaving cream, and she disappears again. "I can't leave. The cruiser will be here in a few minutes."

Clint nods. I walk him to the front and, before he can get out the door, a black and white pulls up outside. When the officer walks through the door, I feel something shift in the room, and I don't like whatever it is. To my dismay, I feel Clint stiffen beside me; he's picked up on it too. I'm trying to figure out what it is when the officer starts to speak, and I try to answer his questions as best I can when Clint interrupts. "I'm going to get the things we talked about. I'll be back in a few minutes. Call if you need me." I nod and the door closes behind him as the officer and I start again.

In a matter of seconds, Clint comes back through the door and there's a look on his face that I've seen before, but I can't figure out what it means. "Forgot something. Be right back." He disappears into the hallway and we try one more time.

The cop makes a few more notes before he looks up. "So let's take a look at this woman and I'll see if I can find out more about her. Where is she?"

"Back here. My daughter-in-law is helping her get cleaned up." For reasons I can't explain, something feels off.

We head into the common room, only to almost run headlong into Clint. "Be right back," he says, that weird look still on his face, and jets out the front door."

We start down the back hallway to my office and I notice that the light is off in the locker room, so I turn it on and call out, "Hey! Trish? Where are you?" I march on into the locker room, but there's no sign of the two women. My office is empty, and I go from private room to private room, checking through the monitor windows; no Trish or Olivia. That's when I notice it: The back door is propped open. I work through it all in my mind. Clint's odd look. The two women gone. The back door open. Something is wrong, and I can't figure out what it is, so I decide I'd better smokescreen until I can find out what the hell is going on. "She must've bolted on Trish. You guys should probably go look for them."

"Will do." The officer jogs back toward the front of the building and out the door. I notice that there's another black and white out front, and they talk together for a couple of minutes before they get in their cruisers and drive away in opposite directions. I'm still standing there scratching my head when my phone rings.

"Dad?"

"Yeah! What the hell . . ."

"Trish and Olivia are in the trunk of your car."

"What?"

"I'll explain in a little bit. Are the cops gone?"

"Just left. But Clint . . ."

"Trust me on this one. Wait until you know they're gone for sure. Then go out and get them and bring them back inside."

I can't figure out what the hell is going on, but I answer, "Okay. I will. Are you . . ."

"Going to get her some clothes and some food. We've got to make some kind of decision when I get back and they're back inside. In the meantime, make it look like you're going to your car for something, to look in the trunk for something, and open the lid and tell them that you know they're there and everything is going to be okay. I'll be back as fast as I can."

"Okay, son. I will. Hurry."

"Will do." With that, he hangs up.

I grab my gym bag and head out the back door. As soon as I open the trunk lid, two anxious faces peer back at me. "It's okay. I'm pretending I'm looking for something. I'm keeping lookout and as soon as I know they're gone, I'll come and get you." Trish nods at me and I notice she's got her arms around Olivia, who looks like a frightened child. The younger woman's face is buried in Trish's chest and she's shaking. I wish Clint would hurry up and come back.

Ten agonizing minutes of constant surveillance later, I go out and open the trunk lid again. "Quick! Get inside!" The two of them scramble and run back through the door, Olivia in a long tee that Trish must've found in the men's locker room. Once inside, I turn to Trish. "What the hell?"

"I don't know. All I know is Clint ran back here and said she was in danger. He found your keys, hit your trunk release, and shoved us in before he took off again. I have no idea what happened."

The three of us sit in my office. Trish pulls one of the chairs in front of the desk up against the other one, and the two women sit in them, Olivia leaning into Trish. It's at least another fifteen minutes and I hear footsteps coming through the building. I'm about to close and lock my office door and turn off the light when I hear a voice say, "It's just me. Don't panic."

Clint steps through the door carrying two fairly good-sized bags, probably of clothes. He also has a sack from a fast food restaurant in one hand. "Here. Clothes. And something better than potato chips!" He smiles at Olivia, who doesn't return the gesture. "Baby, why don't you take Olivia to the locker room and help her get dressed? Then take her to one of the private rooms and let her eat there, okay?" Trish nods and takes Olivia's hand, then lets Clint load her other arm with bags as they pass him on their way out.

Once they're out of earshot, I turn to Clint. "What the hell was that about?"

His face is almost gray when he starts to speak. "There was another cruiser out front. When I passed it, the officer was on his phone and I heard him say, 'Yeah,

I'm guessing it's one of those homeless whores we had that little "party" with last week. We've gotta keep them quiet or god knows what'll happen.'"

The horror starts to sink in and I collapse into one of the chairs. "Oh my god. Do you think they . . ."

"We've got to keep her away from the cops. That means no homeless shelter, no social worker, no nothing. We've got to handle this or no telling what will happen to her. I bet they'd kill her to keep her quiet. Just one more dead 'whore,'" he says, using air quotes around the word for emphasis.

"What the hell have I gotten myself into?" I moan, my face in my hands. I look up at Clint and find him looking back at me, just a hint of a smile on his face.

"It's not you. It's us. I'll commit us to helping you and her however we can. Let's try to come up with something, okay? Steffen and Sheila will be right here with us if we need them – you know that."

Somehow that doesn't make me feel one bit better. Boy oh boy. I've gotten myself into some fixes in my lifetime, but this one really takes the cake.

<hr>

"Welcome to *casa* Adams." I drop my keys into the bowl by the front door. Olivia follows me in, still clutching Trish's hand. "It ain't much, but it's all I've got."

"Olivia, let's find you a bedroom so you can get some rest, okay?"

Never releasing Olivia's hand, Trish looks to me. I just tell her, "Clint's old room."

"Gotcha. Come on, honey. It'll be okay." Trish leads her past and Olivia gives me a hard stare as she heads down the hallway. I hear Trish saying, "Dave will give you a big tee shirt to sleep in. You'll be fine." Her voice drones on and I look at Clint.

"What do I do now?"

Clint shrugs. "That's what do 'we' do now, and I don't know. What are the rules here?" He's grinning when he asks that question and plops down on the sofa, waiting for me to sit down too.

I'm so wired that it's hard to breathe. My elbows on my knees, I lean forward and put my face in my hands. "Well, rule number one would be to not sleep with her for any reason. I don't think that one's going to be too hard to follow."

Clint chuckles. "Well, I'm glad to hear *that*!" Then he sobers again. "I'm going to have Trish go and get her some more things tomorrow. She needs more clothes, another pair of shoes, some pajamas, a robe, things like that."

"I'll pay for them. I don't mind."

Clint shakes his head. "No. It's all right. It's not like she's going to Nordstrom's or anywhere like that. Just Walmart or Target or somewhere. It won't be that much."

I hesitate, then ask, "What about some jewelry? I mean, just cheap stuff, but women like that kind of thing. And maybe some makeup? What do you think?"

A thoughtful look passes over Clint's face. "Yeah. That might be a good idea. A few things that would be considered a luxury to her. Give her some hope, some stability. Maybe even get her to open up a little, tell you about herself."

I nod. "Yeah, I've already decided I'm going to tell her that I'm not planning to ask any questions, that I'll just wait until she's ready to tell me."

Clint nods back. "Good plan. Let her relax a little, get comfortable."

I sigh deeply. "You do realize that she might be a serial killer and she could murder me in my sleep or steal everything I have for all I know?"

"The thought had occurred to me." Clint smirks.

"I'm trying not to think about it." Then something hits me. "I've got an idea." I start down the hall. When I get to the bedroom doorway, I smile.

Olivia is in Clint's old bed, sheet pulled up to her neck, and Trish is sitting on the side of the bed, speaking quietly to her. From time to time, Trish brushes a hand absent-mindedly over Olivia's hair, and the younger woman closes her eyes as though she enjoys the simple touch. When Trish hears me, she turns. Her tiny little reaction causes Olivia's eyes to pop open, but she calms when she sees that it's me. "Hey, honey, can I ask you a question?" Olivia lies stone still and says nothing. "I'm going to try to get you some money, but do you know your social security number? I'm going to need that to find your money. That and your last name."

She stills completely and just stares at me for a moment, but then she starts rattling the number off so fast that I'm having trouble catching it all. I whip out my phone. "I'm making a note here. Tell me again." Once it's typed into my notes, I tell her "Good girl. I'll see what I can find for you. You get some sleep, okay?" She nods, and I head back to the living room.

"Got it."

Clint looks up from the newspaper. "What?"

"Her social security number." I snatch a note pad from the coffee table, open up the note in my phone, and write the number on the paper, then hand it to Clint.

"What am I supposed to do with it?"

"Call Steffen. Give it to him. He can find out who she is."

"Oh yeah! That's good thinking. I'll call him in the morning." Not only is Steffen a member at the club, he's a regional manager for a large banking chain. He'll be able to look her up based on credit reports. We can at least get a little information that way. "I think I'm going to collect my sub and take her home. You gonna be okay here with her?"

I shrug. "Guess we'll find out come morning."

⟨⟨◦◦◦⟩⟩

I'm almost asleep when I hear a voice. The house had gone completely silent, and I'd heard nothing from Olivia since Trish and Clint left, but I'd intentionally left my bedroom door open so I could try to detect movement. Now, in my addled sleeping mind, I hear, "Hello?"

I roll to face her. "Hey! What's up, honey?"

"May I use the restroom?" She looks terrified again.

I nod. "As long as you're staying here, it's your bath-

44

room too. Do whatever you need to do."

"Thank you. Thank you so much. Thanks." She keeps thanking me as she walks down the hallway and I hear the bathroom door close. The toilet flushes, the door opens, and she stops in my doorway again. "Thank you. Thank you so much. Thank you for letting me use your restroom."

As she turns to go back to the other room, I call out, "Olivia, would you like to talk? I'll always listen. I hear I'm a good listener."

She stands in the doorway again, her head hung. "No. What would I talk about? I don't have anything to say."

"I just thought, you know, maybe you'd like to tell me more about yourself. Or I could answer questions about me. I don't mind at all. I'm not very interesting, but I'll tell you anything you want to know."

She shakes her head. "That's okay." I'm pretty sure she's going back to the room, but she continues to stand there. Finally, she says in a low whisper, "Please don't call the police. Please?"

I feel tears come to my eyes. "No, honey. We're not going to do that. That's why Clint put you guys into the trunk of my car. The police were out front. And no, they're never going to hurt you again. I'll see to it."

She doesn't smile, but she also doesn't look as stressed as she'd looked five minutes before. "Thank you. Thank you for helping me. Thank you so much."

A grin stretches across my face. "Oh, quit thanking me! It's just a twin-sized bed in Clint's old room. This isn't the Radisson. It's just a little house on a city street."

Her head shakes slowly. "No, it's a very nice house. Very nice. You're so lucky to live in a house. Some people don't have anywhere to live."

Okay, that does it – my heart is officially broken. I decide to try something. "I know. Not everyone has a place to live. What happened to your house?"

Very quietly, she murmurs, "My dad's medical bills were too high. The court took it and sold it."

Ah – *now* we're getting somewhere. I forge ahead. "Oh! So did you live with your parents?" She nods. "Did you always live with them?"

She sighs and leans against the door facing, the first somewhat-normal thing I've seen her do. "No. I had a condo in Jasper. And a job and a car."

"Wow. That must've been nice." I wait and, when she doesn't say anything else, I sit up and pat the foot of the bed. "You can come and sit down if you want. It's okay."

To my total surprise, she does just that – sits on the foot of the bed and crosses her legs yoga-style. But she doesn't say anything else. Finally I ask her, "So how did you wind up here?"

"My parents were sick. Then my mom died. So I quit my job and sold my condo to come and help my dad. I hadn't had my condo very long, so there wasn't any equity and I lost my down payment and everything. Then my car quit, so I just drove his. He couldn't drive it anyway."

"Do you mind me asking what was wrong with your

dad?"

"COPD. It's terrible." A far-away look passes over her face. "He was only fifty-three. That was three years ago. I was twenty-six."

"Oh, Olivia, honey, I'm so sorry. That's horrible. Is that how you wound up without a home?" I was trying to piece it all together, and I was failing.

"Yeah. He had a lot of medical bills and the bank foreclosed on the house once he died. I couldn't pay the payments. And once I lost the house, I had no address, so no one would give me a job."

I know that to be common, and it makes me furious. How in the hell is a homeless person supposed to not be homeless anymore if they can't get a job? It's a convoluted, fucked-up world we live in. She invades my thoughts when she says, "I lived in the car, but one day I went into the mall to wash up and when I came out, they'd found it and repossessed it. Everything I had left was in that car and I never got any of it back. I stood there on the mall sidewalk, looking at the spot where my car had been, watching shoppers walk back and forth, and I thought, 'Now I'm one of those people I used to give money to on my way to the office from the parking lot.' I remember that I stood there for about four hours. I didn't know what to do or where to go. That was the first night I slept outside." She stares at her lap, not crying, just staring, completely still.

Every paternal Dominant trait in me kicks into high gear, and my head drops in shame. This woman has been abandoned, deserted, used, abused, thrown away, and ignored. All I want to do in that moment is get one of those beautiful rocking chairs from Cracker Barrel and rock her in my arms. She doesn't deserve what happened to her. She tried to do the right thing, and she's been punished in every way possible for her love and sense of responsibility. Before I can stop it, a tear rolls down my face and drips off my nose, and I sniffle.

"Don't cry. It's okay." Her soft voice fills the room. "I don't have anybody. If I'm not around anymore, no one will know. There's no one who'll be hurt. It's okay, really. I'm not afraid anymore."

And that's all I can take. This woman has lost everything and *she's* comforting *me*. When I manage to pull myself together, I look up at her and say the thing that is cycling in my head. "I'd know, Olivia. I'd know you weren't around anymore. I'd miss you. I really would."

And there it is – a tiny little smile, shy but beautiful. "Thank you. Thank you for saying that. Thanks so much." Every time she's thanked me, it's been over and over. A tiny kindness. A pleasant word. A small smile. A gentle reassurance. I take so much for granted, and this woman is appreciative of them all. "I should let you go to sleep. I'm sorry for taking up your time like this. You didn't want to hear any of this. I'm so sorry." She rises from the foot of the bed and heads out the door, but she stops in the doorway. "You're a very kind man, Dave. And Clint and Trish are very kind too. Thank you for being so nice to me. I'll leave whenever you want me to." Before I can say a word, she disappears and I hear the bedroom door close.

And now I just want to know more about Olivia.

Chapter Three

When I wake up the next morning, I get the shock of my life.

I stumble into the kitchen, confused because I can smell coffee, and the sight that greets me is unbelievable. Yes, there's coffee. Plus, on a platter, there's bacon, sausage, and hash browns. While she's cooking the eggs, she's also babysitting the pancakes on the griddle. I watch in amazement as she handles it all with ease. When she turns to put the eggs on the platter, she jumps. "Oh! I'm sorry! I hope this was okay. I wanted to show you how much I appreciate you. I hope it's all right that I cooked this food."

I'm still in shock. "Uh, yeah, that's fine. Great, in fact. I'm just . . . wow. I just don't know what to say."

"If you'll tell me what you want, I'll serve you. I don't mind at all." She gives me something that might pass as the beginnings of a smile, the first expression like it that I've seen from her, and I get a weird sensation in my chest.

"No, no, I'll get it. I should be serving you since you've cooked all this. Wow. This is awesome!" *I could get used to this,* I think, then tell myself, *Dave, you old dog, forget about it. Not gonna happen.* I get a couple of plates out, set one on the counter for her, and fill the other one, then take a seat at the table. One bite and I ask, "What did you put in these eggs? They're ridiculous."

Her face falls. "Oh, no, are they awful? I'm so sorry!" She reaches for the platter, and I stop her by pulling it toward me.

"No-no-no, they're ridiculously delicious! That's what I meant! You're a helluva cook, little girl!" I'm grinning from ear to ear, and I see her facial muscles relax as she takes a deep breath.

"Okay. I'm sorry."

"Olivia, why do you keep saying you're sorry?"

She shrugs. "I don't know. I guess I don't want you to be mad at me." Now she just looks sad.

"Can I ask you something?" She nods. "How long has it been since someone has hugged you? I mean really, really hugged you?"

Her expression is flat when she says, "Three years. I mean, Trish kinda hugged me last night, but not really. She just put her arm around my shoulders. Nobody's hugged me in three years."

I don't even know what to think about that response. Somebody is hugging me all the time. If it's not Clint or Trish or their kids, it's Sheila or Steffen or one of theirs, or a sub, or Marta or Angela, or one of the Doms at the club, or *somebody.* The idea that someone would go three years without the barest minimum of human contact and affection is hard for me to comprehend. I shudder internally before I ask, "Would you like a hug? Can I hug you?" I remember something Trish said. "Trish says my hugs are magic. Want to see?"

She just stands there, and I realize she doesn't know what to say. Faced with the possibility of caring and attention, she freezes. I get up and make my way across the room to her, where I put a hand under her chin and turn her face up to mine. "I'm going to hug you. If it's too much for you, let me know." I open my arms, then step up against her and wrap them around her.

Her arms don't move, but I feel her melt into my embrace, and then it happens: She starts to sob. I grip her even tighter, and finally her arms wind around my waist. Three years of bottled-up anguish pours out, soaking the front of my tee and making my knees feel weak. Instinctively, my face tips downward and I kiss the top of her head. She's still crying and I realize she can't stop, so I scoop her up and carry her to the living room, then sit on the sofa and hold her on my lap where she just keeps crying and heaving. I stroke her hair and make a mental note to myself that she needs it trimmed to get rid of the splits and frizzies. Then she does the one thing I wanted to do myself, but I knew better. Problem is, she doesn't when she lifts her face to meet mine.

And she kisses me. Something inside me breaks open and I feel lighter somehow. I know I should pull back, but I just can't. I think about her age, my age, what she's been going through, and I wonder what's going to happen next, how badly one or both of us is going to get hurt, what the hell I'm doing in this predicament, but I can't make my lips leave hers. When I manage to get my wits about me, I grab her upper arms and push her back to look into her face. The look there takes my breath away, so much fear and desperation and pain, when she whispers, "Please? Please love me? Please? I know I'm dirty and I'm trash, but I'm a really good person, really, I am. Please love me?"

She's a child and she's a woman, and in that blindingly bright second I fall in love with both. I just pull her to my chest and hug her tight, and she wraps her arms around me and squeezes for dear life. "Oh, Olivia. I want to, I really do, but honey, you're twenty-nine and I'm sixty- . . ."

"Stop!" She peers up at me. "Dave, please? I need you! Please?" To my horror, she leans back and starts tugging at the bottom of my tee shirt, and I grab her hands and hold them together in front of her.

"No! Olivia, no. I can't do that." My heart is racing and I'm almost panting. "That wouldn't be right."

She cries even harder. "No one wants me! I'm such a mess! I'm no good for anything!"

That just makes my blood boil, and I shout out, "THAT'S NOT TRUE! Stop it, Olivia! You're a beautiful girl. You deserve to have someone love you, but I won't take advantage of you like that. I respect you too much. Let's just take a deep breath, honey, please?"

She stops struggling against me and sucks in air, a look of sad resignation passing over her face. "I'm sorry. That wasn't right of me. I'm such a slut."

"I told you, stop it! You're not a slut! You've been

used and abused and taken advantage of. I don't want to be one of the people who does that to you when you're vulnerable and alone and afraid. We'll figure all of this out, but let's eat breakfast and see what we can do today that'll take you another step closer to being whole, okay?"

It's a small victory when she nods. "Okay. Okay, I understand. Thank you, Dave. Thank you so much for taking care of me. Thanks."

I chuckle. "Do you know how flattering it is for you to do that? I'm an old guy and you're . . ."

"Now it's MY turn to tell YOU to stop it!" Then I hear it for the first time.

She giggles.

I start to laugh. "Why should I stop it?"

"Because you're not old. You're very, very distinguished."

"Translation: Old." I'm still laughing. Now she's laughing too.

"No. You're very, very hot. And you're very sweet too." Now she's blushing.

"Let me ask you something. Trish was going to shop for you later, but would you like to go with her to shop? Then you could get things *you* like." There's a moment of fear on her face, so I add, "And I'll go with you if it would make you feel better."

"Can Clint go too?" Ah. She wants to make sure there are plenty of us with her. Makes her feel safe, I assume.

"I don't know. He may have work to do. But if he

doesn't, I'm sure he'll come. We can have lunch too. What do you think?"

She gives me a tiny little nod. "I haven't eaten in a restaurant in a long, long time." Then she blurts out, "Oh my god! This food is ruined! We didn't eat it."

I'm afraid she'll burst into tears again, so I say, "Hey, it's just wonderful that you actually cooked for me. I'm impressed."

She nods again. "I can earn my keep."

I just chuckle. "Girl, all you have to do to earn your keep here is to pay me in smiles."

And I get my first payment right that second.

<hr/>

"No. I can't." Trish hands her three tops and Olivia shakes her head. "Just one."

"No. All three. Go." Trish points to the dressing room, and Olivia stares at the door. "Go on. You need to try them on. You don't want to buy them if they don't fit."

"But I can't, you can't . . ."

"I can do whatever I want, and I want to buy these for you. Now GO!" Trish practically shouts. When Olivia gives a little jump, Trish shrugs. "Sorry. But stop being difficult and do it. Please?"

A sheepish Olivia heads off into the dressing room. Clint is across the aisle in the men's department, but when I look up again, he's even farther down the aisle in lingerie, and I see him grin and hold up a very sexy bra when Trish looks around for him. I have to chuckle.

"Who knew this shopping trip was going to turn into foreplay for the two of you?"

"It's not!" Trish laughs. Then she says, "Well, not yet anyway. I don't know why he's showing me those. I have a drawer full." About that time, Olivia comes tiptoeing out of the dressing room.

"Well, would you look at that!" At my words, Trish turns to see. "Don't you look cute as can be?"

Olivia stands staring at the floor, and the top she's wearing is so adorable I can't even think. I hear Trish say, "Oh, Olivia, that color is beautiful on you!"

In a voice so timid that we can barely hear it, Olivia mumbles, "Thank you." She looks up to smile at me but, just as she does, I see her glance over my shoulder and then turn and bolt back into the dressing room. Of course, I wheel to get a look at what she saw.

Two police officers. They appear to just be walking through the store, not really doing anything, maybe shopping on their lunch break or headed to the food court. I hear Trish say, "I need to go see about her." She disappears into the dressing room.

Just as Trish is out of sight, Clint wanders up. "Where'd Trish go?"

I turn and point discreetly in the direction of the officers, who've stopped and are looking at some shoes just a couple of dozen feet away. "In the dressing room doing damage control."

"Shit." He turns with his back to them. "You do realize one or all of us are going to have to discuss this with her, don't you? We've got to talk to her, try to find out if she can give us names or at least who to avoid. I think that's imperative."

"I doubt we'll get very far. I think she's locked up tight on that one."

"We have to try. She can't hide in dressing rooms and car trunks forever. Besides, not all police officers are bad. Matter of fact, most aren't. There are just a few bad ones mixed in there, like there are bad ministers, and bad car salesmen, and just about anything."

"Bad dominants?" I chuckle.

"Big, bad dominants. There's a difference," he guffaws back. When we look again, the police officers have strolled back out into the actual mall, and Clint marches to the dressing room doorway. "Trish? The coast is clear."

She appears in the doorway leading to the hallway of dressing rooms. "She won't come out."

"What do you mean, she won't come out?" Clint snaps.

"I mean she won't come out. She's sitting on the floor, curled up into a ball in the corner, and I can't get her to even talk to me." She finds my eyes and gazes into them. "You try."

"Well, okay. I'll give it a go." I wander down the hallway until Trish nods, and then open the door. And it's exactly as Trish said. She's in her jeans and a tee, and she's knotted up on herself in the floor of the dressing room, scared and shaking. "Olivia? Hey, little one. They're gone."

"They'll come back," she whimpers.

"No. They're gone. Besides, you were safe. Clint and I are right here with you. No one's going to hurt you."

"Yes they will. The police will hurt me, and you and Clint can't do anything about it." She's trembling.

I ask gently, "Will you let me touch you?" She doesn't respond, so I ask her again, "Olivia? Please, may I touch you?" After what seems an eternity, she nods. Thinking about it, I sit down in the floor cross-legged and, once I'm settled, I tell her, "Okay. I'm going to draw you over into my lap. I just want to hold you, that's all. I'm not going to hurt you." Even though she shakes her head, I pull her to me anyway.

She's rigid as a board in my embrace. Poor thing. Clint's right: We've got to talk to her about what happened, and the sooner the better. I finally feel her sigh and relax a little against me, and I whisper, "Baby, we need to leave. Let's go."

"No! I'm scared!"

"No need. I'm right here. Clint's got his gun with him; he always does. You're perfectly safe with us." I press her body away from mine and look into her face, but she won't meet my gaze. "Come on, Olivia. We've got to go." Once she's standing, I tell her, "You have to change out of that top. We'll get it for you, but we have to take it to the cash register." She just pulls it off over her head and hands it to me, then picks up her own top and puts it back on. "Ready?"

"No." I take her hand and lead her out of the dressing room area and back to Clint and Trish. I can tell she doesn't want to go – she's pulling back with every step –

but we can't stay there forever. Her eyes won't leave the floor long enough to look at either of them.

"I think we've had enough shopping for today," I announce. "I'm paying for this stuff. Trish, can you take Olivia to the car, please?"

"Sure! Come on, sweetie. It's okay." Clint and I watch them walk away hand in hand and I head for the nearest checkout.

"By the way, you're right." The cashier has taken everything out of my hands, and I'm getting my card from my wallet when Clint makes that pronouncement.

"In what way?"

"We've got to talk to her. Should we try it when we get back to the house?"

"No time like the present."

She still needs bras and underwear, and a few more pairs of shoes, but that can wait. Right now we've got to get down to what happened in that circle of officers. It's her only chance to heal and our only chance to get through to her.

<hr>

"Okay, Miss Olivia, come right over here and sit down." We've gotten everything carried in from the car and drinks poured all around so we can talk without being disturbed. The kids won't get out of school for another hour and a half, so we've got enough time. I try to get comfortable but, frankly, there's no way to get comfortable when you're about to ask someone about being ruthlessly violated by the very people who should've been protecting her. "Sweetie, we need to talk about the policemen." She shakes her head violently. "Yes, we do. We have to. We need to know for sure what happened."

"No."

Trish tries. "Olivia, we can't help you unless we know what happened to you."

"No."

Right at that moment, Clint's phone rings. He steps outside the front door to talk on it, and Olivia looks me dead in the eyes. "Who's he talking to?"

"I have no idea. Probably business." She's eyeing the front door suspiciously. "I can tell you who it's *not*. It's *not* the cops. I'm sure of that." Unfortunately, that doesn't seem to help.

Once he's returned and taken a seat, Clint smiles over at Olivia. "Honey, our friend Steffen found your money. Looks like you had some that was deposited into your bank account, and when it didn't have any activity for awhile, it went to the unclaimed property roster at the state capitol. Steffen's trying to figure out where it came from and exactly what it is, but it's definitely yours." Her eyes are round and wild. "It really is yours, Olivia. I swear. We're going to try to find a way to get it all back to you."

"How much?"

"It's not much. Maybe four hundred dollars?"

"Oh my god, that's a lot of money!" she gasps out. I suppose it is to someone who hasn't had a penny to their name for years. I can't help but think, *Yeah, you probably paid that much for a purse in the past.*

"We'll get it back to you, I promise. But for right now, we need to talk about the police."

She shrinks again. "I really don't want to."

When I take her hand, I figure she'll snatch it back but, instead, she grips mine. "We really don't want you to have to, but it's the only way we know of to help you. We want you to be safe."

She shakes her head. "I'll never be safe."

"You're safe here, aren't you?" I point out.

"Only because I'm inside. If I go outside, I'm not safe. And I can't stay inside forever; I'll have to find a place to sleep."

"Maybe I haven't been clear about this, but I think it's time I set you straight." I put a hand on either of her cheeks and turn her face to mine. "You're not going back out to sleep outside. Ever again. Get that idea out of your head. Your life has changed. I know it's hard to believe, but Clint, Trish, and I are dedicated to seeing you get back on your feet, both personally and financially. We won't stop until we've done that, do you understand?"

Bewilderment fills her eyes. "Why? Why would you do that? Why would you care?"

Clint takes her other hand and, to my surprise, she doesn't lurch away from him either. "Because we do. Dave's my dad, as far as we're all concerned, and he raised me to care about others. You fell into our lives for a reason, little one. I'm not sure why, but you're here to stay. Got it?"

"I still don't understand."

I smile at her. "You don't have to understand every-thing, just accept it. We want to help you. We care about you and want you to be safe and happy."

"But why?"

How do you explain this to someone who's been so beaten down and abused? Abandoned and alone? Afraid and penniless? I search my brain, and then I finally say, "Because. Because at some point in all our lives, we've needed help, and someone's been there for us. And we want to do the same for you. Does *that* make sense?"

She nods and in a tiny voice says, "Do unto others."

"Exactly!" I drop her hand to put my arm around her shoulders. "Now we need to talk about the police."

Eyes on her hands in her lap, she picks around her cuticles and tries to avoid our eyes. "So what do you want to know?"

"I want to know: Is that where you got the marks on your body?" She doesn't answer, so I try again. "Looks like they hit you with a nightstick and burned you with cigarettes." She starts to shake all over. "Olivia, did they beat you with a nightstick and burn you with cigarettes?" Still getting no answer, I try again. "Baby, if they hurt you with . . ."

"They raped me with a baton."

Trish tears up immediately and Clint's face goes pale, but not mine. This was pretty much exactly what I was expecting her to say. "How many of them, baby?"

"About ten." It takes everything I have not to gasp.

"Okay. They raped you with a baton. Did they beat you with it too?" She nods. "And the burns?"

"Yes. Cigarettes. They burned one girl's, um, privates, with cigarettes because they said she was diseased and they needed to disinfect her with fire."

Now we're getting somewhere. "They tied you up, didn't they?" She nods. "Rope?" Another nod. "Handcuffs?"

She shakes her head. "Zip ties."

Bastards. But we're getting closer. "So, did they beat you while they had you tied up?"

"Yes. Over and over." She stops for a second and, in a voice so quiet I can barely hear it, she says, "They killed a girl."

I knew it. Clint heard right. My god. They're using the homeless female population as their personal sex toys. I have to ask it, don't want to know the answer, but have to ask. "Olivia?" When she doesn't answer, I take her chin in my hand and pull her face up, then scrunch down until I can look up under those lashes. "Baby, did they rape you?" No answer. "Olivia, answer me. Did they have sex with you?"

A huge, shuddering sob escapes her lips, followed by a wail the likes of which I've never heard before in my life. There's no way to fight it off – I grab her and hug her to me as tightly as I can. This poor child. Who does this to someone this lovely and fragile, someone who's already been dealt the worst hand luck has? Before I can say anything else, she sobs out, "Yes. They said we were their bitches. They said they were going to breed us like bitches in heat until we couldn't walk. My friend Elizabeth was older. They kept at her with that baton until there was blood coming from, well, you know, down there," she says, pointing to her lap, "and then they left her. And the next morning, she was dead. They beat Mrs. Sullenger in the head with the baton until she couldn't move, and then they raped her and raped her until they finally just threw her on the ground. And she never woke up. I guess she starved because she was unconscious." The horror I feel only grows when she says, "Sometimes they'd tie up fifteen of us at one time. And they'd make the homeless guys have sex with us too, and watch them and give them money for doing it. They'd say, 'You take this money and if anybody asks, you don't know anything about any of this.' So the other guys would do it for the money. And the sex." Now it's pouring out of her like oil, and it's fast becoming the hardest thing I've ever had to sit through. "One night, they tied me to a post down by the interstate and eight of them . . ." She stops and just freezes. It's like she's suddenly catatonic, like she can't move.

"Olivia?" I get no response. "Olivia, honey, hey." Then I reach up, catch a wisp of her hair, and push it behind her ear.

The minute my hand touches her skin, she lets out a shriek that makes the rest of us jump a foot, drops to the floor, and skitters off across the room and under the dining table. It takes me a minute or two to get my wits about me, but I hear Clint whisper, "PTSD." Sliding across the room, the hardwood slick under the knees of my jeans, I reach for her.

"NO!" she screams.

"Olivia, it's Dave. It's okay. You're fine. Come on out, honey."

"NO! Don't touch me!"

A voice behind me says, "Dad, let her calm down."

So I sit and wait. Eventually, Trish gets up and starts a pot of coffee. Clint starts taking tags off the things we bought, but I just sit there. She's been rocking to and fro, and she finally stops and looks at me. "Dave?"

I smile. "Yes, sweetie."

"Don't let them hurt me."

"I won't, baby. I'll never let them hurt you again." I've never said words that I meant more than those.

"You promise? You swear?"

"Absolutely. Clint, I keep my promises, right?"

"He does, Olivia. Always."

She eyes me suspiciously and doesn't say anything. Finally, I hear Clint say, "Olivia, we're going to have to go. Our kids are getting out of school, and we have to pick them up. You'll be fine here with Dave. Right, honey?"

Trish's voice calls back, "Oh, absolutely! Dave will take good care of you." She wanders into the room, then bends down to talk to Olivia under the table, her hair dropping and swishing on the floor. "You're perfectly safe here with Dave. And if you need us, he's got our phone numbers. All you have to do is call."

The timid little, "Okay," that slips from her lips sounds like it came from a five year old.

"Good girl. Can you come out and give me a hug before I leave? I'd love that." Trish straightens and steps back about two paces. Sure enough, Olivia slides out from under the table, stands on shaky legs, and throws her arms around Trish, who hugs her back and strokes her hair. "Now see, that wasn't so hard, was it?" Olivia shakes her head in reply and Trish grins at her. "You take care of Dave for us, please? He's always alone. He needs someone to watch out for him."

"Okay," she whispers back. As they start to the door, she calls out, "Thank you, Clint. Thank you, Trish. Thanks for being nice to me. Thanks so much."

A warm, genuine smile crosses my son's face. "You're quite welcome, missy. You take care of Dave and take care of yourself too, okay?"

"Okay." She gives them both a tiny little wave just before they close the door behind them, then turns to me. "I'm so sorry, Dave. I'm really, really sorry. Please don't be mad at me."

This beautiful woman breaks my heart. Her whole world is so fragile and tenuous, and I know she thinks anything and everything will come crashing down around her at any moment. I have to find a way to let her know that everything's going to be fine, but I don't know how. And before I can make her believe it, I've got to believe it myself. Trouble is, I don't know how to do that.

Then I realize: Shit. I've got to be at the club at six thirty. What am I going to do? I can't take her there; she'd be horrified. But I can't leave her here alone. She'll just have to come with me. I'm going to have to explain things to her, but right now, we've got to have something to eat. I go and root around in the refrigerator until

I come up with some sliced ham and sliced cheese, and there's a loaf of bread on the counter. I'm standing there, looking at my meager offering, when she walks up behind me. "Ham sandwiches. I love ham sandwiches. May I fix them? Please?"

I just shake my head in disbelief and tell her, "Sure! Knock yourself out. I don't have any chips, but I have popcorn."

"That sounds like fun." She finds the mayo and mustard and sets about putting together two sandwiches, then watches as I pop the popcorn in the microwave. Her voice is tiny and sad when I hear her say, "I remember doing that."

"Doing what, honey?"

"Popping popcorn. I had a microwave. And a refrigerator, and a sink, and a living room. I had all of that." Her face drops toward the floor, her shoulders quaking with stifled sobs, and I do what I always do – I just wrap my arms around her and she melts back into me.

I'm unable to process what's happening before she lifts her lips to mine and kisses me again, just like the night before. And this time, even though I know better, I kiss her back.

This is not what I wanted. It's not what I need. It's an unexpected complication that is going to cost me money and time and sleep, I know, not to mention worry and frustration and heartache. I don't want to want her, but I do, damn it, I do. Everything in my brain is on red alert, but everything in my body has a big green light glaring and I know I shouldn't act on it, but I can't seem to stop myself. What is it about this woman? She's barely more than a girl. Worse yet, she's wounded and scarred and torn apart by acts perpetrated against her while she was in the most vulnerable state she's ever been in, and yet here I am, up to my earlobes in trouble, kissing her like there's no tomorrow.

I play with subs all the time. I play with Marta and Angela. They're mature, experienced women, and they know how to satisfy a man. But this girl? This slip of a thing? There's nothing there that tells me she would ever know how to handle a man like me, but I'm so attracted to her that I can't think straight. Hell, I can barely breathe. Her body is pressed against mine and it feels like nothing ever has before, like someone custom-ordered her to fit against me, to take up space where I have it and retreat where I have a ripple or bulge. Puzzle pieces. The parts in the assembly package. A drawer in a dresser. It all fits, every inch of her against every rock-hard inch of me, and I can't think about pushing her away. All I want is to hold her to me tight and never let go.

We devour each other, and then she pulls away. There's a light in her eyes that I haven't seen before, and she puts a finger to her lips when I start to speak. On tiptoes, she leans into my ear and whispers something I'll never forget.

"I was made for you, Dave. I know it like I know the sun will come up tomorrow. And you were made for me too." I look down into her face as she steps back, and there's a smile there that takes my breath away.

Shit. I'm in trouble – deep, deep trouble.

My god, I'm glad we got those sandwiches down without any more complications. She sat at the table and hummed the whole time we ate. But I'm still glowing and my brain's buzzing from that kiss when we pull up in the parking lot of the club, then drive around the back. Once I park the car, I tell her, "I'm going to tell you what you can and can't do as we go along. Do not buck me, do you hear me? Do. Not. Buck. Me. When I tell you what to do and when, I mean it. Got it?"

"Yes, sir," she says with a flourishing salute. Great. A smart ass.

"I need to show you around, show you what goes on here without anyone here, okay? I don't want you scared." We stroll into the building and I turn lights on as we go. When we get to the big room, she looks around. "Ask any questions you want. But here's what we do. We practice bondage and discipline here. We apply punishment. We refine sado-masochistic behaviors here." When she gives me a blank look, I point at some of the equipment. "This equipment was intended to have people strapped to it so they can be disciplined or punished. Those implements," I say, pointing to the racks on the walls, "are intended for bare skin."

To my utter shock, all she says is, "I see."

I decide to go on. "We don't allow blade or needle play, but pretty much everything else goes. And there is sex out in the open here." Nothing registers on her face, no pain or confusion or fear or even excitement. "Any questions?"

"Men or women?" I wasn't expecting that to be the first question.

"Both. In any configuration. There are sadists here and there are masochists here. Dominants and submissives. I think we may only have one couple who practice a Master/slave kind of relationship."

She gives me a pointed stare. "And you?"

I've got to be honest with her. "I'm a Dominant."

She nods. "And you cause the pain?"

How to explain? I just say, "No. The pain is already there. I cause enough of another kind of pain to make the first one go away, at least temporarily."

"Do you have sex out here?"

I almost chuckle, but that wouldn't be appropriate. "I used to, but not so much anymore. I have to run the club. I occasionally get to play with a sub, but not often."

It's obvious she's mulling over all of this in her head. Finally, out of the blue, she asks, "So, I'm guessing you'd like to know if I'd be interested in any of this."

"I, well, um, you know, I never . . ."

"The answer is no. I've been tied up one too many times. I can't do that again." She just stops with that and continues to look around.

"Would you see yourself as being the one to mete out the punishment or discipline?"

She shakes her head. "No. I've had that done to me. I don't want to do it to someone else."

"Remember," I tell her, "these people came here of their own free will. They want this. So it's not like they're being forced to do anything."

Her shoulders lift in a shrug. "Still, not interested."

"Uh-huh. Okay. Just wanted to ask."

"Thank you for asking." She wanders around for a little while longer, then takes a seat on a bar stool. "So do you want me to stay out here with you tonight?"

"Will that make you uncomfortable?"

She nods. "Yeah. Sorry. Just the truth."

"Then you can stay in my office. I have a laptop back there, and you can play games or send email or . . ."

She giggles. "Who on earth would I send an email to?"

"I don't know. Anyone you wanted, I suppose."

"Hmmmm."

"Members will start coming in before long. Let's get you settled back there." I lead the way back to the office and point at the desk. "It's in that drawer there. Just pull out the drawer and you can use the laptop. My bathroom," I point behind her, "is right back there. There's stuff to drink in the fridge over there. And I'll lock the back door so no one can get in and surprise you. Nobody should be coming in through there anyway."

"Is there a phone?"

"Yeah. It's right there." I point to a small, older cell lying on the desk. "It's old. I just keep it for emergencies."

"Oh. Okay. But it's okay if I call someone?"

Who in the hell would she want to call? "Sure. Just not to China. Definitely not to China," I grin at her.

"Okay. No China!" she laughs.

"Good deal."

"Hey, Dave?"

"Yes, blossom?"

"Can I have Trish's number?"

"Sure." I jot it down on a piece of paper. "But they may very well be here tonight, so if she doesn't answer, she may actually be here. If they show up, I'll tell them you're back here – I'm sure they'll come back and say hi. Oh, here. This is *my* number. If you need me, just call it. Unless you can handle walking past all of the scenes going on out front." I scribble it under Trish's.

"Got it. Thanks, Dave. Thank you so much. Really. Thanks."

"Stop it." Both hands on the desk, I lean down toward her as she sits there. "You're welcome. Always. More than. Now entertain yourself. We're going to be here for quite some while, so get comfortable. And if you need anything," I say, pointing at the phone, then head out the office door.

"Sure. Dave?"

Wheeling to face her, I smile.

"I meant what I said earlier."

"I know you think you did. This is all new to you, baby. It'll all look different in a few weeks."

"No. It won't. But nice try." She shoots me a lopsided grin and I chuckle out loud, then make my way through the crowd to the bar.

We haven't been open more than thirty minutes before Clint and Trish come through the door, and they're both wearing grim expressions that I can't read. Trish walks right up to me, leans in, and asks, "So have you done anything with her?"

"What?"

"I mean it, Dave. Have you done anything with her?"

"You mean *sex*?"

"Yes, I mean sex."

"No!" I don't dare tell her what happened earlier. "Why? What's wrong?"

"I got a call from her. Have you checked your trash cans?"

"No. For what?"

"She called to tell me you have no paper towel in your bathroom back there and she needed some. She's bleeding."

It takes me a few seconds to get her meaning, and then I have to shake the cobwebs from my brain. "Bleeding? What the hell?"

"Exactly what I want to know. I'm going back there to talk to her. I'll be back in a bit." I watch her stride across the room and disappear into the hallway.

"What the hell is that about?"

"I have no idea." Clint reaches for the glass of bourbon I've poured for him. "I just know her phone rang and she almost didn't answer it, but I'm glad she did. And the longer she listened, the more worked up she got. But I really don't know what's going on." We sit in silence and wait for Trish. Twenty minutes later, she appears at the bar.

My question is, "Well? What's going on?"

Trish climbs onto a stool. "That's why she wanted to know if she could make a call. She needed to talk to someone, but she was embarrassed for it to be you."

"I can understand that. But what's the . . ."

"Tomorrow I'm making an appointment for her with my doctor. She needs to be seen. She says she's been bleeding since the third or fourth time they raped her and it won't stop. It's not a lot, but it just keeps coming. She needs to be seen."

"Yes she does. I'll gladly pay," I offer.

Trish looks relieved. "Thanks. Because this could be expensive and we have a household budget . . ."

"No. I want to. Don't give it another thought. And I'll want to know what's going on."

Trish pats my hand. "Try to get her to talk to you about it when you get home. Maybe she will. But I'm guessing it's just too embarrassing for her."

I can understand that. And I don't want that for her. I want her to be healthy and happy.

But more and more, I want her to be with me. And that's just not right.

<hr>

"So you called Trish. You guys have a good talk?" We're on our way home, and I'm trying to break the ice.

"Um-hmmm," she answers, still staring out the car window instead of at me.

"Get things straightened out?"

"Um-hmmm."

She's not going to talk to me. I can feel it. So I try a new tactic. "So I like to go to the gym most days. Do you like doing things like that?"

She still doesn't turn toward me, but she says, "Yeah. I used to be a member of a gym. I enjoyed it."

"Well, you can go with me. I'd love for you to come. But no pressure."

"Sure." Well, that's a surprise. She wants to go to the gym! I was just sure she'd say no, but sounds like she's up for it. "I don't have anything to wear, though."

I'm passing Walmart, so I just wheel into the parking lot. "Let's go get you some yoga pants and a couple of tops. And a couple of sports bras." Then I laugh. "And some athletic shoes and socks. And a package of headbands and some ponytail thingies."

"Ponytail thingies," she giggles.

"Hell, I don't know what they're called!" Laughing, we head into the store.

When we walk through the doors, there are two police officers at the service desk, and I feel Olivia bristle, so I grab her arm and turn her to look at me. "Listen to me: Just don't look at them. Pretend they're not there. Pretend it's only you and me in the store and everyone else has gone home. Sing a song in your head until we get out of their sight, okay? It'll be okay, baby. Really. They're not going to hurt you."

I take her arm and power on through the doors and toward the exercise gear. As soon as we wind our way through the ladies' department and they're out of sight, she relaxes. We find stuff – a lot of stuff, so much stuff I have to go get a cart – then go find her some tennis shoes and socks, after which we visit health and beauty and get what she calls ponytail elastics, plus a couple of headbands. Hell, I don't know about this stuff. A lot has changed since my daughter Kathy was a little kid. Before we head up to the front, I suggest that she get some pads or something, just so she'll be prepared; at least that's the excuse I give her. I watch as she gingerly picks out a box of tampons and a box of pads, then puts them in the cart and just refuses to look at me. It's kinda cute.

As we stand in the checkout line, she looks the candy bars over. Picking one up, she sniffs it, then puts it back. "Smell good?"

She shakes her head. "I can't smell it through the wrapper." She picks up another – same procedure.

"Want one?"

"Oh, no, I couldn't . . ."

"I've got a cart full of clothes for you and you don't think you'll let me buy you a candy bar?" I start taking candy off the rack. "Tell me what you want or I'll get one of everything. And you'll have all that candy to eat. You'll eat it until you puke it." The lady in front of me glares at me, but I just grin at her. "So? What'll it be?"

Her eyes dance and sparkle – the "kid in the candy store" analogy doesn't even touch it. It's like Christmas morning and the best thing she's ever gotten as a present. Finally she looks at me and says, "I can't choose. I like these two. Which one should I get?"

I just take them both from her. "No choice. See? That was easy!" Her frown makes me laugh right out loud, but I put them on the belt and pay for them, then hand them to her. The look on her face breaks my heart again.

A candy bar. A bag of chips. A clean place to sleep. She hasn't asked for anything, and everything I do for her is treated like the most wonderful prize anyone ever won.

It's terrifying. It's only been about twenty-four hours, and I think I'm falling in love with Olivia.

———◦◦◦◦———

I manage to get all of her workout wear and all the clothes we bought earlier in the day washed and hung up so she'll have things to wear. She still needs bras and underwear, but we'll take care of that sometime soon.

Bless her heart, she wants to pop more popcorn, so I tell her how long to set the microwave for, then have to show her how it works. It's not because she doesn't know how to operate one. It's because every damn one of them is so different. Once it starts popping, she's practically bouncing up and down as she watches the bag expanding through the window on the microwave.

We have a soft drink and popcorn, and then it's time for bed. Face washed, teeth brushed, hair brushed, and a pair of lounge pants and a tee shirt on, I crawl in between the sheets and take a deep breath. I'm treading in dangerous territory, and I know it. This girl is just that – a girl. I'm a grown man, old enough to be her grandfather. But everything about me, my head, my heart, my cock – they all want her. I'm trying to figure out how best to keep that from being a problem when I hear a soft knock on my door. Shit. I can't ignore her, and I let out a deep sigh before I say, "Come in."

There she stands in nothing but a pair of panties and one of my huge tees. Her legs are beautiful, and she's standing there, so unsure of herself. "Can I talk to you for a minute?"

"Sure, hon. Sit down." She sits on the edge of the bed down at the foot, and I sit up and prop myself up with pillows. "What's up?"

She turns a deep shade of scarlet. "Um, Trish told me I should talk to you about, um, a problem I'm having."

"Yeah?"

"I'm, uh, it's almost like a lady problem but, uh, it's not stopping."

"You mean you're bleeding?"

"Yeah."

I nod. "Yeah, I know. Trish told me."

"Oh." And there she goes, staring at the floor again.

"Honey, she wasn't betraying your confidence. She's afraid something's wrong with you, and she wanted me to know in case you had a problem. That's all. Just a safety thing."

"Oh," she says again.

"Do you have any idea what's wrong?" I'm terrified of the answer.

"Yeah." She hesitates, then says, "I think they hurt me."

"Trish is taking you to the doctor, right?"

"Yeah. I hope tomorrow."

Something crosses my mind. "Are you in pain?"

It happens, that thing that tears out my heart. A tear

rolls down her cheek. "All the time."

God, I want to hold her and tell her everything will be okay. "Oh, baby, I'm so sorry."

"It's okay," she sniffles. "It's not your fault."

"I know, but I'm still sorry. The doctor will help you."

"I hope so. Will you go to the doctor with me?"

My smile is soft and warm, and I choose my words carefully. "Honey, that's kind of a lady thing, and I'm not even related to you. I don't think they'd let me go back there. But they'll let Trish if you want her to, so she's the one to go with you. But it'll be all right. You'll see."

"Okay." She looks so sad. She's been in pain all this time? That cuts me to the quick. How has she been able to stand it? "I think I'm going to bed now. So good night." Standing, she looks at me like she wants to kiss me, then leaves the room and closes the door behind her.

Whew. Crisis averted, although knowing that she's in pain would've stopped me from doing something that would be extremely stupid. But I don't need to flirt with this; I need to nip it in the bud. I snuggle down into my sheets and try to think of something else. I think about Kathy and how I don't see her very often, only when she needs something, but that's okay. I wasn't around for her much when she was growing up. And I think about Clint, what a fine guy he's turned out to be, and how happy he is now, he and the kids, since Trish has been in their lives. I think about Marta and how much I've always loved her, and Angela, that beauty who stole her away.

I'm just about to drift off, dreaming of doing a couple of the subs from the club in a threesome, and I hear a shriek, loud and long. I almost fall trying to get out of bed, and I run down the hall and throw open the bedroom door.

Olivia is standing on the bed, sitting on the top edge of the headboard, hands drawn up under her chin and screaming bloody murder. When I reach for her, she yells out, "Don't touch me! I don't want to do that with you! Please don't hurt me! Please? Please?" I touch her, and she starts fighting my hands away, screaming and banging against the wall behind the head of the bed.

"Olivia! OLIVIA! Wake up, honey! It's me – it's Dave! Wake up, baby! It's okay, really. It's just a bad dream."

It's like she freezes, just goes motionless, and then she blinks a couple of times. Her eyelids flutter oddly, and then she shakes her head a couple of times and moans out, "Dave?"

"Yes, baby. I'm right here. You had a nightmare, but you're okay. Come on, let me help you get back into the bed. Come on. It's okay."

She's shaking like a leaf, trembling from head to toe, and she almost can't make her legs work well enough to drop onto the bed. Sitting in the bed, she whispers, "They were trying to get me. They were trying to make me do things I didn't want to do with them. Please, Dave, please, don't let them get me."

"They can't get you, honey. You're here and you're

safe. Now go back to sleep." I run a hand across her forehead and then lean down to kiss it. "I'll see you in the morning. Go back to sleep." In seconds, she's calmed and rolled over.

But I've no more than gotten the covers back up over me when I hear a soft knocking. "Yeah?" The door opens slightly and she slithers in through the crack. "You okay, honey?"

"Dave?"

I know as sure as I'm lying here what's coming. "Yeah, hon?"

"Dave, can I sleep with you? I'm scared."

Yup – there it is. Oh, god. What do I do now? My mind whirs. If I let her into my bed, I don't know if I can control myself. Wait – something's wrong with her and she's in pain. I can use that to my advantage, tell myself that nothing can happen because it could hurt her. Yeah. That's it. It'll be okay. "Okay, baby. Get on in here." I lift the covers so she can slide in and brace myself for all the things I'm going to feel.

Good thing, too. It hits me all at once, and it takes everything I've got to be able to just let her scoot up against me without touching her in a way I don't want to. Well, okay – that's a lie. I want to. I just don't *need* to. I shouldn't. And I've got to remember that.

But she slides right up against me with her back to me, and then into me so we're spooning. I can't help it; my arms instinctively go around her and I pull her close. Her hair smells like the lavender shampoo Trish bought for her, and I can smell the peppermint of her toothpaste on her breath. Why did I let her into my bed? How can I keep her out of my heart? I know the answer to the first question. But the second one? I have no clue.

After a few minutes, I feel her relax against me and she lets out a deep sigh. Trust is something I don't take lightly, and she trusts me. I can't let her down. The sleep I fall into is troubled, and I know the next day won't be any easier for me. She's gotten under my skin.

Chapter Four

The sun streams in through the crack between the curtains and lights up the room enough that I know it's morning. Olivia's not in bed, and the sound of banging pots and pans echoes through the house. But before I can get up and see what's going on, the door opens and she marches in, a plastic tray in her hands. On it is two pieces of toast, two eggs, and two pieces of bacon. "I had this in the fridge?"

"Yes, you did. And I made it for you, seeing as how I messed up yesterday."

"You didn't mess up yesterday. We just let it get cold, that's all." It's not a big breakfast, but it's more than I'm accustomed to. No one's fixed me breakfast in years, and now two days in a row? I could get used to this. *Stop it, Adams!*, I tell myself. *No. That can't happen.* "So what does your day look like?"

"Trish called me. She got me an appointment, and she's coming to pick me up at ten."

My head snaps around to the alarm clock. Seven forty-one. "Oh my god. It's not even eight o'clock yet."

"So you're up early!"

"I run a club. I'm used to sleeping late because I'm up late."

Instant sorrow hits me as her face turns red and she stares at her hands in her lap. "I'm sorry. I should've asked first. My fault. I'm so sorry."

"No, no, I should probably be getting up earlier anyway. But yes, you need to get ready for your day. Did you fix yourself some breakfast?"

She shakes her head. "No. There wasn't enough for both of us."

I pat the spot beside me in the bed. "Get in here."

"No, I made it for . . ."

"I said get in here. No arguing. I mean it. You need to eat. Get up here and sit down right now." When she finally gets cuddled up against me, I pick up one of the pieces of bacon. "Open your mouth."

"But Dave . . ."

"I said open it." I sit stock still and glare at her until she finally opens her mouth, and then I stick the bacon in until she bites off a piece. Then I take a bite off of it and chew. That makes her laugh, and she opens her mouth again like a baby bird. I give her another bite, then I take another. Three rounds and it's gone.

We eat an egg the same way, alternating with bites of toast, until it's gone, then the other piece of bacon followed by the other egg and toast slice. When I take the last bite of bacon, I smile at her. "Thanks. That was very good."

"You're welcome. I hope you didn't mind me cooking it."

"Mind? Frankly, I didn't even know it was in there. I don't remember buying it."

"Well, it's gone now and you're going to need some food. The refrigerator and cabinets are pretty much empty. You should go to the store."

"*You* should go to the store. Find things you know how to fix. Wait: Do you even like to cook?"

"I *love* to cook! I used to cook all the time. But then, well, I couldn't cook anymore. One time some of the guys stole some stuff from a grocery. They didn't even know what to do with it. I asked them to start a fire and I took all the stuff they'd stolen and made a big meal. It was really good. They were so surprised! And then one of them got knifed by a crazy guy and died, so I never saw them again."

Good god. She just said that like it was an everyday occurrence. That's frightening to me. "So how often did that happen? I mean, something like a knifing?"

"Oh, just about every other day. A knifing, fighting over a blanket or something. Or a car would pull up and people would start getting out and beating the homeless people closest to them, sometimes with baseball bats. It was awful. It was something all the time. I was glad when I got skinny. Made it easier to hide, you know? To kind of slip into the shadows so they couldn't see me. So I'd be invisible."

What kind of hell is that to live in? No wonder she thanked me over and over. She lived in a nightmare. Then I remember the nightmare from the night before. "Do you remember your nightmare last night?"

I see her body tremble. "Yeah. It was horrible. They were all coming toward me and they had their pants unzipped and they were telling me all the things they were going to do to me. It was terrible. I was so afraid."

Without thinking, I put an arm around her and draw her up against me, and she rests her head on my shoulders. She's so precious. A little soft kiss gets planted on her forehead, and then she looks up at me so innocently when she asks, "Dave? Do you think you could ever love me?"

"Olivia, I don't think . . ."

"Please. Don't talk like that. You're so wonderful. I want to stay here with you forever."

"I'm not wonderful." Now my cheeks are scalding. "I own a club where people walk around naked. I enjoy whipping subs until they scream. I'll have sex with pretty much any woman who approaches me in the club. I'm a long, long way from wonderful. I'm actually a pretty horrible guy. My world is pretty dark."

"I want to be part of your world. Please, Dave? Please let me be part of your world?" And she does it again.

She kisses me. This girl has got to stop this. I've got to stop this. I'm trying to stop it, but I can't, and the kiss just grows and expands. Next thing I know, she's flat on the bed and I'm on top of her, my hands in her hair, kissing her, pressing her into the mattress. Her fingertips skate up and down the surface of my shirt, and then I feel them slip underneath it. What was throbbing is now rock hard, and it's difficult to breathe or sit still. God help me, I'm going down and she's taking me. I'm trying to stop kissing her, and I can't. This is too much, it's just too much.

"Olivia." She kisses me again. "Olivia, Trish will be here in a bit," I whisper into her neck. "You have to be ready to go."

"Come with me?"

"No, sweetie. No. You go with Trish." I force myself up onto my hands and look down at her. Damn, I want to bury my dick in her and pump away, but that's not going to happen. I involuntarily let out a groan as I fall to my back on the bed beside her, and she rolls to rest her cheek on my shoulder.

"Dave?"

"Yes."

"Promise me that at some time in the near future, you'll stop being afraid and let me in."

I just stare up at the ceiling – I can't look at her. "Olivia, I can't let you in like that. Do you realize how far apart our ages are? It's not going to happen, sweetheart. I should be treating you like a daughter."

I feel the disconnect, its abruptness palpable. She rises, sits on the edge of the bed for a few seconds with her back to me, then mutters, "I'm a grown woman." With that, she stands and drags out of my bedroom. Five minutes later I hear the shower start. I'm in the clear for the time being. It'll be best if I just hide out and wait until she's gone before I come out to shower.

I must've dozed off because I wake to voices, and I recognize one of them as Trish's. I get up from the bed and stumble up the hallway. "Good morning, sleepy-head!" Trish calls out in her effervescent voice.

"Hey, doll. You doing okay?"

"Great! I'm taking your girl here to the doctor."

There's an overwhelming urge in my throat to say, *She's not my girl,* but I don't. I just say, "Well, you guys be careful. See you when you get back."

"I think we may go for some lunch afterward." She glances at Olivia, who gives her a nod and a smile. "Want to come too?"

"Nope. You girls go and do girl things. You know, those things guys don't like to do," I chuckle.

"Yeah, yeah. Party pooper."

"No, that's Sheila," I laugh.

"Yeah. Well, not so much anymore!" Trish is laughing right along with me. Olivia's face is a big question mark when Trish says, "Oh, long story, honey. I'll tell you in the car." She looks at her watch, and I notice Olivia looking at her bare arm too. "We'd better get moving. Bye," Trish tells me with a kiss on the cheek.

"Yeah, bye." Olivia tries to do the same, but instead, she kisses me right on the mouth. Out of my peripheral vision I can see Trish's brows shoot up. Not good. I'm guessing I'm going to get grilled about this.

I get showered and dressed, and then a crazy idea strikes me. It's something I shouldn't do, but I decide to do it anyway. Why, I don't know. But I get into the car and head for the mall. It shouldn't take me long, and boy, won't she be surprised?

The trash can is almost filled with all the junk I've taken out of the pantry. Olivia was talking about buying food, so I need to get the past-dated stuff out. There's an awful lot of it, and it's weird stuff, like canned cabbage and strawberry pie filling – and I don't bake. Very strange. By the time they walk in, I've pretty much gotten it cleaned out and filled up the dumpster outside to boot.

"Hey! We're back!" Trish strides in and sits down on the sofa. Olivia stands there like she doesn't quite know what to do or say.

"Hi!" I expect a smile, but Olivia doesn't look like a smile. She looks kind of bewildered. "Everything go okay?"

"Yeah, pretty much. Olivia will tell you about it when I'm gone. Right, sweetie?"

She stares at me and shrugs. "Yeah, okay."

Trish stands again. "Well, I guess I'd better go. I have to pick up some cookies for a party at the school and then get over there. It's Hailee's teacher's birthday." She pats Olivia on the shoulder. "Now you've got those antibiotics to take, so don't forget. And she told you what to do for the other thing, right?" Olivia nods. "Let me know when they schedule it and I'll come and take you, no problem, okay?"

"Sure." There's something hollow in her eyes that I can't translate, and it's scaring me a little.

"See you two later. Love you, Dave," she says as she gives me a kiss on the cheek. I squeeze her tight.

"Tell Clint and the kids I said hello, please."

"Will do. Bye." With that, the door closes and I'm

alone with Olivia, whose face still looks like something horrible has bitten her.

After a few seconds, I ask her, "Want something to drink?"

She shakes her head. "No. I had something at lunch."

"Okay then. Want to sit down and talk? Trish said you'd fill me in." Her legs seem a little wobbly as she crosses to the sofa. She sits down in a very prim and proper fashion with her hands folded in her lap, and I'm starting to feel very scared. "Olivia, what's going on?"

About that time, my text messaging goes off. I glance at my phone to see a notification from Trish. It's short and sweet.

Be extra gentle with her. Her heart is broken.

What the hell? The gynecologist broke her heart? This doesn't make any sense at all. "Olivia, you need to tell me what's going on. You're scaring me. What are they scheduling? I don't understand." A single tear rolls down her cheek, but I try to temper my feelings with the way Trish was behaving and talking, like it was an every-day occurrence and nothing to worry about. "Please, baby?"

"I, I, oh, noooo." She leans down with her forehead on her knees and I feel slightly dizzy. "I have to have one of those D&C things."

"Oh! Those aren't that bad. What did they find?" When she doesn't answer, I move to sit beside her and stroke her hair. "Baby, what did they find? What's causing the problem?"

"I was pregnant."

I feel like somebody hit me in the gut. "You were pregnant?" She nods and keeps crying. "I don't understand."

"I had a miscarriage and didn't know it. And there's stuff still in there, and an infection." Her crying quiets just a little, and she adds, "They said it was probably when I got hit in the stomach by that one cop."

"Hit in the stomach?"

"Yeah. He wanted me to get down on my knees and, well, you know, and when I wouldn't, he started punching me in the stomach until I just fell to my knees. And then he made me do it. But they said that's probably when I had the miscarriage."

Oh my god. No wonder Trish said Olivia's heart was broken. Before I can pull her to me and hold her tight, she cries out, "Oh, god, why did all of that stuff happen to me? Why did they treat me that way? What did I ever do that was so awful that people would hate me so much?"

With my arms finally around her, she just dissolves, and all the brokenness and hurt from the last three years, all the bitterness, swirls around her and threatens to drown her. I hold onto her as tightly as I can and let her cry on my chest. Finally, I ask her, "Olivia, if you were still pregnant and we hadn't found you, what would you have done?"

Through her sniffles she whispers, "I don't know."

"So see? Things happen the way they're supposed to

happen. It's okay."

"But if I were, just think: I'm here. You would've been able to help me. And I would have a baby, a child, to love and take care of."

"Olivia, you still don't have a home. How in the world do you think you'd be able to take care of a baby?"

"You'd help me."

"Sweetie, I'm sixty-five. I can't raise a child."

The look in her eyes is foreign to me as she says, "I think I'm going to bed. I'm really tired." With that, she just rises and leaves the room.

I'm still sitting there shell-shocked. My god. How much should one person be expected to take? I manage to get ready for bed and get comfortable when, once again, there's a knock on my door. "Come on in." Before she can speak, I chuckle. "Yes. Get in here." She slides in just like the night before.

"Dave?"

"Yes, sweetie?"

"Thanks for the pajamas. Where did they come from?"

I wondered when she'd ask about them. "I got them at the mall this afternoon."

"How did you know I like butterflies?"

I just smile to myself. "I didn't. I just thought about how cute they'd be on you. And tomorrow morning, be sure to look in your dresser drawer. I got you a watch."

She sighs against me. "You're the best person I've ever met. Ever."

My arms tighten around her and I feel whole with

her there, her body pressed against mine. "I don't know about that, but what I do know is that you'll never, never have to live in fear again, not as long as I have breath."

In a whisper that sounds more like a lullaby, she murmurs, "I believe you." And in ten minutes, we're sound asleep.

I get up the next morning to find homemade Danish and fresh, hot coffee. Olivia is writing something on a piece of note paper from my desk by the front door. "What's up, pretty thing?"

"Writing down this appointment. I used your phone to call them and I used your number as a call-back. I hope that was all right." When I smile and nod, she adds, "They're going to do the procedure next Wednesday at seven in the morning. I've got to call Trish and tell her."

My heart's still tender from the night before. "I can take you."

Her eyes swivel to mine. "You said if I needed to go to . . ."

"Yeah, but this is different. They're going to anesthetize you. You may need someone bigger and stronger than Trish to help you into the car, into the house, that kind of thing. And I'd love to go with you."

Her eyes light up just a bit. "You would go with me?"

"Of course! If you want me to."

"Oh, yes, I do. Please. I'd feel so much better if you were there."

"Then I'll be there." Desperation has set in, a desperation to help her and shield her, to keep her safe and comfortable. I don't want her to go through this alone.

But Trish would be there. Why would it be necessary for it to be me? Now I'm feeling desperation, but of a different kind. I'm getting too attached to this girl, and I know I need to back off, but I can't. She needs me, and I need her. Why? I didn't need her two days ago – I didn't even know she existed. There's so much confusion in my mind, just rolling around and making me question everything.

"But Dave?" Yanked back into the present, into the kitchen with its pots and pans and dishes and towels, I look around to find Olivia standing at the sink instead of sitting at the table, staring out the window instead of looking at me. "If you don't want to go, it's okay."

I snap back, "I said I'd go. Why wouldn't I go?"

"I just don't want you to feel obligated. I've already imposed so much on you and your time." She looks like she's folding in on herself. Was I thinking out loud? Did I say something really stupid?

My coffee cup makes a thud on the table as I set it down and stand at the same time. Only five feet separates us, but in that moment, it's about six feet too many. Resting my hands on the sink on either side of her, I breathe into her hair as I quietly reiterate, "I'll be there. I want to be there. With you. Nowhere else will do. Got it?"

She wheels quickly and our faces are less than an inch apart. Before she speaks, I see her swallow hard, and then I watch her lips tremble as she says, "Got it. Dave, I . . ."

My lips crush hers and all I can think about is my next breath into her. Any common sense I might've had withers, dries up, and blows away, and I run one hand around behind her waist, up her spine, straight up her neck, and into her hair, where I grab a handful and pull her head back to break the kiss. I look down to find her looking back up at me, her eyes lit up with lust, and I hover over her like a cloud. There's no thinking or wondering or deciding, just this moment with this young woman and a need that's rising up inside me unlike anything I've ever known. My mouth covers hers and I pour myself into her like water into a glass while her arms wrap around my waist and tighten. Time stands still; it's just the two of us, and the rest of the world falls away to leave us standing here in this split second in time. Unable to control myself, I feel my body press into hers, press her into the edge of the counter behind her, and I give her hair a tug just to hear her moan into my mouth.

And then the ringing of my cell snaps everything back into place and I'm left wondering what just happened, how much of my mind I just lost, and why I'm standing in my kitchen, kissing a girl who's less than half my age, a girl who's lost everything and trying to find herself with all the odds against her. Without turning loose of her hair, I reach into my pocket and draw out my phone, but I don't look at the screen before I growl into it, "Hello?"

"Dad? You okay?"

Clint's voice draws me back into the room, and I release her hair and pull my body away from hers. "Yeah. Everything's fine. What's up?"

His voice drops to not much over a whisper. "I need to talk to you. Is Olivia there close?"

"Yeah."

"It needs to be away from her. Can you step outside?"

"Yeah. Hang on." I kiss her forehead and ignore the confused look in her eyes. "I'll be back in just a second." When my feet hit the porch deck and the door closes behind me, I breathe out, "Okay, what's going on?"

"Steffen struck up a conversation with someone at the bank, someone who works for him. Her husband is a police officer, and a fine, upstanding police officer at that. When he mentioned that someone he knew had been brutalized by the cops, this woman said her husband had told her there was an investigation going on into some cops who've been sexually assaulting homeless women."

"Shit."

"Yeah. Seems they're working on the case, but there's no evidence. And Olivia could be the key."

I feel my heart start to hammer. "Steffen didn't tell her anything, did he?"

"No, but he fished around as much as he dared; he'll just have to take it slow. We do know who's spearheading the investigation. I want a picture of him to show to Olivia. If the cop in charge is one of the abusers, then we'll know that something's really wrong."

"And how can you get a photo?"

"If Steffen can get the name of the cop, their photos are posted online on the police department's website. If any of the cops working on the investigation are the guys who brutalized them, we'll have to get her out of town. If not, we'll have to get her to talk to someone. Steffen's working on it, and I'll let you know as soon as I know something. Trish told me what the doctor said. She okay?"

"Yeah. I think so. Shaken up and afraid, but okay. Tell Steffen I said thanks and I'll hang tight until you get more info. I'm not saying anything to her until we have a photo."

"Good deal. Thanks, Dad. Thanks for caring about her and taking an interest in her."

My mouth says, "You're welcome. Thanks for being here for her too." But my brain is screaming, *You might not say that if you knew what I was thinking about doing to her.* Because now I know, and there's no point trying to deny it to myself. I want to fuck Olivia Warren. And I want to do it until I know she's mine. I hit END, my mind still reeling, and wander back into the house.

The kitchen is cleaned up except for my Danish and cup of coffee, and Olivia is nowhere to be found. Listening closely, I can hear the shower running, and I head to mine. I shave quickly, then step into the steamy embrace of the scalding water, its healing touch comforting and energizing at the same time. Hair washed, I start my usual manscaping, made easier by the fact that I have a raging hard on, rock solid and throbbing. I manage the trim job, but my erection just won't go away, and I grab my body wash and lather it up. The tension in my spine grows and doubles over on itself as my fingers slide up and down, grazing the tip of the head before they go back down to the base and start all over. I'm wound tight like a panther, and then I see it.

Movement. And I know that she's watching me. I don't have to turn and look; I can feel her there, taking in the view through the shower curtain, and I'm in misery. By the time I'm ready to come, I'm almost frantic, wanting that release that I can't have inside her, wanting her to see what it looks like to be wanted by me. A massive groan erupts from my throat as I come, forced up onto my toes, my back bowed, pearly ropes of cum splashing onto the wall of the shower and running down in the hot water. That's the power she has over me. I'm panting, and not just in ecstatic exhaustion.

It's fear. I know I can't do this, shouldn't do this. Most men would know better, but I feel drawn to her. If it's out of pity, it's wrong, but it doesn't feel like pity. It feels like softness and warmth and something I haven't experienced in a long time. There's a peace that rules that bedroom when she crawls into my bed and rests in my arms. It has nothing to do with sex and everything to do with sex. Slumping back against the tiled wall to catch my breath, I see that movement again and I know she's gone.

Now she knows. Dear god, what does that mean for me?

Chapter Five

It's been awkward, very awkward. She knows, and she's been especially odd around me, which is difficult, seeing as how we're in the same house. The last two nights she didn't want to go to the club, so she spent one with Clint and Trish, and the next with Steffen and Sheila. They all told me she was great with their kids, and they were glad to have her. The "other thing" Trish had mentioned was the wounds on her back and ass, and Trish took a look at them while she was there, proclaiming them much better. That's an improvement.

She wasn't able to have anything to eat last night, so Clint and Trish were careful to eat before she got there, and I ate after I dropped her off. When I make it to the kitchen this morning, she's standing there, looking at the fruit on the countertop like it's spun gold. "Nothing for you, missy."

She shoots me a little shy smile. "What do you want me to fix for you?"

"Nothing. I'm not going to eat in front of you."

"You shouldn't go hungry because of me. Besides, I'm used to being hungry. It's no big deal."

See, that right there – that tears me up. The more I know about her, the more torn up I get. "Nope. I'm not doing that to you. When they take you back, I'll go get something at the vending area in the building."

"Okay." She stands there for a few minutes like she doesn't know what to say or do while I drink a cup of coffee. Finally, she says, "Well, then, I'm going to take my shower."

"Me too. We've got two hours, so we should be fine."

"Okay. Thanks. Thanks so much, Dave, really. Thank you."

Not touching her is killing me, so I motion her over to me, then take both of her hands in mine. "You're welcome for the millionth time. And I want to help you, baby. I want to be here for you as long as you need me."

"I'll always need you. I'll never stop needing you."

I chuckle. "Oh, yeah, eventually you won't need me. You'll get back on your feet, find some handsome young guy, fall in love, and old Dave'll be history. I mean, I'll always be here, grandpa to your kids, friend when you want one, but you won't need me anymore." I'm trying to laugh it off, but inside, the thought of all of those things makes me weep.

"No." She shakes her head. "I'll always need you. I don't want those things. I only want . . ."

I press a finger over her lips. "Go get ready. Dress warmer than usual; anesthesia makes you cold, maybe bring a sweater or something. I'll see you in a bit." There's a hurt look in her eyes that'll haunt me for the next couple of days – only the next couple of days, if I'm lucky – and I feel a stab of guilt cut through my heart. I've gotten too attached to her, and I know it. It isn't natural. She needs a life that doesn't have anything to do with me. That's not what I want, maybe not what she wants, but it's what she needs.

When I'm ready and step into the living room, she's already there, her hair glossy, cheeks rosy from her shower, and wearing her yoga pants, a tee shirt, and sitting with a sweater draped across her lap. She looks so lost and afraid and helpless, and I just want to take all of that fear and uncertainty onto myself so she doesn't have to feel it. "Ready?"

"Sure." She stands without ever looking at me, and I regret that kiss those days before and all that it meant. The trip to the outpatient medical center is quiet, only broken by her asking me questions about particular businesses or buildings along the way. We pass a car dealership. "Lots of cars," she mumbles.

"Yeah." Then I think of something. "Do you drive?"

"Yeah, but I have no license, of course."

"Let's take care of that. Let's get your license back."

She shrugs and still doesn't look at me. "Why? I don't have a car."

"But you will." She just sighs. "You'll eventually get a car. Do you *want* one?"

"I don't know. Maybe. I haven't really thought about it in a long, long time." She's still gazing out, her right temple pressed against the glass of the car window as she watches the world go by. This must all seem so foreign to her now.

The outpatient center isn't very big, and neither is the parking lot, but we get almost to the building and she stops right in the middle of the drive. What I hear coming from her is an odd, "Ohhhhh, ohhhhh, ohhhhh, noooooo, nooooo, please, nooooo . . ." I look around and then I see him.

A security guard. She's gripping my hand so hard that I think she's cutting off the circulation in my fingers, and she's stopped dead and won't move forward. I lean down to her ear, and say, "Honey, he's just a security guard. It's okay."

Her eyes are wide and she's shaking, and that sound comes out again, "Nooooooo . . ."

"Yes. We have to go in. It's okay, really." I think for a second. "Look, just scoot under my arm here and stick to me. I won't let anything happen to you, you know that."

She's panting now. "Police."

"No, he's not police. He's just security." I manage to get her to move toward the building haltingly, and the doors open automatically. He turns to see who's entering and smiles at me, then frowns.

"Miss, you okay?" She buries her face in my ribcage and whimpers.

"She's fine. She's just got to have a procedure and she's a little scared."

"Which doc?"

"Um, Dr. Cavanaugh?"

"Oh, she's so nice! She and my wife are friends; my

wife's a nurse, see." He breaks into a warm smile. "Such a nice lady. And a good doctor too. I'm sure you'll be fine." I look around and he says, "Right over there, to your right."

"Thanks so much. Come on, honey, it'll be all right." I manage to get her shuffling that way.

"Have a good day!" he calls after us. I hear her whimper again, and I just tighten my arm around her.

When the door to the suite closes behind us, I feel her sigh and relax just a little. We choose seats by the window so she can look out, and I go up to the desk and check her in. They make me pay up front for her procedure – it's not cheap, not by a long shot, but she has to have it and it's the only way it'll get done. I don't want her going to some free clinic or something. If they see her wounds, they'll probably start asking questions and then alert the police. We can't have that. She's tapping her foot nervously on the floor until I get back and sit down beside her. Taking her hand, I whisper to her, "They said it'll be about fifteen minutes. Need anything?"

"Yeah. I need to go to the bathroom."

"I think that's it right over there." I watch her go and hope she comes back out or I'll have to go in and get her. But in about four minutes she's back and sits down beside me. She still never really looks at me. "You okay?"

"Yes. No. I don't know." She looks away.

"Olivia." She still doesn't look at me. "Olivia, look at me." Her face meets mine but her eyes don't – they're still focused on the floor in front of her. "Eyes up here, babe."

I'm instantly sorry I did that. The sadness there takes my breath away. What the hell have I done to her? I've got to be the biggest idiot on the planet, but I can't help the feelings I have for her. Still, I shouldn't have acted on them, and now I'm sorry. I'm sorry I did what I did, and I'm sorry that I couldn't help it and I'd do it again. "Olivia?"

Her eyes rotate downward again. "What?"

Soft as a feather, I whisper into her ear, "I love you. You're going to be fine." Before she can reply, they call her name from the front.

I walk to the door with her, thinking she'll be going back alone, but the nurse who greets us tells me, "Oh, you're welcome to come back with her if you want." Olivia's eyes plead with me, and I just let the nurse lead me back with her to a small waiting cubicle. "Gown on, opening down the back. Grippy socks on. You can put your hair back if you want, but they'll put it in a cap back in surgical prep, so it doesn't matter." She looks toward me. "You need to keep up with her personal things. They should be fine, but it's just best if someone looks out for them. If you need anything, there's a restroom to your left outside the door, and the vending machines are to the right, then turn right down the hallway." She looks back to Olivia. "Any questions?"

"Will it hurt?"

"The charge nurse will go over it with you, but you'll have some cramping and a good bit of bleeding for awhile. She'll be in to talk to you in just a few minutes."

Chart in hand, the charge nurse comes in almost immediately. She starts asking the usual questions, and she gets through name and age before she says, "Address?" Olivia looks at me, and the nurse gives me an odd look.

"Eighty-three twenty-nine Hollingsworth Street." She looks at Olivia, but before she can say anything, I add, "We just moved and she's had a little trouble remembering the address."

"Yeah. It's kind of long. Eighty-two forty . . ."

"No, honey. Eighty-three twenty-nine."

She gives me a weak smile. "Oh, yeah. Thanks."

"That *is* kind of a long address. Okay, phone number."

"Lost my phone. Can you take his?"

"Sure." I give her my phone number.

"Okay. So you're responsible for her care?"

Damn. I hadn't really given it any thought, but I suppose I am. "Yes."

"We'll go over aftercare following the procedure. There may be things that will be found or change during, and any instruction I give now could be wrong. So let's just do it once."

"Suits me."

"Well, then, Dr. Cavanaugh is only running about fifteen minutes behind, so it won't be long. Just sit tight and they'll come to get you in just a few minutes." She pats Olivia's leg and leaves the cubicle.

"I suppose you should get into your beautiful gown and your cute little socks and get ready, huh? I'll step out and . . ."

"You don't have to."

"I think I should."

Her head shakes violently. "Please don't leave me."

I let out a deep sigh. "Okay. I'll stay right here, but I'll close my eyes. You let me know when you're done."

"Deal." I sit down in one of the two chairs in the room, and I can hear her rustling around. Seems like it's taking a very long time, so I peek.

I'd only seen her from the back before, there in my office, and when my eyelids crack open, I'm caught off guard. Her breasts are small but full, and her nipples are large, soft, and brown. She's not quite as emaciated as I remember, and I feel good about that – at least I seem to be doing a good job at *something*. Beneath those breasts is a long, smooth drop to her belly, flat as a pancake, and opposite it is a small but round ass that looks totally squeezable. And I want to squeeze it. Her legs aren't particularly long, but her thighs aren't heavy at all, just muscular, and I wonder how much time she spent running away from people who were trying to do her harm. Probably quite a bit, considering the descriptions she's given me of her living conditions and circumstances. I'm so sad and, unfortunately, turned on at the sight before me. I manage to squeeze my eyes shut again before she spins to face me. I hear a slight metallic creaking sound and she says, "Okay, I'm done."

I gather her clothes together and put them into the handled bag they've given me to carry them in, shoes too. Watching her, she seems to be trying to get comfortable in the hard surgical gurney, but I think her greatest discomfort is with what I said to her just a short time before in the waiting area. Dropping the bag into my chair, I walk to the bed and sit on the edge. She still hasn't looked at me. "Olivia, we need to talk."

"Yes?"

"I meant what I said out there."

"I know. And I love you too."

"I know." Taking one of her hands, I stare at the floor. Saying this will be hard. "Olivia, I love you. I wasn't lying. I'd like for this to be a lot more than a friendship, but it just can't be. I'm too old. You're too young. You have far too much of your life ahead of you. Mine is almost over."

"No it's not. You've got a lot of good years ahead of you."

"Compared to yours, yes, it is. I don't have a life to offer you. Do you understand."

She shakes her head. "You do. You have a lot to offer someone."

"Yes, but not someone your age. I couldn't do that for you, offer you the things you need. You'll want kids and a family."

Her eyes light up. "Clint and Trish adopted!"

"I know. That's not what I mean. It's not about *having* kids – as far as I know, there's no reason I couldn't father a child. It's *being* a father to a child. I would never saddle you with a child I wouldn't be around to help raise."

Her face falls. "But I don't care."

"I do." Before she can respond, a nursing assistant comes through the doorway.

"Time to go."

"Dave?"

I smile down at her. "We'll continue this conversation later. Don't worry about any of that now. We just need to get you healthy."

"But . . ."

"No. Go. I'll be right here when you get back." I kiss her on the forehead as I rise from the bed, and she gives me a weak wave as they wheel her away.

God, this is a mess. How in the world did I let this happen? I know in theory that it's a very, very bad thing to let a woman move in with you and be that close to you. It's a bad idea to be in that close proximity with *anyone* if you don't want to have feelings for them, and sometimes that's hatred if it's someone you have reason to loathe. But this is the opposite, and I'm afraid this won't end well. Correction: I *know* it won't end well.

I busy myself getting a soft drink and some cookies while I wait. I check my phone for messages, then send Clint and Trish a text telling them that she's in surgery. The chair isn't very comfortable, but I'm exhausted, and I doze for a little while all slumped over. I'm awakened by a rustling and open my eyes to find that they're wheeling her bed back into the cubicle. Her eyes are closed and she's breathing quietly, and I feel like I should whisper. "How'd she do?"

The nurse laughs. "Don't whisper! Your job for the next thirty to forty-five minutes is to try to get her good and awake. Talk to her. If she's thirsty, they'll get you some ice chips for her. Oh, and she did quite well. The doctor will come and talk to you in just a little while."

When she leaves, I sit on the side of the bed again and stroke Olivia's cheek. She looks like she's twelve as she lies there sleeping quietly, and eventually her eyelids flutter open. Before she can speak, I ask, "Thirsty?"

She nods. "Throat hurts."

"It was the tube. Let me get you some ice chips." Once they bring the cup, I spoon a few in at a time and let her suck on them until she opens her mouth for more.

In about twenty minutes, she's more than alert and aware when the doctor walks in and asks, "How are you?"

"My throat is scratchy. And my stomach hurts."

"That's to be expected." She pulls up a chair and sits down, and everything in my brain screams, *Uh-oh. This doesn't look good.* Putting on her game face, she says, "We need to talk about some things. First, how did you get the wounds on your back and buttocks?"

Olivia looks at me, and I nod. "Um, I was homeless and people hurt me."

"I see." Giving that bit of information time to digest, the next question is, "So what is your relationship with the gentleman here?"

"He's my friend. We met a few days ago. And he and his family have been very nice to me." The minute the word "family" comes out of Olivia's mouth, I see the woman relax a bit.

"Family?"

"Yeah. Son and daughter-in-law. Their children. Their friend and his wife and kids. They've all been so nice to me. I'd still be on the street if he hadn't found me."

She smiles. "Sounds like you were in the cabbage patch!"

Olivia doesn't smile when she answers, "No. The dumpster."

I see the woman's eyes go wide and she starts to say something but chokes. After a few seconds to regroup, she says, "We should talk about what I found. Massive infection. I want you on antibiotic infusion for several days, so you'll be coming back here. And lots of scarring. Were you violated?"

I watch the young woman nod in sadness as she looks at her hands resting on the blanket across her lap. "Yes. Many times. And sometimes with things."

"I see. Beaten?"

"Yes, ma'am."

Dr. Cavanaugh nods. "Well, I have good news and bad news. The good news is that as soon as the infection is gone, you should start feeling better and your abdomen should stop hurting."

"That's great," Olivia smiles, then her face falls. "What's the bad news?"

"I'm sorry, Miss Warren. I doubt you'll ever be able to have children."

The look on Olivia's face isn't what I expected at that news. She looks almost happy. "Okay. That's good to know. Thanks for telling me."

"You're welcome. We'll keep you here for another thirty minutes or so, watch your vitals, get you set up for the antibiotic infusion, and then let you go home. Only acetaminophen for pain. Did your situation lead you into substance abuse?"

"No."

"Good. If the acetaminophen doesn't do the trick, we'll have to prescribe pain meds, but I'd rather not do that if we don't have to. And I'll see you in two weeks for your first follow-up. Any questions?" Olivia shakes her head. "Call if you have any problems and I'll see you in a couple of weeks." As she leaves the cubicle, she mouths a thank-you to me and I nod.

When she's gone, Olivia's eyes light up and she grins. "Problem solved!"

"What?" I don't understand.

"I can't have kids! There's nothing for you to worry about!"

Oh. My. God. I never dreamed she'd go in that direction. "Olivia . . ."

"You said you were worried about kids. Now you don't have to be. It's all okay."

"Honey, that's not what I meant. It's just that . . ."

Her eyes flash. "Did you lie? That's not it? That's what you said."

"That's just one of many reasons." I can't believe she's turned this corner, and now I feel conversely backed into it. "I'm a Dominant in the lifestyle. I'm accustomed to a submissive and . . ."

"I can be your submissive. I can! I know I can."

"Olivia, a submissive isn't something you can be. You either are or aren't, and it's a personality trait, a personal characteristic, not something you can just become. And," I add, "I'm used to having sex with a lot of women. Anytime I want. Usually subs in the club. But that's what I'm accustomed to, and I like it. The idea of being with one woman isn't something I thought I'd ever do again."

"But I can be all those things to you, Dave, I can! You'll see if you'll just give me a chance."

"No. Out of the question."

"It's not out of the question." Her eyes narrow to slits. "I saw you in the shower."

"I know." I watch as her eyes widen. "I knew you were there."

"And you did it anyway?" She turns her head sideways and cuts her eyes at me. "You *wanted* me to see you."

Now I don't know what to say because she's right. I did. "That was a mistake."

"No mistake. I'm in love with you, Dave Adams, and you're in love with me, I know it. And you'll see. This will all work out. You said it: Things happen the way they're supposed to happen."

My own words thrown back at me. Great. I don't stand a chance.

<hr>

While she's getting dressed, I make a phone call, and

then help her into the car. She's more animated and cheerful than she was on the way. I know why, and I hate it. I take a detour and tell her, "Sit in the car." When I come out of the store, I hand her the bag.

"What's this?"

"Your cell phone. You need one. We'll get you home and get you settled, and then we'll work on getting all the contacts into it later. I'll put most of them in from my phone. And then you can put in whatever you like."

"Oh my god! A cell phone! I can't believe it! Is it a . . ." She opens the box and squeals. "Ohhh! It's a smart phone! Thanks, Dave! Thank you so much. Thank you!" She digs around and then yells out, "Oh, a case! It's so cute! It has butterflies on it! Thank you!" There's a lot of cursing and muttering as she sets about putting the case on the phone, but when she gets it done, she holds it up. "See? Oh, it's so beautiful! Thank you so much! Oh, look at this!" Before I can say anything, there's the sound of a shutter.

I blush. "Did you just take my picture?"

"Yes! And I'm going to make it my wallpaper."

"Oh, god, don't do that."

"Yes! I want to be able to see you even when you're not around. Give me your phone. I want to call Trish." Once I've gotten it out of my hand and into hers, I see her rooting around in my contacts. "Who's 'My Girls.'?"

"That's my ex-wife and her girlfriend. Clint's mom."

"Ah." Out of the corner of my eye I can see her digging around, then punching things into her phone. In a few minutes I hear that familiar "whoosh" as a text message leaves.

"What did you send?"

"I sent Trish the picture. And I said, 'Dave bought me a phone!'"

"Nice." *I bet I never hear the end of this.* There's a *ping*.

"Oh, she sent one back!" I hear her giggle. "She says, 'Congrats. And he's as handsome as ever.'" Now I *am* blushing. Another one comes in, and I see her typing furiously. "She wants to know how I am."

"Tell here you're back to your sassy self." She laughs out loud. "Because you are."

Her laughter turns to a mile-wide smile. "It's because of you. I was never sassy before. But when I'm with you, I feel sassy, like everything's going to be okay and it's all right to be happy."

Oh, god. *That's what I want for her, but why do I have to be the catalyst? Why can't it be the phone, or her driver's license, or something like that? Why does it have to be me?* "That's good, I guess." If she catches what I've said, she doesn't say so. She's so busy playing with the phone that she's distracted, and I'm glad. It's just good to see her happy and smiling and having fun. And I decide right this minute that, for the next two weeks, I'm going to do everything I can to make her happy and show her that there's a life out there without me.

───◦◦◦───

Every evening I go and pick up something. I've forbidden her to cook because I don't want her to be on her feet. She's doing great and I don't want a setback.

She gets through all of the infusions fine. Every day for four days I take her in, and every evening I take her to Clint's or Steffen's because she doesn't want to go to the club. She's happily planning things, like lunches and shopping trips, and I think the phone was the thing that did it. That feeling of connectedness was what she was missing, apparently. She's set up social media pages and started friending people who sound interesting, and taking pictures of things to use as her profile pictures or timeline banners. It keeps her busy. I'm contemplating getting her a tablet too; she's read everything in the house and she's looking for more. And going to the library really isn't practical.

It's been nine days since the procedure and she seems to be feeling pretty good. I'm seeing fewer and fewer toilet paper-wrapped items in the hall bathroom's trash can, and that's a good sign, as I understand it. She talks to Trish and Sheila pretty much every day. She announces to me before dinner that night, "Trish and Clint have invited us to dinner tomorrow night. Can we go?"

I shrug. "You don't have to ask me if you can go to their house."

She rolls her eyes. "They didn't invite me. They invited *us*."

Uh-oh.

"Olivia, there is no 'us.' You know that."

She gives me this sweet, knowing smile that surprises me. "It could happen. I have faith."

"Misplaced faith." I wander into the kitchen in need of a beer; hell, maybe two or three.

"Faith in *you*. And misplaced? I don't think so."

I stroll back in shaking my head. "Olivia, we've been over this . . ."

"Apparently you don't understand," she quips.

That kind of pisses me off. "So enlighten me."

"You want me."

I sigh and roll my eyes. "Yes. That's true. Doesn't mean I'll act on it."

"And I want you."

Despite my best attempts, I feel my cock twitch. Damn thing always gives me away. "You just *think* you want me."

"I know what I want. And I want you." There it is again, that damn twitch.

Where's my usual self-control? What's happened to the Dominant inside me? This is crazy, just crazy, and I say out loud, "This is crazy."

"No. It's love."

That brings me right up off the sofa. "Whoaaaaa. Let's stop this right now. I have no idea what you're talking about."

"Yes, you do. You can deny it, but we both know it's true. You love me. You told me so."

"Yes. I did. I meant it like I'd love a daughter or granddaughter."

"Yeah? And do you get excited about your daughter or granddaughter?" she asks, then points straight at the front of my jeans.

Fuck me. Talk about world-class betrayal – the stiff little son of a bitch is pointing right straight up and there's no denying what's going on with him. Little rat bastard. All I can think to say is, "Physiological response."

"I call bullshit." A big, cheesy grin covers her face and it makes me furious.

"I'm going to the club."

"And how do I get to Clint's or Steffen's?"

I toss my beer bottle into the trash and hear it break. "I don't care. Have them come and pick you up. You're not riding in the car with me."

"What the . . ."

"You heard me. Get that notion right out of your head. There'll be no lovey-dovey stuff going on between us, so it's just not happening." I throw the door open and look back at her startled face. "Not happening, Olivia. I mean it. Get over it." I drag the door forward hard enough to make the glass rattle when it slams, and I'm breathing hard when I get to the car.

Plopping down behind the steering wheel, I sit there for a minute. God, she's right, but I'm not about to tell her that. I can't. This can't go anywhere. When I start the car, I see her peeking out the living room window, but I don't acknowledge her, just start out and keep my eyes on my driving.

I'm still fuming when I step out into the common area about an hour after the club opens. And who's the first person I see?

Melina.

"Hey, gorgeous, I was looking for you," she purrs as she takes my arm. "I'd really like to enjoy some of your expertise. Have you given any more thought to a film?"

"Hi yourself. And yes, but Clint said he was hoping I'd forget about that."

"Oh, that Master Clint is no fun." She leans in and gives me peck on the cheek. "Do you need a submissive for the night? Because I need a Dom." The arms she's got wrapped around my waist slide downward and cup my ass, and everything inside me lights up.

"And what do you need a Dom for?" I can't wait for the answer to this one.

"I need to be whipped and then fucked brutally. I need it hard. Big and hard. And I think you've got that covered, right? I know you do." One hand trails around the side of my hip and cradles my balls, and I know I've got something for her, something she'll just eat up.

I look around and spot Gary; he'll watch the bar for me. "I'll set up. You go and get yourself ready. Nothing but your earrings, nose piercing, and belly chain. Oh, and those 'come fuck me' heels. I need those to stay on track."

"Yes, Sir." She trots off and I watch that gorgeous ass sway across the room. And somehow, the image is suddenly replaced with Olivia's backside, burns and all. It's all I can do to force the pictures out of my mind long enough to talk to Gary.

When Melina comes out, I've got a performance area set up, but she starts the show right in the middle of the floor when she drops to her knees in front of me and unzips my leathers. My cock springs into view, and I stroke the back of her head as she licks her lips. "Listen up, little one. All the way down, and I'll stop when I please, so be prepared."

"Yes, Sir. I'll do as you've ordered, Sir." As soon as the words are out, I replace them with my rod and go to town on that pretty pink mouth of hers.

In a few minutes, I grab her hair and pull her back. As I zip up my leathers, I march up to the platform of one of the performance areas and point to her. "Down on your knees again." As soon as I see her drop appropriately, I pull out a set of clover clamps from one drawer in the chest and then I root around in another drawer until I find a steripak. I rip it open and her eyes go wide.

It's a Whitehead gag. Some people call them spider gags because they look like two legs attached to two more by a long strap. Two go on one side, two on the other, and the strap around the back of the head fastens to the metal legs which hold the mouth open. When she sees it, Melina's face goes white. "A little worried, are we?"

"Yes, Sir."

"Good. You're so damn crazy for a fucking that I thought I'd add a little unfamiliar element to your performance. Open wide, slut." I put the metal legs inside her mouth, then start tightening the strap behind her head until it's tight enough that she really can't do much of anything but loll her tongue around. "Look at that. Beautiful." I enjoy pinching her nipples hard enough to get them tightened and the clover clamps attached, and I give them a yank, partly to make sure they'll stay on and partly to hear her scream through the gag. With a hand on the top of her head and one under her chin, I slide my cock into her mouth and keep going, going, going, until it's lodged in her throat. I feel her try to swallow around it and I let out a long, low moan. "Ahhh, my little fuck puppet for the night. Good girl. Suck as well as you can." That's damn near impossible, but I want her to try. After three strokes, I tell her, "This is where I get off – literally. Get ready."

And I use her. I use her hard and ruthlessly. She wanted that, but I think I'm going a few steps beyond that. It's all because of Olivia, and I'm thinking about her the whole time, wondering what it would be like to see my dick disappearing into her mouth, what it would be like to see her naked and kneeling before me, how she'd feel under me in the quiet of my house and my bed. I start to wonder, could I do without this? Without the lifestyle? Without the leathers and the constant parade of subs and watching other people fuck? What would that be like? If I were with her, would the occasional porn flick do the trick?

I feel myself starting to get soft, and I can't have that, so I come back into the moment and watch Melina. I pull out and point to the table. When she climbs up, I bark, "On your back. Head over the edge. I'm looking for a throat bump. You'll deliver, I'm sure." When she's in position, I ram back into her throat and watch it expand every time my cock bores into it. That's a beautiful thing, knowing your cock's doing that, and it keeps me hard. I'm watching her tits bouncing with every thrust, and in a few minutes, I feel myself slipping toward the end. I reach out, grab her tits, and start to hunch into her throat until my balls harden and I pour what feels like a gallon of cum down the back of her throat.

"Keep sucking. I need to be hard again so I can fuck you." She's obedient to a fault, and in no time at all my cock is a steel scimitar, ready to pierce her wherever I like. "Elbows and knees, sub. It's time." Melina scrambles up, assumes the position, and I reach for a bottle of lube. No need – it's like the Pacific Ocean down there, and I have no trouble sliding into her well-used pussy once I've rolled on a condom. I just take my time, leisurely stroking in and out of her, my hands gliding around on that soft, smooth ass, and I'm drawn back to Olivia again and the sight of her breasts there in the holding cubicle. As soon as she crosses my mind, I feel my erection soften slightly. What the hell? I try to redirect my thoughts, but I can't, and I'm slipping, my hardness fading away. Melina turns back to look at me, and I just shrug as I try to keep it up, but it's no use. It's soft and it looks like it's going to stay that way.

I zip up and help her up, then take the gag off and throw it in the bin on the table, along with the nipple clamps. So preoccupied with my thoughts, I completely forget to prep her nipples and do a follow-through so when I remove the clamps, she shrieks, "Dave? What the hell?"

Through gritted teeth I hiss, "Address me properly, sub."

"Yes, Sir. Sorry, Sir."

"Aftercare. Now." I start down the hallway with her trailing behind amid whispers. I know what they're all wondering. What the hell is wrong with Adams? Why'd he go soft? Explaining isn't an option; I'm doing the Walk of Shame, damn it. I close the door after her when we get into a private room, then point to the bed. Climbing in, she waits and watches me to see what's about to happen.

I flop down onto the bed beside her, then reach over for her and pull her into my side. With my other arm behind my head, I sigh. Even though she's probably afraid to squeak, eventually she whispers, "Dave, what's wrong? Did I do something wrong? If I did, I . . ."

"No, baby. It's not you." I stare at the ceiling and imagine that I see Olivia's face in the patterns in the textured paint.

She waits a few more minutes, then says, "If I can help, let me know. I don't know what's going on with you, but I know it's serious from the way you acted out there."

"How did I act out there?"

"Like you had something, or someone, else on your mind."

God, she's perceptive. Should I? This woman screws dozens of guys a day, but she came here looking for me. That's got to mean something, that there's some kind of connection between us besides just the sex. Could I consider her a friend? Yeah, I think I could. Maybe she'd be a good person to talk to. "Melina, you've been through a bunch of relationships, right?"

She laughs loudly. "Relationships! So that's what they're called! I thought it was fucking!"

"I'm serious." She stops laughing and watches my face. "I mean, you've had boyfriends, right? Guys you actually dated? I know you're bound to have."

Her face is sad now, and I'm sorry I even asked. "Oh, yeah. I've had several. Once they found out what I do, though, all they wanted was to fuck. That became all I was good for. So yeah, I've had a ton of relationships, but I'm hardly the person you'd want to ask about that kind of stuff."

"But what if you were in a relationship that you knew wouldn't work?"

She scowls. "You mean like every one of mine?"

"Stop it. But yes, one of those that you know is doomed from the very beginning. You know the kind."

She raises up on her elbow and looks me in the eye. "Dave, just spit it out. What's going on? You can tell me. Hell, we've fucked each other so many times through the years that I feel like I'm your McDonald's." That makes us both chuckle. "Over one billion served."

It's now or never. "I'm in love with someone."

Well, that got her attention. Those perfectly drawn-on eyebrows skyrocket. "Dave's in love?"

"Yes, Dave's in love." How do I introduce this concept? "And there's a problem."

"I gathered that."

"I'm sixty-five." I wait.

"Why do I get the impression that I don't want to ask the next question?"

"She's twenty-nine."

She doesn't say a word, just falls back onto the mattress with an arm thrown across her forehead. After what seems like an eternity, she asks, "How in love are we talking about here?"

"The I-was-thinking-about-her-while-I-was-fucking-you kind of in love."

"Ah! That explains the noodle."

"Yup."

"Hmmmm." She just lies there for awhile, then says, "What's the *real* problem?"

"What do you mean?"

"Just what I said. It's not your age; you can say that, but I really don't believe it." She waits. "Are you afraid of what people will say?"

"No! Absolutely not."

"Hmmmm." There's a long pause again before she asks, "Are you afraid she'll want kids and you won't?"

"She can't have kids." I'm still dancing around it, and I know it. If I say it, it might come true, and that would kill me. It's always been a point of pride for me, and the thought is unbearable.

"Dave?" I look over at her. "Are you afraid that, at some time down the road, you won't be able to perform and she'll want a younger man?" When I don't answer, she says, "Yeah. I wanted to guess that first, but I wanted you to think about it for a minute or two."

A light sweat has broken out on my upper lip. "But really, Melina, what if?"

"And what if you're Iron Dick Adams on into your nineties? Wouldn't it be a shame to miss out on that? A relationship with someone who really loves you?" She hesitates, then says, "Does she feel the same way?"

"Oh, yeah, unfortunately."

"Unfortunately? Dave, real love is hard to find. Nobody really cares about your ages except the two of you. And her mom and dad. How will they feel?"

"They're dead."

"Well, there you go!" She kisses me right on the lips, but it's more like a greeting or goodbye than a passionate thing. "You should pursue this."

"Thanks. I don't know if I can do that, but thanks. Thanks for being my friend."

"Friend with benefits. Don't forget that!"

"You gonna be mad if you can't have those benefits anymore?"

"Nope. But wait: You love the lifestyle. Is she into it?"

"No."

She cuts her eyes back to me. "Uh-oh. Are you willing to give this up?"

"That's a good question, Melina. I'm just not sure." And I'm not.

Chapter Six

I't's late before I get to leave the club. Trish sends a text and asks if Olivia can just stay there instead of having to get out, and I tell her that's fine. And it is. I need time and room to think.

It seems so strange to go home to an empty house now. I've gotten used to her being here, and now the quiet is almost deafening. I get a beer and sit down, then get back up and walk down the hallway to Clint's old room. When the door swings open, I get a whiff of the perfume she bought at the mall. At least it wasn't five dollar stuff. I open one of her dresser drawers and pick up a pair of panties. They're beautiful, all lacy and pink, and they're soft and feminine in my hands. There are a couple of bras too, and I remember promising her we'd go and get more. I should do that with her tomorrow.

The next drawer is socks, not very many because it's been marginal flip-flop weather, but it's getting colder and she's going to need more. We'll have to buy boots too. And a coat and some sweaters. I open the next drawer.

There are weird things in there. There's a button, and

its red and orange face reads, "If you want it, get it at Barlow's." I have no idea what that means. Next to it is a piece of glass, and I recognize it as the bottom of a bottle. It's got a piece of aluminum foil on the backside and then wrapped around the edges of the glass in the front. And that's when I get it.

It's a mirror. These are the things she had with her when I found her. I remember thinking I saw her coming in the back door that night I took her to the club with me, and now I know she must have sneaked out there and retrieved these. There's a white mother of pearl button off a shirt, and a pack of matches, which I'm sure were like gold to her. I try to figure out what the next item is, and then realize it's a piece of an old knife blade. The next item is a tattered coupon for tampons and it just occurs to me that those were bound to be hard to come by. What did she do when she didn't have any money for them, which was most of the time? One pair of ragged socks, an old scarf, a coin purse with nothing in it. They're all placed carefully on a towel that she arranged in the bottom of the drawer. I reach for the knife blade and can tell there's something under the towel, so I feel around under the towel carefully and pull it out.

It's a notebook of some kind. It's horribly ratty and smelly, but there it is. I open it up and start to read. There are entries, but it's not really a diary; it's more like a cross between a diary and a daily reminder. On January 9, she wrote, "It's too cold out here, but I have nowhere to go. I'm saying goodbye to my fingers and toes –

tomorrow morning I probably won't have them." There's an entry on March 13 that says, "I've been in four dumpsters and fifteen trash cans, and there's no food anywhere." The scribbling on May 23 reads, "It's finally warm. I'm so glad. Now maybe I can sneak into the fountain tonight and take a bath." Too curious, I flip to the back of the book. Her last entry was two days ago, and it says, "I'm in love with a man who isn't in love with me. Oh, well – that's my life."

Bitterness rises up in my mouth and I start to put the notebook back, but I flip back three pages and look at an entry two weeks before. And it brings me to my knees.

"I've found an angel. His name is Dave. I'll love him until the end of my life, and then into eternity. I think he loves me too. If he does, my life will be complete."

What the hell is wrong with me? I slip the notebook back into its spot, then look around the room before running back up the hall to my room. I throw open a drawer and look into it: Socks. Lots of them are socks I don't wear. I get a paper sack from the kitchen and start weeding them out. Then I go through my underwear and get rid of everything I don't wear. When I get done, I realize I can put all of my socks and underwear in one big drawer and it leaves two smaller ones empty.

I keep doing this with no regard for the time. I just work until I'm done. When I am, I have four dresser drawers and two chest drawers empty. Then I head back down the hall.

There's an empty drawer for her bras, another for her panties, another for her socks. In the chest, there's a drawer for her night clothes and exercise stuff, and the other drawer will hold sweaters. I attack the closet, get rid of about two feet of stuff I don't wear, and fetch all of her things out of the other closet. Last but not least, I move her shoes in. I happen to think of a decorative wooden box in the living room, and I move it to the dresser, then move all of her jewelry into it. It's not really a jewelry box, but it'll do for awhile.

When I finish and survey my work, it's six thirty and the sun is up. And I don't care. I want her in my room and in my bed.

I'm in love with Olivia, and I know she loves me. We'll work it out. We have to. Otherwise, we'll both die of broken hearts.

Crawling into bed at six forty-five, I hear the door at about seven thirty and it wakes me. She's tiptoeing down the hallway and I wonder what she'll think when she realizes I've moved her stuff. I just wait and giggle a little to myself.

But it never occurred to me that she might not figure out what I'd done. I hear some kind of rustling around and then her footsteps in the hallway again. Before I have a chance to stop her and ask what she thinks, I hear the front door open and close, so I go into Clint's old room and look.

The drawer with her stuff, the mirror and knife blade and notebook, is empty. Her phone and keys are on the dresser, and her bag is gone, the one she loves and wanted so badly from the mall. And I figure it out fast – she thinks I'm planning to kick her out.

I manage to throw on a pair of lounge pants and a tee shirt, then grab my all-weather mocs to slip on. When I hit the front door and throw it open, she's disappearing around the corner at the end of the block, so I grab my keys from the bowl by the door and take off for the car. I'm sure the neighbors wonder why I'm peeling out of the driveway this way, but I don't care. By the time I round the corner, I don't see her anywhere and I start to panic. But I drive another block and see that headful of dark, glossy hair turning right on Iroquois Drive, and I hightail it down there. When I pull up to the curb ten feet in front of her, she stops, then turns and goes the other way, but I'm already out of the car and running toward her, and I'm yelling, "Olivia! Stop, please! Please? Olivia, honey, stop!"

Wheeling past her and spinning to face her, my heart breaks at the sight of her tear-stained face. "I left all of the stuff you gave me. I didn't steal anything."

"Honey, that's not what's . . ."

"I get it. All my stuff is gone. I won't bother you anymore." She pushes past me, but I grab her arm.

"No. That's not what's going on here. At all. You don't understand."

"No, I get it. I really do. And I don't want to be a thorn in your side. You're not responsible for me. I can take care of myself." She tries to shake her arm loose from my grip, but I won't let go.

"Olivia, get in the car. You don't understand."

"No!" She tries again to break loose, and a man who's come out to pick up his newspaper stares at us.

"Just stop! You don't have to explain. I get it, really."

"No you don't. Baby, I wanted to surprise you."

"Well, you succeeded."

I guess I'll have to spill the beans. "Olivia, your stuff isn't gone. It's in my room."

That stops her dead in her tracks. "What are you talking about?"

"Baby, get in the car. We need to talk."

"Dave, I . . ."

"Please. Just get in the car and we'll go home and talk, okay?"

I see her face soften, and then she says, "Okay, okay. Let's go." She lets me open the car door for her, and we drive the five blocks back to the house in silence.

I open the front door and she makes a beeline for the bedroom. Just as I suspected she'd do, she starts opening drawers, and then slings the closet doors open. I finally take her by the hand and lead her back to the living room, then point at the sofa, and she drops onto it. I sit down on the coffee table in front of her and take both her hands in mine. "We need to talk. I was at the club last night."

"I know."

"And I fucked one of the subs there."

The corners of her mouth turn downward. "I wish you wouldn't tell me things like that. It hurts."

"I know, but just listen to me. I was up there scening with her and something happened that's never happened before." She waits, and I feel the heat creeping across my cheeks when I say, "I went limp."

Her face is a mask of pain. "And why are you telling me this?"

I stare at the floor, then force myself to meet her gaze. "I couldn't keep it up because while I was fucking her, I was thinking about you." Her eyes pop open wide and her mouth makes an *O*. "It's true, babe. I couldn't perform. All I kept thinking about was you, and it just knocked the wind out of my sails. And then afterward, we went back to a private room for her aftercare, and we talked. I've known her for a long time, scened with her a lot of times, and we're really pretty good friends. We talked about it, I mean, about you and me."

"And?"

"And she told me she thought I should take a chance."

A single tear rolls down her face. "And then?"

I feel one well up and trickle down my cheek too. "I came home and cleaned out the bedroom so there'd be room for your stuff. I wanted to surprise you. It never occurred to me that you might think I wanted you to leave."

I watch the tension disappear in her shoulders as she starts to sob. "I did! I thought you didn't want me here anymore! I don't want to be where I'm not wanted, so I was leaving. You scared me so bad, Dave. I thought I didn't have a home anymore."

"You've got a home here, little girl." I move to the sofa, then pull her up into my lap and wrap my arms around her. With my lips against her cheek, I whisper, "I love you, Olivia. I want to see if this can work."

"I love you too." When she faces me, her lips find mine and I find myself falling into her like an Olympic swimmer off a high dive. It's frightening and exhilarating all at the same time, and I want more. "My doctor won't clear me for sex for a couple more weeks. Can you wait?"

I chuck her under the chin and grin. "Baby, I've waited all my life for you. I can wait a little longer, I promise."

I still don't want her to cook. I know it's been four weeks and her doctor says she's doing very well, but I don't like the idea of her standing like that for an hour or two. She says I'm spoiling her. So what? I like that idea.

The pizzas show up and then everyone else does. I've bought some games for the kids, and all five of them are having a blast in the little den on the back of the house. I've also loaded them down with chips and pretzels in an attempt to avoid the sugary stuff so no one kills me the next day. Once they're back there and busy, I tell our four guests, "Come in and have a seat. We need to talk."

With everyone comfortable, Clint looks at me out the corner of his eye. "Okay, I know something's going on. I could tell when I walked through the door. Spill."

Without looking at Olivia, I just tell them matter-of-factly, "Olivia has moved into my bedroom."

Trish looks ceilingward and sighs. "Well, finally. I thought you'd never get with the program."

"Whaaaa . . ."

There's a snort from one of the chairs. "Oh, for god's sake, Dave. We all knew." Steffen is grinning from ear to ear.

"Yeah. The two of you are perfect for each other," Clint says in agreement.

"You really think so?" I'm dumbfounded.

"Absolutely!" Sheila is beaming. "Look at you. You're the perfect complement to each other. And you're obviously crazy about each other."

"Obviously?" Now I'm really struck.

"Yes. Obviously. The way you look at her makes it more than obvious. There's just one question." Clint leans forward and stares me straight in the eyes. "What about the lifestyle? You've been in it for a long, long time. You're used to having a bevy of beauties available at your momentary whim. Unless the little lady over there is very accepting and accommodating, that'll be a thing of the past." He glances over at Olivia, and we all turn to see her shaking her head. Clint directs his gaze back at me. "So, there's the big question. How will you deal with that?"

"I have no idea. I've got to navigate these waters a knot at a time, just like everyone else. I don't know what to say or do, just that I'm willing to try."

Sheila directs her attention to the young woman on the sofa beside me. "Is that enough for you, Olivia?"

"It is. As long as we're both willing to try, I think it'll be fine. I love him and he loves me. Whatever's supposed to happen will happen."

"Speaking of what will happen, I'm glad we're all here together. We have something to show you." Steffen pulls a piece of paper out of his pocket and unfolds it. "Take a real good look at these and tell us if you recognize any of these men."

When she realizes it's a picture of police officers, Olivia snatches her hand back, then reaches shaking fingers to take the sheet of paper. We watch her study it carefully, then look up and around at us as she says, "I've never seen any of these men."

A huge cloud of nervousness seems to just drift away from Steffen and Clint as Steffen says, "Good. Those are the men on the task force who are investigating the things that have happened to the homeless women over the last few weeks." He stops and takes one of her hands. "Olivia, they're going to want to talk to you. They've had no luck with the women still on the streets. They're too afraid."

She's started to shake. "I'm afraid too."

Steffen's eyes are pleading. "Olivia, honey, so far they've found nine women dead with signs of the same kinds of assault you suffered. And there'll be more if someone doesn't help them."

Bless her heart, she starts to cry, and I hug her into my side. "Why does it have to be me? Why can't it be someone else?"

"Because, honey, the women who are still out there are too afraid. They have no one to protect them. You've got all of us and you'll be fine. Don't you want this to stop?"

"Yes! But I'm too scared!" Now she's almost screaming and my heart is breaking. I shake my head at the
guys, but Steffen says the magic words.

"Olivia, just think: If Dave hadn't opened that back
door and seen you there, that could be you. Tonight.
Tomorrow night. Last week or the week before. You
could already be gone. Think about what they did to you.
You can keep them from doing it to another single
person. Help the cops help your friends, please, honey?
We're doing this because we love you and we want to see
you get justice, you and your friends that those animals
have already murdered."

Her tear-filled eyes look around the little group gathered in the room before she whispers out, "What do I
have to do?"

I hug her. "That's my girl. It's all going to be fine.
They're going to contact the task force first, feel them
out, see what they say before you ever talk to anyone.
We're not going to just take you in there. And we especially don't want any of the bad guys seeing you walking
into the police station." I kiss her cheek. "Baby, I'm not
going to let anything happen to you. You know that." I
feel her nod against my shoulder and I know everything's
going to be just fine.

All the kids are gone and I finish cleaning up the
kitchen, then find her sitting in the middle of my bed.
I've got to quit thinking that – it's *our* bed. She's just
staring into space. "Whatcha thinkin' 'bout?"

"About how scared I am."

"I know." I trace a finger up and down her arm. "I'll

be right there the whole way, I promise."

"I know you will or I wouldn't do this."

"Good. Let's get some sleep. I don't know when this is going to take place, so there's no point in losing sleep over it. And if Clint and Steffen don't get the kind of reception they're hoping for, it may never happen. They won't let you go in there if there's any question about your safety." Dropping a kiss on her forehead before I stand, I tell her, "You're one of the bravest people I've ever met. Now, I'm going to brush my teeth and get ready for bed. See you in a minute."

She's gone when I come back, but in just a minute or two she joins me and cuddles up against me. There's something about her that sets my heart on fire. I don't know if it's the way she needs me, or her softness and vulnerability, but I need her here with me.

Bless Melina's heart. She was right. Love always deserves a chance.

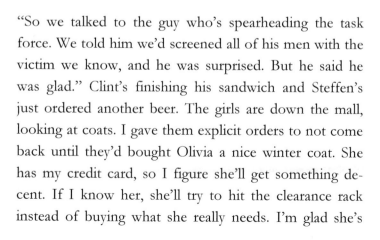

"So we talked to the guy who's spearheading the task force. We told him we'd screened all of his men with the victim we know, and he was surprised. But he said he was glad." Clint's finishing his sandwich and Steffen's just ordered another beer. The girls are down the mall, looking at coats. I gave them explicit orders to not come back until they'd bought Olivia a nice winter coat. She has my credit card, so I figure she'll get something decent. If I know her, she'll try to hit the clearance rack instead of buying what she really needs. I'm glad she's not here for this conversation.

I've got to admit, for the first time since this all start-ed, I'm nervous. "Are you trying to arrange a meeting for them with her?"

"Yeah, but we're being very careful. It'll be a public location, there'll be plenty of guys around who know us, and she'll be in a disguise. And we don't want you any-where near. They might be able to track her back to you. If they do that with us, she won't be in our homes, so they won't be able to find her," Clint explains.

"That sounds good, except you're going to have trouble convincing her to do this without me present."

"I know. We'll just have to work on that." Steffen rises and throws a twenty on the table. "I've got to get back to the office. I'm sure one of you will make sure my wife picks up my kids on time, right?"

"Absolutely." He takes the hand I extend and shakes it. "Thank you for doing this, for caring enough about her to help."

"Dave, listen, that girl is precious. She's got a good heart and she's brave. She'll be fine, but I'm glad to help be a part of her healing. I'll talk to you soon." With that, Steffen heads out, and I wrangle Clint into going and finding the girls.

As we walk, he tells me, "Oh, and by the way, while Olivia was at our house one night and you were at the club, she was asking Trish about being a submissive." I guess I must look more than shocked because he throws in, "She was asking what that meant to Trish and to Sheila. She wanted to know if I 'hit' Trish," he says with appropriate air quotes.

"And what did Trish say?"

"She said no. That's not part of our dynamic. Same for Sheila and Steffen. She seemed surprised somehow, and Trish took that as a good sign."

I just shrug. "Honestly, I don't know what to do with that information."

Clint shrugs too. "I don't know. Just file it away, I guess. But she's curious."

I'm still pondering that when I send Olivia a text telling her that we're looking for them and, according to the one she sends back, complete with emoticons – god, that girl loves that phone! – they're in one of the department stores. We can see them across the store, and Clint and I are strolling toward them when I see something that sends me into a spiral of panic.

The girls are moving toward us in the aisle, and there's a woman and a large man walking the opposite direction. When they near the girls, they move slightly to the side. But a look crosses Olivia's face that I recognize – it's the same look as the one on her face the morning she saw the security guard at the outpatient center. And to my horror, the man turns, looks back at her, and puts his hand under the back of his jacket.

I manage to squeeze out, "Did you see that?"

"I did. You start away from them so they'll follow you. I'm going around the other way and intercept the guy, see if I can watch him for a little while. Get them out of here, all three of them." Clint takes off at a fast walking pace around the perimeter of the store. I take a look at the girls, make a gesture for them to come to me, and head for the nearest exit door.

I stop when I get out into the main part of the mall and wait. Within seconds, they shoot through the door, and Trish and Sheila are practically holding Olivia up – she's pale and shaking like a leaf. Trish instantly asks, "Where's Clint?"

"Keeping an eye on him until we can get out of here."

Olivia's starts to cry. "Dave, that was . . ."

"Trouble. That's what that was. Whose car is the closest?" It takes us only a couple of seconds to figure out that Trish and Clint's van is closest to where we are. Once we're out of the mall and in the van, I feel much better. Trish texts Clint, telling him which mall door to go to for a meeting spot, then runs Olivia and me to my car. When we're in the car, I try not to drive like a maniac out of the parking lot. Attracting attention is the last thing I need to do. In less than five minutes, my phone rings, and I pull over and answer. "Yeah."

"I'm guessing he's one of them?" Clint asks.

"Not a doubt in my mind."

"Okay. I got a really good look at him a couple of times. I'll go and check out the website, see if I can find his picture. She okay?"

"Yeah, shaken up, but okay. We're going home."

"Good. We're dropping Sheila off at home and then picking the kids up from school. Call me when you get in and settled down."

I smile over at Olivia, who's still tense and shaking.

"Will do. Thanks, son." Ending the call, I look at her. "Everyone in this family is looking out for you, angel. It's going to be okay."

She shakes her head, and then a fierce look works its way into her eyes. "I want to talk to those cops, and I want to do it soon. I want that asshole off the streets, and I don't want him to hurt anyone else."

I reach over as I drive and take her hand with my free one. "We'll be right there with you, baby. You can count on that."

<hr/>

"We're here and settled."

"Good. Let me tell you what I found." Clint is rustling papers around. "His name is Mark Falco. He's been with the force for seventeen years. I did a little research, found out he has a wife and three kids. I have no idea if the woman with him was his wife or not but, based on her appearance, I'd say if he were going to have a girlfriend, she'd be much more of a looker than that."

"Okay, so now what?"

"Well, I saw the two out in front of the club that night. It was dark, so I didn't get a real good look, but I've thought about it and thought about it, and I think I've figured out who they were. Do you remember much about the one who came in and took the report from you?"

"No, I don't. I was so shaken up that I don't really remember much."

"That's okay. You can bet if they do this together

while they're on duty, they pal around together off work. We'll catch up with them, I guarantee. Is she feeling better?"

"Clint, she wants to talk to the cops. She wants to get this over with."

"Really? Okay. I'll talk to Steffen and we'll figure out what to do from here."

"Thanks again, son. I appreciate it."

"You're quite welcome. Talk to you later." I turn to Olivia and take her face in my hands. "His name is Mark Falco. We know who he is. And with that information, we can keep you safe. It's going to be okay, baby, I promise." My lips meet her forehead and she sighs as I kiss her, down the bridge of her nose, off the tip, and then on to her lips. They part for me, and my tongue seeks hers out to play, dipping and slipping and stroking. I'm more than aroused; I'm moved for this woman, and she is a woman. Every day I'm made more aware of that fact, and I'm looking forward to the day when I can discover everything about her that makes her incredible and amazing and unbelievable. "When's your doctor's appointment?" I manage to groan out.

"Two days."

"Any more bleeding?"

"Nope. No pain either."

"Olivia, I . . ."

She kisses me again hard, then whispers into my mouth, "I want you too. God, baby, I want you too."

It takes me only an instant to wrap my arms around her waist and take her down onto the sofa, my weight on top of her, my mouths crushing hers. Her hands travel up my back and into my hair, and her fingers on my scalp drive me wild. I want to bond with her. I want us to become one. There's no one else in the whole world for me. Just her.

"Let's see if we can get in a little nap before I have to go to the club tonight. And you're coming with me this time. If anything happens, I want it to be at the club where we're surrounded by big, muscled-up Dominants who know me and will defend me to the bitter end – you too because you're mine." I smile, then repeat those words that warm my heart. "You're mine. And don't you forget it."

"Not a chance, love, not a chance. Let's go catch a nap. Two more days, Mr. Adams."

Two more days. Two more very, very long days.

<hr>

"Sit out here at the bar with me. I want to be able to see you."

She lets out a little exasperated laugh. "I'll be fine back there in the office!"

"No. I want you out here. I mean it. Don't you leave my sight."

"Okay. All right. I'll stay right here." I lean over the bar and give her a peck on the cheek, then go back to readying everything.

Twenty minutes after the club opens, I find myself in a predicament when Melina walks in and sits down at the bar. "Hey, stud! Wanna play tonight? I'm jonesing for that big old cock."

The look on my face must've been telling because she says, "Oh. Just kidding." Intuition intact, she turns and looks at Olivia. "I don't think we've met. I'm Melina. And you are . . ."

Olivia holds out her hand. "Olivia. I'm Dave's girl-friend."

I haven't heard her call herself that before, and I thought if she did it would be frightening, but it's oddly exciting. I'm somebody's boyfriend. It's been so long since I was a boy that thinking I'm a boyfriend is really funny to me. "Yes, Melina, I think I mentioned Olivia to you."

"Yes, you did! You're just as lovely as Dave said." Her eyes sparkle with mischief, and I hope she can behave herself.

"Thank you. So what do you do, Melina?"

Oh, this should be good.

"Well, I'm in the entertainment business."

"Really? What kind of entertainment?"

"Adult."

To my surprise, Olivia is calm, cool, and collected. "That's interesting. So are you a model or a dancer or . . ."

"Film star."

"Ah! I hear there's good money in that."

"There really is! I got involved in it about eighteen years ago when . . ." Melina launches into a history of how she got involved in porn, and I've never heard her talk about it before, but it's really quite interesting. She actually did shows for the automotive industry, the big automotive shows. Someone from the adult novelty business saw here there and hired her to do fully-clothed demonstrations for adult product companies, like condom manufacturers and the companies that make sex toys. From there, a porn producer saw one of her spots. They did a screen test with her, liked her, and cast her in two movies. The movies did so well that they kept calling her back. ". . . and last year I made over three hundred grand!"

"That's amazing! Isn't that amazing, Dave? That's just amazing. I'd love to see one of your movies."

"Oh? I'd be glad to bring you one and sign the jacket insert."

"I'd love that! Please!" I'm watching Olivia, and she's not being a smart ass; she's genuine in her interest in Melina's work. I know Melina can see it too.

Melina smiles at Olivia. "So what do you do?"

"Um, well, right now, nothing. But I'll be looking for a job when we get a little business taken care of. But I like to make things. Hang on – let me get something. Is it okay if I run back to the office?"

"Yeah. Just go back there and come right back." She jets off down the hallway and Melina grins at me.

"Very classy young lady."

"Thank you and, yes, she is."

"Keeping her reined in pretty tight, huh?"

"No, actually, she's in some danger right now, but we're taking care of that."

"Angry boyfriend?"

"No. No big deal, just something we have to take care of."

"I see. Well, I think she's a keeper." Her sentence is interrupted by Olivia's return, and in her hand she has a legal pad. "So what's this?"

"It's not much. It's just some scribbles." She hands the legal pad to Melina and I hear the porn bombshell gasp. When I turn and look, it's all I can do to not break down.

It's me. I think I must've been asleep on the sofa, and she apparently sat and drew me. And it's me, right down to every pore. If it were on something other than yellow paper with blue lines, I'd swear it was a photo. "Babe, I had no idea you could draw like that."

"Oh, it's just a hobby."

"The hell you say, hobby. That's beautiful."

"Very, very impressive," Melina echoes. "I've never seen photo realism done quite so well."

Olivia's cheeks turn crimson. "Thank you. I'm not very good, but I enjoy it."

"No, you're not very good," Melina breathes out and, before I can correct her, she says, "you're awesome."

"I'd like to draw you sometime. I can't pay you to model, but would you think about it?"

"Think about it? No. I won't think about it. I don't have to. The answer is yes. You just let me know when and I'll be here."

"Tomorrow night?"

"No." When they both stare at me, I say, "Two

nights from now. I'm taking you to the hobby store to get some proper supplies before you do this drawing. You know, drawing paper, charcoal pencils, anything you need."

Olivia's lip starts to tremble, her eyes fill, and she struggles to say, "Oh, thank you! Thank you so much! That'll be so awesome. I can't wait!"

"Sound good to you, Melina?"

"Sounds great to me! I'll be here." She stands. "I suppose I should get home. Early morning casting call and I've got to look my best. It was lovely to meet you, Olivia." Melina leans in and gives Olivia a little kiss on the cheek, and my girlfriend grins and turns pink.

My girlfriend. I have a girlfriend. I can't wait to make her mine.

Chapter Seven

"How are you feeling?" The doctor is looking up Olivia's kootch, and I'm sitting in the corner trying to entertain myself, just listening.

"I'm feeling good. No more pain and no more bleeding."

"All of the infection seems to be gone, and your external wounds have healed nicely." With a gentle smile, she adds, "Someone's been taking good care of you."

"Hear that, babe? She says you've been taking good care of me."

The doctor eyes me suspiciously, but I don't let it faze me. "Yes. Thanks! I've tried very hard."

"Have you adhered to your restrictions?"

"Yes, ma'am. I've been very good. So does that mean I can go back to doing whatever I want?"

"Yes, matter of fact, it does. Just be careful and take it slow and easy." She won't look at me, but I decide there's something I have to ask her.

"Dr. Cavanaugh?"

"Yes?"

"We're trying to find the men responsible for Olivia's injuries. If we do, would you be willing to testify in court against them as to the injuries you saw?"

Her eyes fly open and then she smiles. "I absolutely would! I'd be glad to. So you're looking?"

"Well, me, my son, and his friend are. We're determined to find them and bring them to justice for my girl here."

She nods and finally gives me a warm, genuine smile. "That's great. She's lucky to have you, and it sounds like you've got some extended family too," she says as she turns back to Olivia.

"I do. And sort of grandkids, I guess." Hearing her say that makes something inside my gut twist, and I'll have to come to grips with that later.

"That's wonderful. Okay, just go on out to the front desk and they'll check you out. You're released from my care. Just call if you need anything or have any problems, but everything looks good."

"Oh, thank you!" Olivia is beaming at the doctor, then turns to me and grins. I know what she's thinking.

I'm thinking it too.

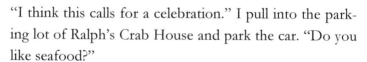

"I think this calls for a celebration." I pull into the parking lot of Ralph's Crab House and park the car. "Do you like seafood?"

"I *love* seafood! You kind of have to if you're going to live here, right?" I walk around and help her out of the car, then take her hand and head to the building.

The hostess seats us and, to my delight, we get a table by the window. We chat and laugh until the server gets there, and he addresses us immediately with, "Oh, how nice! Father/daughter night?"

I'm sure I have a ridiculous look on my face, but before I can say a word, Olivia snarls out, "He's my *boyfriend*, not my dad. Frankly, I would think a gay man would be more sensitive to others."

The server blushes a deep scarlet and it's all I can do to keep from laughing. While he's trying to compose himself, I tell him, "We'll have a bottle of sparkling white. And yes, she's of legal age."

He finally manages to blurt out, "Oh, sir, I'm so sorry, I didn't mean to . . ."

"Ah, it's okay. Doesn't bother me. When you're my age you'll be wiser too."

"Um, thank you sir. Uh, um, a bottle of sparkling white. Yes sir." He turns and beats a hasty retreat, leaving me and the beautiful woman across the table from me laughing so hard we can barely breathe. When I finally manage to stop my snickering and snorting, I give her a serious look.

"You know we're going to hear a lot of that, right?"

She pulls a bite off a breadstick and talks around it. "I don't care."

"You're sure?"

"Positive. Does it bother you?"

Honesty is important in the lifestyle, so I tell her, "Yeah. A little. Not a lot, just a little."

"You'll get over it."

"I think I probably will. There are a few things you

can do to help me get over it."

"Oh? And what might those be, Mr. Adams?"

"What do you think, Miss Warren?"

She leans across the table toward me and says, "I think I'd like to . . ."

"A sparkling white and two glasses. And I brought you two glasses of water." Damn. This boy has shitty timing. "Ready to order?" We place our orders and watch as he disappears, thankfully.

"Oh my god, this has got to be the funniest thing I've lived through in ages," I manage to whisper coarsely.

"And awkward. Don't forget awkward."

"Very."

While it's delicious, the rest of the dinner is uneventful, thank god. We're still laughing about it when we make it through the front door. But as soon as it closes, Olivia spins to face me and wraps her arms around my neck. "God, I've waited for this and I want it."

I smile down at her. "Me too. I just don't want to hurt you or scare you."

"If you're concerned about that, then I know you won't." She stretches up on her tiptoes and kisses me, and everything inside me comes to life. In a flash, I've got her in my arms and I'm headed for the bedroom. I dump her on the bed, then start pulling off clothes. "Wait! Wait!"

"Oh, great. You get a clean bill of health and your first sexy words to me are 'wait, wait'? Seriously?"

"No! It's just that I want to go in, get freshened up, all that, you know? I want to feel good about myself

before you make me feel good about you. And myself."
She's grinning from ear to ear; I take that as a good sign.

"Okay. Go do your freshening or whatever it is that
you do and get back here. I'll go do the same."

In just a few minutes, we're both back, and she's
wearing a big, fluffy robe. "What the hell's up with that?"

"Oh, nothing. Just trying to keep warm." She steps
to the edge of the bed and throws the robe off.

Oh. My. God. She might as well not have anything
on. She's wearing a red stretch lace cami and thong set,
and I can see everything, and I mean *everything*, right
through it. And it's a glorious sight, oh yes it is. All I can
manage to squeak out is, "Sweet mother of god."

"You like?"

"No. I love it. You look amazing." And that came
out almost in a pant.

"Thank you. I hope it looks even more amazing on
the floor." She winks and kneels on one knee on the bed.
"And what would you like to do first?"

"I want you in this bed. I'll decide what we do and
you'll love it, I promise. Anything you just can't handle?"

"Yeah. I can't stand to have my eyes covered. Makes
me feel claustrophobic."

"Okay then. No blindfolds for you."

"Yep. Anything else should be fine." *Well, not anything*, I think. *There are some things I'd never try to do with you.*

"Great. Let's start with you down here with me, how
'bout that?"

"A workable plan." She throws the covers back and
slides in beside me. Once our arms are wrapped around

each other, she looks up into my eyes. "Hi."

"Hello, beautiful." I give her a tiny, quiet kiss, then ask, "Are you sure you're ready?"

"Oh, god yes. Absolutely. Bring it on, Mr. Adams."

I don't need another invitation, and I've always been a self-starter and a leader, not a follower. I know exactly what I want to do with her, have been thinking about it for weeks now, and it's finally going to happen.

We cling to each other and kiss for the longest time. It feels like we're finally connecting, finally making that bridge from one body to another, that warming and meshing that I've wanted with another person. I haven't had that since Marta, and apparently what I had with her meant more to me than to her. That's not the case with Olivia, but I have to admit, it wasn't her who fell first. It was me.

The night I opened that back door and looked into those eyes, I was gone. I know that now. Along with the fear and anguish raging within them, there was a luminosity that startled me. It was as though I knew that, with or without me, she'd survive and eventually thrive, but I wanted that to happen with me. Being the one person that it happened with was and is important to me. I want to see her blossom, to really come into her own without all the worry and terror swirling around her and hanging over her head. She doesn't deserve that. She deserves to be loved well by a man who'll take care of her and adore her.

That would be me.

My hand slides down her back and cups one ass

cheek, its tenderness feeding my growing arousal. I feel her toying with one of my nipples, and I can't wait anymore. I've got to take something of her into myself, and give her something of me. I grab the edge of her cami and pull it up, and she helps by sitting up slightly, taking it from me, and pulling it completely off.

And there they are, two perfect tits, big enough for my liking, but instead of the large, soft nipples I spied at the outpatient facility, these nipples are puckered and hard as rocks, and they might as well have my lips tattooed on them for all the restraint I have. I draw one into my mouth and smile around it as her back arches and her breath comes in small, quick huffs. My other hand stimulates the other nipple, and she cries out as I pinch and tug on it. God, she's responsive as hell, and she wants more, I can tell. I make a big production out of shimmying out of my boxer briefs, and I hear her gasp when she gets a look at my family tree. Son of a bitch is practically a California redwood at this point, and it's aching so badly that I wonder if it'll ever stop. She's moaning and writhing, and I put my hands on her waist and hold her down. Feeling her body moving against mine stokes my fire, and I can feel precum seeping from my slit.

Almost as though she could hear my thoughts, her hand finds my cock and starts to stroke it, gently at first, and then more aggressively. She stops, and I feel her fingertip slide across the head, stop at the slit, and then drag across. What she does next knocks the wind out of me – she puts her finger to her lips and kisses it, then shoves it into her mouth and sucks. I crawl down between her legs, and I love the way the big, long, hard thing pokes me in the belly when I bend at the waist. She's watching me with a mixture of love and pure lust, and I drag her thong off.

And there it is – Nirvana. I can feel my fingers twitch as they scramble to touch her, and I wrap my hands behind her knees, pull her legs up and bent so her feet are flat on the mattress, and then press them apart until she's opened up like a butterfly. I hear her moan out, "Oh, god, Dave," and run her hands down her chest and over her tits until she traps her nipples in between her fingers and starts to work them over.

Damn. I wanted to eat that pussy, and all I can think about is being inside her. But I want her to come for me so I know she's ready to come *with* me. I open her slit with my fingers and grin. God, that's a gorgeous slice of female, all pink and buttery and waiting. I press my face into her folds, then let my tongue drag up her slit until it lands on the one thing I'm looking for. I back it down, run it into her pussy for just a few seconds to feel her squirm, then slide it back up and suck her clit into my mouth.

This girl tastes like joy, smells like rainbows, and looks like happiness. I look up her mound and belly to the undersides of her tits and find her looking down at me. "Oh, god, Dave, please, don't stop, baby, don't stop." *Not a chance!*, I think. "Dave?"

"Um-hmmmm," I hum from between her thighs.

"You love me?"

I stop, lift my head, and look straight into her face. "Hell yeah, baby. I love you like I've never loved anybody in my life."

"I love you that way too." Her face turns a little pink and she whispers, "Fuck me."

"I'm finishing what I started and then you'll have me inside you until you're sick of me." As I bury my face again, she whispers to me again.

"Me sick of that? Never happen."

I tie into her like a wrecking ball. I'm seriously concerned that I'm going to come before I ever make it inside her. I don't care how old she is, I can tell she's gonna fuck like a porn star, and that's more than I could've ever dreamed of; way, way more. The smile she shoots me is come-fuck-me dazzling, and I work her over in earnest, giving her everything I've got, using my tongue to tease her like she's never been teased in her life. It's coming closer and closer, and I hear the growl in her voice as she cries out, "Oh, god, oh, god, daaaa-yummmmm," and her body turns loose, her pelvis bucking wildly as I try to hang on and make her ride it through. Her hands slip into my hair and pull, and I feel like the rodeo star who just won the gold buckle. I hear her scream, "Baby, stop! Oh, god, please! No more! No more!"

That's it. I'm ready, past ready, hard enough to bore through oak. When I crawl up and put a hand on either side of her shoulders, my body suspended above hers, I take in the sight of her face, flushed with sex and blazing with desire. "Are you ready? Really ready?"

"God, yes. I need you. Please, Dave, please?"

"I'm making you mine. Right now. You belong with me from this point forward. Understand?"

"Yes. I understand. Please?"

"If it's too much, tell me. I don't want to hurt you."

A whine comes from her lips as she cries, "Please, god! I'm all yours. Just fuck me, Dave, please? I need your cock."

Hot damn. She talks dirty too. How'd I get this lucky? I position the head of my cock at her entrance and rub it up and down in her juices to lubricate it. And she's wet – so wet I'm pretty sure there's a puddle underneath her. Then I slide into her in one firm stroke as I hiss out, "God, Olivia, I love you."

There's a shriek of, "Oh, god! Oh, god! Damn!" Almost on cue, her legs come up with her knees against her chest and she begs me, "Deeper, baby, deeper. All the way. Please? Deeper, please? Oh, god, fuck me, Dave."

Christ, she's tight. I'm struggling to maintain my control, but as I watch her, I'm completely caught up in the expression on her face, the way her body's moving, the words that her lips are forming even though no sound comes out. I rise up enough to put my hands on her chest and let them trail down to her tits, and I pull and twist to listen to her cry out. Her hands return the favor, fingers trailing up and through the hair on my chest to find my nipples and tweak them, and I feel almost weak.

In a few minutes, I move to kneeling and lift her until she's sitting on my cock, and it's forced even farther into her pussy, making her practically scream. "Ride me, baby. Come on. Show me how much you love it." Hands gripping my shoulders, she puts her feet flat on the bed and starts to lift and drop on my hardness. While she does, she tosses her head and her hair flows back and down over her shoulders. I moan out, "Oh, god, angel, fuck me. Yeah, that's it." My hands encircle her tiny waist as I help her rise and fall, and I swear she gets tighter by the minute. "You're a goddess, baby. Your body is pure sex. I want to fuck you until we can't move."

"Look. Look at where we're joined, Dave. Look. It's beautiful, huh?"

I stare downward at the point where my dick disappears into her tight sheath and smile. "It's the most beautiful thing I've seen except for you."

And then she kisses me. She's still moving on me, and the kiss is powerful, long and hot and ball-hardening. I manage to groan out around her lips, "Oh, god, I can't hold back anymore. I'm gonna come, baby. Are you ready to come with me?"

"I will be." She takes a hand from my shoulder and reaches down between us to stroke her clit, and it's a sight that drives me wild. God, sexy, sexy, sexy, this girl is beyond sexy and all mine. I harden to the screaming point and she grinds down onto me as she cries out, "Oh, god, Dave, I'm coming, baby, I'm coming, oh, damn, damn, damn, DAMN!" Her body convulses against me as I pour into her, all salt and heat and wetness shot into her precious warmth, that instrument of pleasure that she's shared with me so freely.

I've never felt like this, so overwhelmed with love and passion for a woman, and I've had my share, but none have ever had this effect on me. I hold her against me, kneeling there in my bed, and whisper into her forehead, "You're mine forever. I love you, Olivia."

"I love you too, Dave. I've never had a man make love to me this way before."

"Aw, babe, we're just getting started." I manage to drop both of us back down onto the bed, and I pull her close and hold her against me just to feel her heart beat. I'd love to freeze this moment and come back to it over and over. I feel her twist and reach out. "What are you doing?"

"This." I look to see her phone in her hand and, before I can stop her, she holds it up over us and clicks a picture.

"God, Olivia, really?"

"Yeah. I mean, you're not mad, are you?"

I chuckle. "No, I guess not. I just haven't ever had a woman take a picture of me holding her after I've fucked her."

She draws back just a little. "Was any of that love-making? At all?"

"You're so cute."

"Answer my question, Dave Adams."

A chuckle rumbles out of my throat. "Yes. It all was. I just say fuck because it sounds sexier."

She tips her head back and laughs, and I love that sound. "I guess it is! Look." She turns the phone around and shows me the picture.

And there we are – sated and happy and in each other's arms. Well, arm. She's got one up in the air, taking the picture. But whatever. The intent comes through loud and clear. It's two people in love, and I'm one of them. An old man and a young woman.

And oddly enough, in that picture, we look like we belong together.

<hr/>

"Hi, angel. Sleep well?"

"Yeah. What time is it?"

"It's about nine."

"Really? Huh." Eyes rubbed in early morning fashion, she asks me, "How many times did you come last night?"

"I lost count. I'd wager you did too."

"Yes I did. Damn, that was good and I'm sore."

My cheeks pink, I say, "Yeah, I have to admit, I am a little too."

"What? 'Mr. I-Have-Twenty-Subs-At-My-Disposal' is a little sore from some sex with a barely-legal girl?"

Rolling her, I tickle her for a second and look into her face. "First, you're a grown woman. You've been legal for quite a while. And second, I haven't had twenty at my disposal. Eighteen maybe, but not twenty." She smacks me with a pillow and laughs. "Besides, you're better than seventeen of those."

"Oh, is that right?" Now she's laughing and tickling me. "I'm better than ALL of them," she announces.

"Know what?" I tap the end of her nose. "You are.

Better than any and all of them. Seriously. I didn't know what to expect last night, but that wasn't it."

"Then what *were* you expecting?"

I shrug. "I don't know, but not that. I guess I thought you'd be a bit more, um, virginal maybe?"

That really gets a laugh out of her. "I know I've been hurt and abused, but I had several boyfriends in college and *lots* of sex. I'm not inexperienced, just out of practice."

"We'll fix that." I kiss her again, and she slides down my body like a penguin on ice. "Damn, girl, what are you doing?"

"I'm gonna suck your cock."

"Right now?"

"Morning wood?"

I grin. "Well, yeah, but I didn't expect you to . . ."

"See? I'm constantly exceeding your expectations!" She disappears down the length of my body and in just a few seconds, the heat and wetness of her mouth draws my shaft in and I'm ready to beg her to stop. She slides up and down it with ease, then moves downward slowly and lets the head press down into her throat. I almost come unglued. She doesn't say anything, just keeps working slowly and deliberately until she's got me wriggling and cussing. There's some hand action added to the job, and in a few minutes I yell out, "Fuck yeah!" and fill her throat.

She licks my cum off her hands, then smiles up at me. "Yummy!" That makes me laugh again. "What? You don't believe me? Here – you'll see."

Sliding back up the bed, she kisses me with wide open lips, and I can taste myself on her lips and in her mouth. "Wow. I do taste good – if you like the taste of cum. And I don't especially." Giggling as she goes, she heads to the bathroom, and I hear her morning wee hitting the surface of the water in the toilet bowl. When she comes back out, she poses in the bathroom doorway and looks at me on the bed.

"You are without a doubt the sexiest man I've ever seen in my life."

"I do okay for an old guy."

Kneeling on the bed, she leans down into my face. "You are the sexiest man I've ever seen in my life," she says again. "It has nothing to do with your age. Look at that body. You're muscled up just right in all the right places. No love handles, no beer belly. Nice, nice, nice, and that cock of yours? Oh my goodness, Mr. Adams. It's quite the instrument of pleasure."

Propping myself up on one elbow, I grin at her. "You are a true gift, you know that? I feel like the luckiest bastard in the whole world."

She snuggles up against me. "Yeah?"

"Yeah. You make me the luckiest man alive because I get to wake up here with you." Halting my next word, my phone rings – Clint's ringtone. I reach for it and growl into it, "Hello?"

"Hello! Is this Dave I-Got-Lucky-Last-Night Adams?"

"Why, yes it is, nosy Nellie. What's up with you?"

"Get your cock outta that girl and listen up. We're

meeting with the chief detective on the case at two o'clock. I'll let you know how it goes immediately afterward. Sound okay?"

"Yeah, sounds great. And listen, son, you and Steffen, you be careful, you hear me?"

"Will do. Thanks, Dad. And congratulations."

"Wait. How do you know about this?"

"I think it was that sweet post-coital pic Trish got this morning."

"Oh my god." Olivia is giggling against me, and I look down at her. "You didn't." She nods.

Clint laughs, and I can tell he's not laughing with me; he's laughing *at* me. "Yep. She did. Very nice. You should have that framed, use it for the family Christmas cards. All that stuff."

"Smart ass. Talk to you in a bit."

"You know it. Bye, Dad."

I stare down at Olivia. "You sent Trish that picture? Of us post-fuck?"

"Yeah! I was proud of it."

I just shake my head and grin. Ah, the age of technology. Sharing the fact you've just fucked your woman, and doing so at the speed of light. How nice.

Actually, I'm kinda proud too.

<hr>

I hear the door open and I know who it is. It's about four o'clock and I call out, "Guys?"

"Yeah!" Just as I thought – Steffen and Clint.

"Be out in a minute." Olivia's asleep, but I wake her.

"Hey, baby, Clint and Steffen are here. You need to come out here and talk to them."

"Yeah, okay. I'm gonna brush my teeth and hair and I'll be right out." She retreats to the bathroom across the hall. I brush my teeth and hair and head out into the living room.

Steffen's shaking his head. "Wow! Late night or late morning?"

I grin. "Yeah." That makes Clint moan. "So what did you find out?"

"I'm as sure as I'm sitting here that the guy heading up the team is straight as an arrow. He said he didn't care if he never met Olivia, as long as he had a statement and she was willing to testify. That makes me feel pretty confident," Clint says.

Steffen throws in, "Plus I'm a pretty good judge of character, and I didn't detect anything fake about him. He seems very, very set on bringing these guys down."

"Did you give him Falco's name?"

Clint shakes his head. "Didn't have to. When I told him about the encounter at the mall, he said, 'Big guy. Dark hair. Mark Falco,' so apparently he's the one they're watching. He was very forthcoming with information. At one point, he called the chief and told him that they have someone reliable as a witness. I was impressed. The chief even talked to me on the phone. He didn't try to get me to give him Olivia's name or anything, just told me he was grateful that someone seemed to want to stop this, and if she's willing to testify, he'll do everything he can to make it comfortable and easy for her."

About that time Olivia joins us. "Hey, guys. What's going on?"

They tell her everything they just told me. Clint finishes with, "And I think we need to set something up to let you talk to him."

"Okay. I'll do whatever I need to do. Just let me know." I'm a little shocked at her willingness, but I try not to show it. I'm glad she feels safe enough with all of us to even try this.

"Good deal. He also suggested that we use you as bait to try to force their hand."

That's when I interrupt. "Absolutely not. They'll have to catch them some other way. She's *not* being put in that position."

"But honey, wait. If they need me to . . ."

I shake my head – hard. "No! And I mean that. No discussion. It's not going to happen, you hear me? I won't have it."

"Dad, you know we'd be . . ."

"I said no. End of discussion. Pick another way, because that one's not happening."

Steffen pipes up. "Okay. Well, we're still going with the meeting in the disguise, all of that. Will you agree to that?"

Clint interjects toward me, "Yeah, but you can't be there. Remember? We discussed that."

"Yes. I don't like it, but yes, I think that could happen. But there'd have to be plenty of safeguards in place."

Steffen nods. "We'll have it well covered. I'm thinking I'll enlist the help of some of the Doms at the club. Gary, Bruce, some of the other guys. I think they'd help if they knew what was going on."

"I'm sure they would." My hand finds Olivia's. "I just don't want anything to happen to her. At all."

"Neither do we." Clint reaches over and slaps my knee. "None of us want anything to happen to you, Olivia. We're watching out for you. Always."

"I know. Thanks." Her face is flushed and she's staring at her lap. I know this is overwhelming for her, and I hate that. "So when?"

"Early next week. That be okay?"

"Sure. I'll do whatever I need to."

Once they're out the door, I sit back down beside her. She's looking a little flushed and shaky. "Baby, if this gets to be too much for you, all you have to do is say so. We'll all understand."

"I've got to stop them. For my friends."

I'm so proud of her. I hope when the time comes she knows that.

<hr />

"Hey! Wake up!" The sun breaks through the window as I pull open the drapes, and she squints against the light.

"What? What's going on?"

"Come on! We're getting some breakfast and doing something fun. And I've got just the thing."

Making her get going is harder than I thought, but she's pretty perky and chipper by the time we get to the pancake place. She orders the biggest mess of pancakes I've ever seen – chocolate chip, raspberry, and pumpkin. What a weird combination, but she seems to love them. As we head out again, she stares over at me. "Where are we going?"

"You'll see." I just keep driving. We talk about little things, things we've seen on TV, stuff around the house that probably needs to be done, and places we'd like to go in the next few weeks. I finally turn down a little gravel road and drive as far as I can, then park. "Come on. Get out."

"Where are we?"

"You'll see."

"You said that before."

"And I meant it. Come on. It's not far." I take her hand and we walk along the quiet trail, listening to the birds and crickets. I can see the water through the trees, but I don't think she's put it together yet. When we round the bend, she sees everything and gasps.

"Oh my god. It's like a fairyland."

Sitting there at the edge of the water, there's a cabin, small but pristine, with two rocking chairs on the porch. "What is this place?"

"It was my grandfather's fishing cabin. When he died, he willed it to me. For a lot of years, I just let it fall down, but about a year ago I got interested in it and started working on it. I think I've made a lot of progress." We step up onto the low porch and I open the door. "After you."

It's lovely. The rough-hewn logs just bring out the

natural beauty of the old handmade quilt, and the cabinets have red speckleware stored in plain view. A stone fireplace dominates the other end of the room, and anyone who's in the cabin could enjoy a fire in it, even from the bed. She looks around. "Bathroom?"

"Um, outhouse."

She sets her jaw and slams her hands onto her hips. "You're kidding, right?"

"Nope."

"Snakes?"

"I guess they might be in there, but probably not."

"Nice. Where is it?"

"Right out the back door." I point and she leaves, then comes back in a few minutes.

"Hey, that's cool! That water thingy in there made water to wash my hands and flush the toilet. I like that."

"Thanks! I invented it more or less."

"Well, it's brilliant, more or less." That gets a grin out of me.

We spend the afternoon sitting on the porch, rocking in the rocking chairs; well, most of the afternoon. At one point we wind up inside in the bed, and we fuck each other to the moon and back before we dress and go back out to rock. As we sit there, she asks quietly, "So, do you think you'd ever want to get married?"

I don't look at her, but I answer, "I didn't think I'd ever want to again, but I've been thinking about it lately. It sounds like a lovely proposition in some ways. Let's just get this thing with the police behind us and see where everything stands, okay?"

"Okay." She stops, then asks, "How many times have you been in love?"

I look out over the water. "Oh, twice. I still love Marta, but it's like a friendship kind of love. And then there's you." Turning toward her, I smile. "I love you, Olivia. I know I say it, but I hope I show it."

"You've more than shown it. I hope you can tell how much I love you too." She gets quiet for a minute, then says, "I think I want to go back to work. Not just yet, but sometime soon."

"Doing what?"

"I don't know. But something. I feel like I need to contribute to the household."

"You don't have to," I tell her quietly.

"I know, but I want to. I do. And without kids, I need something to keep me busy. Of course, then the problem is that you're working at night and I'm working during the day and we never see each other. So I don't want that. But I would like to buy a car, get my license back, all of that stuff."

"You can do that without going to work. I have a good pension and my share of the club's profits."

"I know, but I feel like I should work for some of what I have, if not most."

I shake my head. "Well, okay. But I really don't think you should."

"When the time comes, we'll figure it out." *Damn, that sounds like something I'd say,* I mumble in my mind.

The sky is still plenty light, but I don't want to get caught out here in the dark. "Let's go, okay? We can stop somewhere on the way back and get something to eat."

"Sounds good. And Dave?"

"Yeah, baby?"

"Thanks for bringing me here. How many women have you brought here?"

My heart is so full of love for this woman that I can barely breathe. "Just one."

Hands on waist, she looks up at me and says, "Then thank you."

"You're welcome. Thanks for coming with me."

Arm in arm, we head back to the car. An hour and a half and three hamburgers later, we pull into my drive. "This was a fun day."

She nods. "Yes. It was. I almost felt normal."

"Good. We'll do it again."

"I'd like that." She climbs out of the car and I walk behind her to the house.

Twenty minutes later, we're cuddled up in my big bed, soaking up each other's body heat and thinking about the coming winter and what it will mean for us. I keep thinking about this thing with the police, and I like it less and less all the time. I'm just praying that it'll be all right. I don't want to lose this girl.

She's my heart and soul.

Chapter Eight

You know that feeling that you get sometimes when you wake up, like the day is going to hell and you just know it? You don't know how, but you just know it's going to. And before too long, those tell-tale signs start showing up, the ones that let you know your gut was right and you're so fucked that you'll never be able to sit down again.

This is one of those days.

I've had a weird, uneasy feeling in my stomach ever since this all started with the cops, and now I'm almost sick. I know she feels like she has to do this, but I truly don't want her to. Something just feels wrong. Sure, it's probably just fear, but I can't help it. This girl is too important to me. If anything happens to her . . . well, it just can't.

Trish and Sheila show up early, and they're carrying all kinds of stuff. "What the hell is *that*?" I ask Sheila.

"I did theatrical makeup in college for the drama department. It's a contouring kit. I can make her up so that you won't recognize her at all. Seriously. You'll be amazed."

"Good. I don't want anyone to recognize her."

They pull her hair back and get started. Honestly, I'm so upset that I just leave the room. I can't watch. I don't want to be part of this, and I don't want her to be part of it either. It needs to be over, and I hope this does it, at least until there's some kind of court proceedings. With any luck, the guys will plead guilty and there won't even be a trial. That would be the absolute best resolution to the problem. Of course, I don't expect that, but I can still hope for it.

"Dave? Dave, come in here and look," Trish calls out. I walk into the kitchen and I'm shocked.

Sitting at the table is a woman I've never seen before. Her lower jaw is square, her forehead almost Cro-Magnon wide, and she has half-rotted teeth. They're fitting a wig on her head over her brunette hair, and it's a kind of shaggy-looking thing with gray and blond in it, kind of a dirty salt-and-pepper mix. She looks up at me and grins. "Hi, honey!"

"Holy shit."

Sheila smiles. "See? I told you that you wouldn't recognize her."

"Holy shit. That's pretty amazing."

Sheila hands Olivia a hand mirror. "Oh my god, I'm so ugly!"

"Yeah. Amazing what the wrong makeup can do for a girl, huh?" Trish laughs.

"Now, for the rest of the getup. Let's go." Sheila picks up a huge bag and heads to the bedroom. "Come along, Dave. We may need some help." Once we're in the bedroom, she starts spreading out a bunch of stuff that I can't identify. Then I see something that makes me feel a little better – a Kevlar vest. If this is part of the disguise, I'm pretty happy about that.

"Okay, let's get these on," Trish instructs. Olivia pulls off her jeans and works her way into the bottoms. They're these padded things like you'd wear under a Halloween costume, and her ass looks huge. She's handed a pair of sweats to put on over them. Then the Kevlar goes on, followed by another thing that's kind of like the bottoms, only not as thick. It has bulky sleeves, and it's topped with a zippered hoody. Trish is tugging and pulling. "When you get there, pull up the hood and pull the drawstring. Let some of the hair stick out. You'll have on sunglasses too, so that'll help. Just before you leave, we need to put makeup on the backs of your hands so they'll be dark like your face."

"Put these on," Sheila orders and hands her a pair of almost-worn-out work boots, complete with mud.

I can't help but be sarcastic. "Can we do that at the door? I don't want vacuuming to be on our list of things to do before the funeral." Olivia's eyes rotate to me and go wide. "Well, I'm serious. I still don't like this."

"It's going to be fine. I have faith in everyone who's working with this. They haven't let me down yet." She's staring at the boots. "These are kinda big."

Trish scowls. "That's the point. They need to fit poorly. You're supposed to look like a homeless person."

Olivia's face goes blank. "I could just go back to being me. That would make me look like a homeless person."

The air crackles with tension at her words, and Trish immediately says, "Honey, I didn't mean it like that."

"I know. I'm just not sure how you meant it."

My daughter-in-law squats in front of my girlfriend and looks up into her eyes. "I meant you need to look like what people *think* homeless people look like. Does that make sense?"

Olivia nods as she looks at her hands in her lap. "Yeah. Sorry. I'm just kind of sensitive about it."

"I understand. I'm sorry if I offended you. That wasn't my intention," Trish tells her with a sad smile.

"It's okay. I know what you meant. Don't worry about it." She stands and looks in the mirror at herself all fattened up and frumpy. "I look like Griselda." When we all give her a weird look, she explains. "We called her Griselda. She was down under the bridge with us. She couldn't remember her own name, so that's what we called her. She had this Hollister hoodie she loved."

"What happened to her?" I ask.

In a voice so tiny that we can barely hear it, Olivia says, "We don't know. She just disappeared one day and never came back."

And then I understand. She's doing it for Griselda, for all the people she knew and tried to make into a family, the ones who disappeared without a trace or died in violent ways. Something happens to me in that moment that I never expect. "'Scuse me," I manage to mumble and go across the hallway to the big bathroom. Once I've got the door closed and locked, I sit down on the toilet lid and do something I've never done, not in my entire adult life.

I cry. I'm terrified that something will happen to her, but I also understand how much pain and heartbreak she's been through. It's something I've never experienced, and I hope I never do. My sobs are silent; I don't want them to hear me. But then I see something slip underneath the door. When I pick it up and open it, it tears my heart apart.

I love you. If anything happens to me, know that the last few weeks have been the happiest I've ever been. I've been loved by the finest man I've ever known. You'll always be the one true thing in my life. – O

I just clutch that little scrap of paper to my chest and cry. The fear is overwhelming, but so is the pride. What's happened to me? I've never been this needy or emotional or attached to anyone. But I can't deny it.

This is the one woman I'm destined to be with. I know that now. If I can keep her alive, everything will be okay.

The towel is soft against my skin as I splash water on my face to soothe my swollen eyes, and I walk out to find the women in the living room. Clint and Steffen join us in just a few minutes. "Conference," Clint calls out. When I step into the room, he takes one look at me. There's a knowing in his eyes, and he gives me a slight nod to let me know he's with me. I take a seat at the table and turn my chair around. We're all here. "I was just on the phone with Detective Roberts."

"That's his name?" I can't help but ask. I want to know who all the people are, who to hold responsible if anything goes wrong, so names are pretty important to me.

"Yeah. So here's the deal. I got some of the guys to come along. I've got Bruce, Gary, Tim, Cody, and Austin. Greg will be joining us at the site. They'll be scattered around, looking like they're just there like everybody else. Matter of fact, Bruce is bringing Valerie – she wanted to come and help. And I think Tim is bringing Leslie. So they'll look like couples just out for a nice afternoon. Detective Roberts will be wearing a wire that's strong enough to pick up Olivia's voice too. He'll have three men out there at each of the four corners, keeping an eye out and watching. They don't want our guys there; I told them it's this way or no way."

I breathe a tiny sigh of relief. "Good. Because that's how it is. We have no one on the ground, she doesn't go. End of discussion."

"We've got it under control, Dad. I think it'll be fine. Olivia, listen to me." He locks eyes with her, and she's giving him her total attention. "Behind where you'll be, there's a low retaining wall and some shrubs. If anything goes wrong, drop off the back of your bench and roll up against the retaining wall. Understand?"

"Yes."

"Don't forget this. When you get there, take a good look and you'll see what I'm talking about. Remember, drop off the back of the bench and roll up against the retaining wall. Triangle of life style." Living here where earthquakes are always a possibility, we've all been schooled on the triangle of life, so I know she understands. "We all set?"

"No." They all wheel around at the sound of my voice. "I want to speak to her alone. Please."

"We'll wait in the car. Don't be too long. They're expecting us." Clint shepherds everyone else out the door, and the house is quiet again. The young woman in front of me stares up at me, and even through the ghastly makeup, I see that spirit shining through. My god, if I lose her, what will I do?

"You remember everything you're supposed to do?" She nods silently. "You remember who loves you, right?"

"You do. And I love you."

"And I want you back here in a couple of hours. And I'd kiss you, but I don't want to mess anything up."

There's that grin, the one that melts me down into a puddle. "I know. I'll be back, I promise. Gotta go." My heart is sinking into my stomach as I watch her open the door, wave at me, and disappear.

No. Not without me. I grab my keys and run out the door, catching her before she closes the van door. "I'm going."

"Dad, we've had this conversation and . . ."

"I'm going. I go or she doesn't. I mean it." Clint and Steffen look at each other and then back at me.

"Then you'll do exactly what you're told. No variation. You'll put her life, hers and Detective Roberts', in danger if you don't. Do you understand?"

My nerves are shot and I have no self-control left when I snap, "I'm not fucking deaf."

Clint snarls back, "You were told you couldn't go, so maybe you are."

"Guys!" Trish's voice cuts through the racket. "Look, this is tense enough as it is without you fighting. Dave wants to go. I can understand that – surely both of you can understand that. I want him there too. Olivia wants him there, right, honey?"

"I want to do whatever we've got to do but, yes, I would prefer it."

"Fucking get in," Clint sighs. "And I've got a call to make." He gets out of the van and we watch as he walks back and forth in front of it, then gets back in. "I've got a place for you to be." When he turns to look at me, he snaps. "Out of the way. And you'd better stay there, you hear me?"

"Yeah, yeah, I hear you. And I'm sorry if I've messed everything up. It's just that . . ." My voice trails off because I can't finish the sentence. It's Steffen who saves me from myself.

"You're scared. We get that. We're all scared. Matter of fact, the one person who should be the most scared is Olivia, and she seems to be the calmest." He reaches a hand out to her and she takes it. I see her squeeze it, and he squeezes back and smiles at her. "You're a brave woman, little one."

"Thank you." Dropping his hand, she turns to stare out the window, and then reaches blindly over for mine. That soft hand in mine makes my stomach churn even harder. God, I'm afraid. I'm afraid of losing her, afraid of her being hurt and suffering, afraid of someone else getting hurt. I'm afraid of everything to do with this little operation. This detective had better be good and be on the ball, because we can't do this again. Fuck everybody else; I don't think I could survive it.

We pull up to a modern-looking building, and I'm not sure why. As we enter, a security guard nods to Clint, and he nods back. The sleek, modern elevator takes us up to the eighth floor, where Clint opens a door. "The cops don't know it, but I've got use of this suite for the day. The building belongs to one of my clients. We can watch from up here."

"You're going down there with her, right?" Is he trying to tell me he's sending her down there?

"No. I'm staying inside. Everyone else is staying here. Steffen and I can't go out; we've been in and out of the police station, so he could make us. And he saw me at the mall that day. He'll know something's going on if he sees one of us."

"You can't send her down there by herself!" I know I seem frantic, and that would be because I am. Holy shit. This is not happening.

"She has to go. It's the only way. But trust me, I'm going to be in that alley. When she's done and she leaves, I'll be at the back corner of this building to meet her, you can bet on that." Clint pulls out his forty-five and checks the chamber. "The only time she'll be alone is when she's going from the back door to the commons. No other time."

Everything inside me is screaming when Steffen pulls me to the window. "Look." Olivia starts toward it, but he barks, "No! You can't see where they are. You might accidentally look at them and jeopardize everything. Turn with your back to us." When she's turned around, he points. "Look. There's Tim over there. And over there is Bruce. That corner is Gary. This corner is Austin. Greg's over there where you can't see. Cody's out there on the far side. And look again; there are cops out there too. See that big red bush? There's a cop there in camo, and another one over here by the trash can. Roberts will come in from the other side, so that's where Falco would come in if he's following. He won't see them over here."

"I don't feel any better." And I don't. I'm a wreck.

Clint watches. "There he is. The guy with the white hair." We watch as a tall, white-haired man walks out into the outdoor seating area and looks around like he's looking for someone. He glances at his watch, and then he sits down at one of the concrete tables. True to the plan, he's facing the outside and the concrete retaining wall; if she has to, the wall is right there to shield her. He's got something in his hand, and it looks like a bag from a fast food restaurant. "Okay, honey. It's time."

She hugs everyone until she comes to me. "Promise me you'll wait right here for me. I'll be back in just a little while."

My voice is more of a whine, but I don't care. "Baby, *please* don't do this, please? I don't want you to do this, Olivia. Don't."

"I have to. I have to do this for Mrs. Sullenger and Griselda and Elizabeth. They're counting on me. I've got to go." Her eyes gaze steadily into mine when she says, "If anything happens, I love you, Dave. I'll always love you." I watch her and my son leave the room and the door closes behind them.

My heart wants to stop beating. My lungs want to stop breathing. My god, I don't know what to do. Full-blown panic consumes me, and my knees get shaky. Trish gets me a chair and Sheila fans me with her jacket. When Steffen stoops beside the chair and looks into my face, I can barely speak when I whisper out, "Cothran, I beg you: Stop this right now. Go down and make this stop."

"I can't. This is Olivia's decision. It's what she wants to do. I'm not going to argue that point with her. She'll be fine. Come over here and watch."

It's not what I want to do, but I feel compelled by an unseen force. Can they see me if I press my hands against the window? I decide I don't want to take a chance. A woman comes out from between the buildings, her too-big boots causing her to kind of stumble along. She looks around, approaches the table, and stands warily at a distance while the man tries to persuade her to sit. When she does, he holds out a bag, then takes it back when she reaches for it and begins a conversation.

This is it. I hope she's telling him everything this time, everything he needs to know. If not, I can't go through this again. I see the two of them chattering, her making arm gestures, him continuing to ask questions. He opens the bag, hands her a couple of French fries, and then takes it back again.

It seems like forever. Is this never going to end? How much information can he need? They talk and talk and talk. Finally, he hands her the bag and I see her clutch it to her chest. He rises to leave and leans across the table to shake her hand. I see her struggle to get up in all the crap she's wearing, but she wobbles a little and lands on her butt. He's still standing there, hand outstretched, when I hear the "pop."

And he falls. Backward. A red spray goes everywhere, and I try to make sense of everything as I see a flash from a muzzle, then another. Clint hasn't come back up, and I wonder where he is and if he's safe, but I can't see Olivia and I'm terrified. Where is she? What's happening? That's it. I can't do this. Before Steffen can stop me, I've sprinted for the door and I'm down the stairs.

I take them two at a time. It's eight floors, and I contemplate taking the handrails down, but they're those damn fire stairs where every level has a landing, and that won't work. I'm out of breath by the fourth floor, but I can't stop. If I could've skydived out of the upstairs window down to the ground, I would've. Nothing could get me there fast enough.

When I burst through the downstairs door, Clint is right there. "No! We've got to wait for them to clear the area! The cops have to sweep it. Stay put."

"Where's Olivia?"

"Dad, just hang on."

"NO! I want to find her NOW!"

Clint's doing everything in his power to hold me back, and I almost manage to break free when I hear a voice yell, "CLEAR!"

I'm done with this. I break out of his grip and run faster than I ever thought I could, and I manage to get all the way to the edge of the seating area before a cop catches me. "Sir, this is a crime scene."

"I'm well aware of that! LET ME GO!" I struggle against him and I feel hands all over me. Next thing I know, I'm looking up at the sky and a big, brawny guy has his knee in my chest.

"Hi, Dave!"

"Bruce? What the hell? Let me up!"

"Calm down. You're going to give yourself a heart attack."

"I can't. Where's Olivia?"

"Talking to the cops. She's fine, really. Calm down."

She's fine. That's all I care about. "I need to see her right now."

"Okay. But don't get all crazy, okay? They left me in charge of you and I don't want to get hauled in because I didn't do my job." His knee lifts from my chest, and he reaches a hand down to help me up. When I'm upright, he points. "See? She's right there and she's fine."

Sure enough, she's standing ten feet from where the detective was shot. "I'm going down there."

"No. Let them finish. She's fine."

"What happened?"

"The shooter's dead. One of the cops got him. And your girl did exactly what she was supposed to. Dropped off that bench and rolled up against the wall. He couldn't shoot her; he couldn't see her."

Thank god. She finally turns and sees me, and I hear her say something to one of the cops before she starts toward me at a dead run. Before I can say shotgun, she's in my arms. I just hold her tight and try to release some of the tension knotting my muscles and fogging up my brain. "You okay?

"Yeah. Yeah, I'm okay. I was so scared." Her face rests against my chest, and I don't care if she's getting makeup all over me. "Take me home, please?"

"They finished with you?" I don't really care if they aren't; she's going home. But we're not doing this again, so they might as well be.

"They said they are. The recording device Detective Roberts had on got the entire conversation. If he hadn't shown up, we would've met, talked, and then gone our separate ways. But now the bad guy's dead, and so is the good guy. And I don't know what that means."

"I don't know what it means to them, but to me, it means your part in this is over. And we're going to have a little talk at home."

"Okay." Her voice is tiny and soft, and I know she was scared. I'm proud of her, but I'm still so enraged that I don't know how long it will be before I finally calm down.

With a nod from the cops, we all load into the van and head back. I speak to no one. Clint tries to ask me a question, but I just snap, "I'm not talking to anyone here. Leave me alone." Out of the corner of my eye I see him and Steffen glance back and forth and a look passes between them. I don't acknowledge that look.

We get out at home and I storm to the front door. I think she's behind me, but I'm not sure. I wait until I hear the front door close and then I wheel on her. "What the HELL did you think you were doing, agreeing to this? I swear, Olivia, the next time I tell you no to something, I mean NO! Do you understand me?"

Head bowed, she whispers, "I'm going to take a shower and get all of this stuff off. We'll talk then."

As she walks past me, I grab both of her arms. "No. We're going to talk now! I'll have nothing like that going on ever again, do you hear me? Nothing like it. I tell you no, it means no."

Under all that hideous garb, two luminous eyes look up at me. "Dave, I'm your girlfriend, not your sub."

I feel a cold fury pass through my body, and I tremble at what it could mean. "What did you say to me?"

"I said, I'm your girlfriend, not your sub. I have a mind and a free will."

"This is what I get for everything I've done for you?"

The instant the words pass through my lips, I know what I've done. I see her shutting down and pulling in on herself, see the same look I saw that first night when her eyes met mine out by the dumpster as it clouds back over their clearness. But I can't stop myself. "Go shower. Stay in your room until I come for you." My hands leave her arms and she leaves me standing there without a word. As she disappears into Clint's old bedroom, I halfway expect her to slam the door, but she closes it very quietly and I don't hear another sound.

I make it back to the living room, drop onto the sofa, and plant my face in my hands. Dear god, what almost happened today? She was very nearly killed, and I let that go on. I should've put my foot down and insisted that she forget about it.

I said, I'm your girlfriend, not your sub. I have a mind and a free will.

And that's the moment I check myself. I've been treating her as another submissive all along, and now I know it. I don't think I've ever once asked her what she wanted to do for the day; I've just planned what I want-ed to plan and expected her to come along. I ordered her to buy a coat. I ordered her to eat her dinner.

I've dictated her life. Is it because she's so young? Or is it because I see her as a submissive? My mind is a jumble, all craziness and mind-numbing fear, and I don't know what to do. I love her, but I can't keep her like a bird in a cage. It's a terrible thing, what I've done to her. She's not my girlfriend. She's the daughter I took to raise.

She's a submissive. I'm her Dom. And no one thought to tell her. They most certainly didn't ask her permission.

Everything crashes down around me. I've made a huge, huge mistake by stepping into this relationship. I should've followed my instincts and pushed her away when I had a chance. Now my heart will be broken, and so will hers. I'm such an idiot, so bigoted and chauvinistic. She needed to be nurtured and given a place to grow, not sequestered and told how to live her life, and I just walked in and took over. I've got to fix this and there's only one way to do it.

I have to let her go.

The sofa isn't all that comfortable, but it's okay, and I stretch out to wait until the wildness inside my chest gets quiet. My phone rings and I glance at the screen: Clint. I'm not talking to him right now. I'm not talking to anyone. I'm done. He tries again, and I ignore him again.

A couple of hours go by before I finally get up and drag down the hallway. I give a tiny rap on the door and I hear her voice say, "Come in."

In nothing but a towel, she's on the bed, curled up in a fetal position. The face I'm accustomed to is back, no grimy, dark makeup on it, just that porcelain skin I've had the privilege of touching, her hair all wet and stringy. When I sit down on the edge of the bed, she scoots away. I tell myself it's to make room for me, but I'm not sure that's true. "Olivia, honey, we need to talk."

"I'm sorry. I was wrong. I was wrong about everything. I'm sorry."

"Baby," I start and reach for her, but she jerks away when I touch her, and I realize what I've done. There's no fixing this. It's permanently broken, and I'm the one who destroyed it. It didn't have a chance from the start. "Olivia, let's talk, okay?"

"I'm sorry. I'm really, really sorry."

"Stop it. Stop saying you're sorry. I'm sorry. I've

done something horribly, terribly wrong. I've been telling you what to do and when to do it. I've ordered you around like a puppy. Yeah, like a submissive. I might as well stop kidding myself. That's what I need, and that's not you. And it's not fair to ask you to become something you're not."

Her shoulders quake with sobs. "I'm sorry, Dave. Please. Don't say things like that. You're just upset."

"Yeah. I'm upset with myself. I don't know what I was thinking taking on this relationship. It's not fair to you, and it was wrong of me."

Her sobs quiet and she just lies there. Is she waiting for me to tell her I was just kidding? Or does she understand that this isn't going to work and she's just accepting it? I can't tell. When I rise and reach for the door, I look back at her there on the bed.

Every fiber in my being wants to hold her. She was scared and alone. She sat two feet from a man and watched him be killed. She watched her friends be beaten and raped and left to die; she took beatings and abuse at the hands of those monsters too. She needs to be held, to be comforted, to be told she's in the right place and everything will be okay. But I know nothing will ever be okay again.

⋙◦◦◦⋘

Someone's beating on my front door. Or is that my head pounding? I got a bottle of scotch and a glass and locked myself in the bedroom last night. Then I realize: All of her clothes are in here. She's had nothing to wear all night. And there it is again: The pounding. Someone *is* beating on the door.

I unlock the door and look around, but the other bedroom door is closed, so I stumble up the hall and yank the door open. "What do you want?"

Clint is livid. "What the hell's going on? I've been trying to call you since last night and you haven't answered. I've been worried sick."

My hand reaches for my cell phone and I hold it up. "Not on. I don't want to talk to you. Can't you get that message?"

He wrinkles his nose at me. "You're drunk."

"Not anymore. But I was last night."

"Where's Olivia?"

"I think she's in your old room. That's the last place I saw her." When he brushes past me, I tell him, "She probably doesn't have anything on."

"I've seen naked women before. I'm more worried about her than thinking about what she might or might not be wearing." He raps on the door once. "Olivia?" When she doesn't answer, he opens the door gingerly, but I step up behind him and just slam it open.

She's on the floor behind the bed, towel still wrapped around her, cowering against the closet door. Her eyes have that same wild look I remember from the night before, the ones I saw out back that first night, and she's shaking like a leaf. In a heartbeat Clint's on the floor beside her, smoothing her hair, but she pushes with her feet to scoot her butt across the floor and winds up in the corner by the closet door, trying her best to get away from him. "Olivia? It's Clint. It's okay, honey. Come here." She shakes her head, her hair swinging back and forth in ropes because it was never brushed after it was washed. "Baby, it's okay. Come here and let me hold you, honey. It's all right." She just shakes her head again and hides her face in the corner.

Clint stands, strides out in the hallway, and closes the door gently behind him. Next thing I know, he's got me by the shirt collar, dragging me up the hallway, and I yell, "Hey! What the hell do you think you're doing?" I'm shocked when he slings me onto the sofa and towers over me.

"What did you do to her?"

"I didn't do anything to her."

"Yes you did. What did you do?"

"I told her the truth. I told her I'd been treating her like a sub and I shouldn't have. I told her I'd made a mistake accepting our relationship. I told her to go to her room and not come out."

"*Your* room is her room."

"Not anymore. I told her I wouldn't accept her disobedience." His eyes go wide. "She needed to be held last night and I wouldn't hold her. This has to end. It's not fair to her and it's not going to work."

Clint just stands and stares at me. After what seems like an eternity, he says, "I've looked up to you, loved you, and respected you almost my entire life. And right now, I can honestly say I despise the man I'm looking at. Honesty. Integrity. Respect. Dignity. Dependability. Trust. Over and over and over, as a man, as a Dom, as a friend and a father. You've driven into me the idea that those were the things real men were made of. And look at you. You take this girl from the gutter, give her a home and shelter, tell her you love her, use her body, and then just push her away when she does something you don't like."

"I told her not to do it."

"That's not your call! She's a grown woman."

"I know. My mistake. I've been thinking of her as a little kid. And I can't take on a kid to raise. So this has to end."

Clint's still staring at me. A sick feeling grows in the pit of my stomach. This is my son, the boy I raised from the age of seven. He's just told me that I'm everything I've ever preached against, and he's right. It's all because I couldn't deny my heart and my body what I knew was wrong, and I'm ashamed and angry and tired. He turns away from me and pulls out his phone. "Baby? Yeah, I need you to take the kids to Steffen and Sheila's and come over here to Dave's. Yeah. No, it's bad. Yeah. Thanks, baby. See you in a few." Phone back in his pocket, he wheels and points at me. "You. Get some clothes on and get out of here. I don't want you back here for at least four hours. If I have to clean up your mess, I shouldn't have to trip over you to do it."

"Fuck you."

"Yeah, well, fuck you too. I don't care if it's your goddamn house, get out. Don't come back until," he looks at his watch, "three o'clock. I mean it. I don't care where you go or what you do. Just go."

Well, isn't that nice? I drag on some jeans and a tee shirt, put on socks and some Nikes, and head out the door. I don't turn around to look at him or wave or anything. I just leave. My car seems to have a mind of its own, and I don't realize where I'm going until I'm there.

I park and get out, then walk the rest of the way. When I can see the water, something inside me starts to crack. I stumble along the path until I reach the cabin and by the time I hit the door, I'm wheezing with sobs. The bed is there, its quilt straightened and neat, and I remember that day not so long ago when I made love with Olivia right here in this bed. I pull one of the pillows into my arms, clutch it to my chest, and cry.

It's ruined. And it's going to stay ruined. She needs a chance to grow and spread her wings, and she's never going to get that with me.

<hr />

I wake to the sound of chirping and singing. One glance at my watch and I realize it's morning – I've been here all night. Besides being thirsty as hell and needing to pee, my eyes are caked shut and I feel like I've been kicked in the gut.

Hell with the outhouse – I just let 'er rip off the porch, then find some bottled water inside. I cup my hands and splash it on my face, then drink the rest of it. Finished with it, I go out to the water's edge, fill the bottle full of rocks and dirt, screw the cap on, and throw it as far out into the water as I can. I watch the ripples hit the bank, colliding and disappearing, and I think about how that's my life now. Washed up. Petered out. Over.

The radio gets turned up as loud as I can get it, and I sing along mindlessly as I drive back home so I don't have to think. Home. Not much of one. I wonder what'll greet me there.

I don't have to wait long to find out. Dropping my keys in the bowl by the door, I see a note propped up on the kitchen table.

Dave,

I had Trish take Olivia to our house last night. After she left, I moved all of her things back into my old room. We'll try to talk to her tonight, maybe get her some help, but I don't know if she'll come back there or not. It took us an hour to get her into the car.

Spectacular. They're all ganging up on me. Then I realize that, considering the circumstances, Olivia needs them a lot more than I do. I haven't been home ten minutes when my phone rings. Clint – who else? "She was gone all night and you haven't even called to check on her. What the fuck?"

"Maybe that's because *I* was gone all night."

"Sounds about right."

"Hey, before you go getting all cocky on me, I was at the cabin. I needed the peace and quiet." I wait, but he doesn't say anything else. "Well?"

"Well what?"

I sigh. "Is she coming back here?"

"I don't know. I'm not sure how long she'll be at the hospital."

Fear grips my chest. "Hospital? I thought she was all right. I thought she wasn't hurt."

"She wasn't – physically. She's at the psych ward. They're treating her for PTSD."

"From the shooting?"

He hesitates, then says, "Among other things."

Now I don't know what to say. What else is there? The relationship that never should've been is over. She's getting help from someone who can really help her, not some over-the-hill Dominant who wants to bully her into submission. It's all for the best, this disaster that's not over yet. My voice is shaky when I manage to stutter out, "I'm . . . I'm glad she's getting some help."

"Yeah? Can I give you a little advice? You need to get some too. I think you've lost your ever-loving mind."

"Alzheimer's."

"Fuck that shit. Blame it on whatever you like, but we both know the truth." And the phone goes dead.

I take a shower, get dressed, and fumble around the house for awhile. Dinner is microwave popcorn and some French onion dip I find in the fridge. I drag a kernel through the dip, chew for a second, and then swallow. It's not very good, but it's here. I don't want to go out. I don't want to go anywhere. And then I get an idea.

I grab my tablet and start researching. Olivia needs a new home, and I've got to find the right one.

Chapter Nine

Sunshine is creeping in the bedroom window, and I turn to pick up the phone. It's a number I've never seen before, and I hit DECLINE and lay it back down, then bury my face in the pillow. It chimes for a voicemail; I'll listen later.

At two o'clock that afternoon, I remember the call while I'm gathering up the garbage, so I check it. Probably some salesperson or something.

But the voice in the message hits me completely unawares and I'm riveted to the spot. "Dave, it's me. Olivia. Remember me? I'm at the hospital. I don't want to be here. I want to come home. Please, can I come home? I'll do whatever you say, I promise. I just want to come home. Please?" There's a voice in the background and she says, "I've got to go. It's someone else's turn. I love you. Please come and get me. I miss you." There's a noise that's an old-fashioned phone receiver being hung up and she's gone.

I run the message back and listen to it over and over, tears coursing down my face. God, I want to hold her, but I can't. It's not right. I've hurt her too much and I can't go back to where we were. It would just be too disastrous when it fell apart again, and it *would* fall apart again.

I get a call the next morning, and the next and the next. At the club every evening I go through the motions of doing the things I've always done. It's been exceptionally quiet. Bruce and Valerie, Gary, Austin, Cody, and Tim and Leslie haven't been here since it all went down. I heard a rumor that Bruce was trying to buy The Catacombs and clean it up, turn it into another version of Bliss. I don't care. Nothing matters now.

A month goes by. My house is a damn wreck. Clint isn't speaking to me, and I don't blame him. I miss him and Trish and the kids. Steffen has come by a couple of times, but I told him I didn't want to talk to him, so he quit coming by. Secretly, I'd love for him to stop again. I'd like *someone* to talk to, but I don't deserve it.

On a random Thursday, I get a different kind of call. I recognize the prefix, but it's not the same number Olivia's been calling from, so I answer it to hear a voice say, "Mr. Adams?"

"Yes?"

"This is Dr. Cooper, Miss Warren's psychiatrist. How are you, sir?"

"What do you want?"

"Well, um, sir, I'd really like for you to come in for one of Miss Warren's sessions. I think we all need to talk."

"Nothing to talk about."

"Sir, I don't think that's quite accurate. Miss Warren

says that the two of you . . ."

"There is no two of us. She needs to get that out of her head. Thanks for calling, but you're only hearing one side of the story, and it's all you need. My side doesn't matter. Please don't call me again." Before he can say anything else, I hang up.

Two weeks later, out of the blue, I open my front door and there stands Clint, Trish, Steffen, Sheila . . .

And Olivia.

I feared this day would come, but I'd prayed it wouldn't. I was hoping she'd just fade away and I wouldn't have to deal with her. I see they're not going to let that happen. All I manage to choke out is, "Yeah?"

"We all need to talk."

"Nothing to talk about."

He ignores me and pushes the door open, and the five of them come straight into the house. Trish and Olivia head directly to the spare bedroom, and I know she's collecting the few things still left there. The other four of us sit and wait in silence until they come back, and when they join us, Clint looks around the group and then straight at me. "Olivia's been released from the hospital."

"I see that."

A scowl is directed at me, and then he says, "We need to know what you want to do. Does she have a home here? I need a straight answer so we can help her figure out what to do next."

"I think coming back here would be a bad idea," I tell her, looking right into her face. I can't read her expression, and then I realize I've seen it. Those dogs on the commercials for the ASPCA, sad and abandoned. My heart is being ripped from my chest, but I try to look like I don't give a shit.

"Okay. Well, at least we know how to proceed now."

Clint starts to stand, but I tell him, "Not yet. I've got something to say." They all look at me expectantly, and I get an envelope from the desk and open it. The brochures are colorful and glossy, and I hand one to each of them. "Share them around. Each one is different because they're about different aspects of the program."

Steffen stares at me. "My god, this is what you've been doing?" There's a look of total disgust on his face, and I deserve it.

"Yeah. I've looked around, and this looks like the best one."

Trish's voice is shrill. "What the hell is this?"

"It's a home. Well, not a home like some kind of facility, more like a school. It's a group setting where they house students while they learn a vocation. You go through the program, and when you're done, they help you find a job, housing, transportation. And it's in Denver. It's really pretty there. I think you'd like it," I say directly to Olivia.

Her eyes are empty, but her lip trembles when she whispers out, "Dave, I love you. Please don't send me away."

Everything inside me melts, and I know if I want to save my soul from the eternal fires of damnation, I have to show her my heart right this second. I kneel in front of her and take her hands. "It doesn't matter if you love me or I love you. It's . . ."

"Do you love me?" Her eyes dart back and forth as she looks into mine, and I know she's watching for some shred of caring and compassion. I need to give her something, but I need to be careful.

"That doesn't matter. It's time for you to find a life for yourself. I took yours and didn't give you anything of value in return. This will help you get a fresh start in a new city with people who are trained to get you that fresh start and do it right."

"You *did* give me something of value. You gave me your heart."

"And I shouldn't have. That was wrong of me. I was expecting you to be something you're not, and that's not fair to you. This will right that wrong and you'll be surrounded by people who really can help you. You won't have to worry about them being cruel or mean-spirited or letting you down. They're professionals and they'll do right by you."

"I just want to be in a home. This home. Our home." Oddly, she's not crying. I find that a relief even as it's a curiosity. I would've expected that, but instead, she's very calm and rational. Probably meds. "Weren't we happy?"

"It wasn't real, honey. It was just us trying to make the other person be what they needed them to be, and it didn't work."

"You're exactly what I want."

I shake my head. "I'm not. I'm a Dominant who was

looking for a permanent submissive. You're not a sub-missive."

"No. I'm not." Now I'm shocked. I just knew she'd say that she could be whatever I wanted her to be, but this takes me completely by surprise. Then she adds, "I don't think that's what you really want either."

"You don't know that because you don't know me that well."

"I know your heart."

I shake my head again. "It's black, baby. Black as coal."

"No. It's not. I've seen it and it's beautiful." Her face is sweet and calm, even as her lip keeps trembling.

I give up and turn to Clint. "I've already paid for the program. They just need to know when she's coming and to make transportation arrangements. I've given them the money for that too. They don't know when to expect her, but they *are* expecting her."

Clint slaps his knees and stands. "Well. That's taken care of, looks like. Thanks for that. We'll be going now."

Steffen mumbles out, "Clint, I . . ."

Clint snaps at Steffen, "No." Then he glares at me. "No. It's all taken care of. Do you want me to let you know when she's leaving so you can say goodbye?"

"Probably not a good idea, but if it'll help, I'll come."

Shaking his head, he snorts. "Wow. Thanks for that. Come on, baby. You girls get in the van and we'll go get some ice cream or something. Anything." As they all file out, Steffen gives me an odd look and follows everyone else, then closes the door behind him.

Well. That's done. Everything can go back to normal. Yeah, right.

<hr>

I haven't seen or heard from Clint for three weeks when I see his name pop up on my phone. I just answer, "Yeah."

"Dave? I just wanted you to know that she's leaving tomorrow. About two o'clock. We're taking her to the airport. I'd really like for you to be there and at least pretend you care something for her. She's doing very well. It's the least you can do."

"Son, I do care something for her. I love her and I want what's best for her."

"Gotta tell ya, if that's how you love her, now I'm worried about all the times you've said that to me." Ouch. But I deserved that.

"Look, I'll try to be there. But don't tell her I'm coming in case I decide not to. Please."

"Wouldn't dream of disappointing her again unnecessarily." Then he hangs up on me.

I keep wiping down the bar. A few people mill around in the commons area, but no one is scening. It's almost time to start decorating for the holidays, but I don't really care about it this year. I don't want to be reminded that my heart is broken by being around people jostling me in the malls and getting crabby in the lines at the grocery. I don't need that.

During the night, I dream, and in my dream we're right back here in my bed, my arms tight around her. I kiss her and she kisses me back, and then she whispers, "I love you, Dave. You're my dream come true." Her lips are like caramel on a hot summer day, and her hair is a silky wave of chocolate drifting down her shoulders and across the pillow. I draw one of her nipples into my lips and listen to the moan that rises from deep in her chest. It's perfect and cozy and so, so right.

Waking with a start, I sit bolt upright in the bed and look around in the dark. The realization that it was just a dream is a bitter pill, and I slump back down into the bed and pull the covers up to my neck. I never expected a broken heart to hurt this badly, but it's excruciating.

Every minute without her is the most painful minute of my life, only to be replaced by the next that's more painful still. Remembering her arms, her smile, the touch of her hand, it all sends me into a spiral I don't think I'll ever surface from, and I'm lost in all the memories. We had so little time together, but it meant so much. And now it's gone, and it's not coming back.

Halfway through the morning I decide that, out of decency, I should go and see her off. I paid for the program, I drove her to this point, and I should at least go and show her that I care. I pick out something I think really says "me," a button-front crew neck, and draw my brown leather jacket over it. I don't know where they'll be or when, so I just drive to the airport and park in short-term parking. The board inside the front door says there's a plane departing for Denver at three o'clock – that's got to be it. I head for the gate and look around.

They're standing in a cluster, my son, daughter-in-law, grandkids, and Steffen, Sheila, and their two. Olivia's right in the middle of them, and she's smiling and laughing, teasing the kids and jumping into Sheila and Trish's conversation. She looks different somehow, kind of settled and calm and . . .

Grown up. She looks all grown up. She's not the fragile, frightened little thing I rescued from the garbage. Her hair is glossy, her skin and eyes are clear, and she's got a smile on her face. My chest aches with the knowledge that I couldn't help her get there. Someone else had to do it, and it looks like they did a very good job. For that, I owe them my eternal gratitude.

I stand and watch them, wondering if I should just leave. They'd never know I'd been there. But just as I think I should do that, she looks up and locks eyes with me. And I have to go to her. I can't help it. They all part their little circle and she stands there in the middle, waiting. Stopping in front of her, I look around at my little family and ask, "Could you guys give us a second, please?" Without a word, they all drift away toward a hot dog stand across the concourse and leave us standing there.

Face to the floor and staring at my shoes, I manage to mutter, "Wow, this is awkward."

"It's not for me. Thanks for coming. I'm glad to see you. And thanks for doing this for me."

My head snaps up. The look on her face tells me that she genuinely feels what she's saying, and a wave of relief washes over me, followed by regret so enormous that it threatens to swallow me. "I'm glad to see you too. I just wanted to come and tell you how sorry I am about . . ."

Her finger presses against my lips and she smiles. "Let's not go there. I'm just glad that you came to say goodbye."

I eye her suspiciously. "This is weird. I was sure you'd beg me to let you come back."

The smile that slips out is sad. "I wouldn't do that because I know it's not going to happen. I love you. You don't love me. That's just how it is."

"I *do* love you, Olivia."

"No, you feel obligated to help me. I consider this our day to say that we're even. I gave you what you wanted from me insofar as I was able. You gave me what I needed from you until you just couldn't anymore. So we're good. But there's something I need to say to you."

My eyebrows arch. "Okay. Go ahead."

She reaches for one of my hands and takes it in hers, then looks into my face. I see the girl I fell in love with, and the love I feel for her is deeper than the ocean and wider than the sky. I want to tell her that, to grab her and kiss her, but I can't. That wouldn't be right, and I know it. I just wait and she starts to speak.

"I just want you to know that I love you. I love you just as much as I ever did, maybe even more. I know you didn't act the way you did toward me because you hate me; you did it out of love, and I respect that. I'm not what you want, and that's okay. I'm just glad I had your love for a little while. No one ever loved me like that before, and I thank you for that." She draws my hand to her lips and kisses the back of it, and I feel like I'm going to faint. Then she looks at me and says, "And now it's time for you to go." She immediately drops my hand and smiles.

I've been dismissed. Whatever she's done in the last few weeks, this girl has become a woman, a strong, determined, self-sufficient woman who only needs a little help to have the life she deserves. I'm the poor schmuck that broke his own heart when he couldn't get his shit together, and that's something I'll regret for the rest of my life.

I stammer out, "Well, uh, okay, I'll be going. Have a great time, I mean a good life. I care about you, Olivia. I hope you get all the wonderful things you deserve."

"Thanks." She doesn't move to touch me again, hug me, anything. After the most uncomfortable minute of my life, I just turn and start to walk away.

Then I remember something and turn back. "Hey, how did all of that with the police work out?"

"Ask your son. He loves you, Dave, and you've treated all of us like shit. Fix your relationship with him. And Steffen. With the whole bunch. Apologize to the guys at the club. That's all they really want, to be treated with some respect."

Lower than whale dung, I smile a weak smile. "I'll do that. Thanks for the advice."

"You're welcome. Anytime."

I don't wave to Clint or the rest as I leave the terminal. It's over. I can go back to the life I had before she stumbled into it. I've been there less than thirty minutes, so I owe parking nothing, and I head home and try to think of things to fill my time now that she's really gone. And it's true.

She's really gone.

⸻◦◦◦⸻

"What?" Clint's voice isn't angry, just cold and distant.

"Son?"

"What?" he repeats.

"Could we go to lunch sometime this week? I'd love to sit and talk to you."

"I don't think so. I'm really busy." That little statement comes with dead airspace behind it, so I try again.

"Clint? Before she left, Olivia asked me to make things right with all of you. I'm trying to do that. Would you be willing to meet me halfway?"

There's a deep sigh before he says, "I'll come a third of the way. The other two thirds is yours to make."

"I'll accept that."

"Good. Where and when?"

"I'm asking you, so that's your choice. Your convenience."

I hear him rustling some papers or something. "How about Tuesday? Twelve thirty? Tequila Mike's?"

"Sounds good. And Clint? For what it's worth, I'm really sorry about everything."

"Save it for Tuesday." With that, he's gone. Then something occurs to me.

I haven't talked to Marta and Angela for a very long time, since before all of this started up. I punch Marta's contact and wait. Then I hear, "Well, look who's still alive!"

"Haha, very funny. Sorry about that. I was wondering: Would you by any chance have some time for me?"

"In the sack or out?"

That's a valid question, coming from Marta. "Out. Just to talk."

"Sure! Why don't you come over tonight for dinner, about six. Angela's trying out a new recipe on me, and it would help to be able to spread the love, if you know what I mean," she chuckles.

"That sounds great. And thanks."

"You're welcome. I always love your company." I hang up and smile. I don't know how we've managed to stay such good friends, but she knows me better than anyone else, and I'm thankful she's at least speaking to me.

I step into the house to find an intoxicating aroma of chili peppers, vinegar, and cheese of some kind. "Wow. I don't know what's going on in here, but it smells fine."

"I hope it tastes just as good." Angela crosses the kitchen and hugs me, then pulls back and looks into my face. "What's up with you?"

"What do you mean?"

"You don't feel very, um, sexy. You feel kinda tired. To me, I mean."

"You're very perceptive."

"Um-hmmm. Okay. Back to cooking for me. You should talk to Marta."

The smile on my face looks fake, I'm sure. "I fully intend to."

As if on cue, Marta comes bee-bopping into the kitchen. "Hi, handsome!"

"Hi yourself." She gives me a hug and then leans back to look in my face. "What's wrong, honey?"

"You won't believe me when I tell you."

"Try me."

"After we eat. It's a long story."

She twirls a strand of her hair around her finger. "I've got plenty of time for stories."

I try to help Angela clean up after dinner, but she stares at me like I'm possessed. "No, honey, you just go on in there with my baby. I got this, really. Go. Scoot."

Marta's in the living room with a glass of wine in her hand. She grins as she says, "I'd offer you a glass, but for some reason I get the feeling you drinking right now would be a mistake."

"Huge mistake."

She waits. When I don't begin, she asks, "Dave, baby, what's wrong? You look like somebody tore your heart out and stomped on it."

"I did. It was me. I tore my own heart out and stomped on it." My hands have started to shake. I can't hide anything from Marta, and I knew I was coming over here to talk to her, but talking out loud about what's happened is going to be harder than I ever dreamed. "So I met a woman. A homeless woman. She was living out by the dumpster at the club."

"Yes. Clint told me about that."

"Well, I took her home with me. Got her straightened out, cleaned up, secure and cozy. Helped her do something she really needed to do. And fell in love with her."

"Yeah?"

"And then I made her leave."

Marta takes a sip of wine before she says, "I get the impression that a lot of things happened between the falling in love and the pushing her away."

"They did." And it happens. It all starts pouring out of me like water, spilling everywhere, wetting everything down, gushing out like a broken main, threatening to drown me. I finish with, "And when I walked away in the airport, I knew I was walking away from a woman who'd grown up because of the horrible way I'd treated her. I sent her away, Marta. I broke her heart and mine too." Without warning, the real, honest to god water-works start, the tears falling so fast I can't hope to mop them up. Marta moves to sit beside me and puts an arm around my shoulder.

"Dave, I want to ask you something."

I'm sobbing and still manage to choke out, "O-o-o-kay?"

"Baby, if you could do anything differently, what would it be?"

"To never fall in love with her or tell her that I love her."

Marta snorts. "That's a bald-faced lie."

I straighten and wipe my eyes. "No! It's not! If that hadn't happened, neither of us would've gotten hurt."

She gives me the evil eye. "Admit it: You fell in love with her the minute you saw her."

My brow furrows. "I did not! That's not at all what . . ."

"David Nathaniel Adams! Do not lie to me. Don't think you can. Remember who you're talking to. Now, I'm going to ask you again, and I want you to think about your answer instead of just giving me some flip-pant mumbo-jumbo that's just bullshit. If you could do anything differently, what would it be?"

My mind goes in fifty different directions, and then it settles on one very clear truth. It's hard for me to admit, but I have to. Almost reverently, I say, "I would've stopped seeing her as a homeless woman I was helping and respected her as a person."

Marta slaps my knee. "And the truth shall set you free."

I feel the weight of fifty elephants lift from my shoulders. That was it, in a nutshell. And it was so ironic. I knew how she lost everything, and it was through no fault of her own. It was most certainly not from stupidity or laziness. If anything, she deserved my respect for managing to survive as long as she had. She'd slogged on through being shelterless, cold, wet, hot, hungry, sexually abused, and more things I probably couldn't even imag-ine, and still made it with some shred of dignity. I should've celebrated her resiliency, not played on her insecurities. She deserved to wear the labels "strong" and "determined," and instead I'd branded her as weak and powerless.

What a fool. The woman I'd waved goodbye to at the airport was the real Olivia. She'd just needed some help coming back from the dark corners she'd been shoved into by poverty and despair. She wasn't the woman I'd originally met; that had just been an automaton existing on autopilot, an empty shell that needed to be filled. The real Olivia was a lovely, intelligent, well-educated woman.

Woman. She was a woman, and I'd treated her like some petulant child when she needed to do what was right. My tirade at her the day of the shooting hadn't been because I was worried about her – it had been because I was embarrassed that the possibility of her being hurt made me afraid. And my response was to push her away so I wouldn't have to face those feelings again. I'd made yet another hideous mistake.

I only have one saving grace, and that's sending her away to a better life. She would've gladly stayed with me where I would've continued to treat her in the same condescending way. At least now she has a chance to make a good life for herself with someone who'll treat her the way she needs to be treated. It's all swirling through my head, and all I can manage to say is, "Oh, god, Marta, I messed up so bad."

"You sent away the love of your life, didn't you?"

All I can do is nod and sob. That's exactly what I've done, and I can't undo it. She's gone. And for her sake, it's got to stay that way.

We've always had such a good relationship, and now all Clint's managing to do is be civil to me. He doesn't talk to me while we're looking over the menu, even though I try to make small talk. All he does is grunt. Once we've managed to order our food, I try again. "Clint, I just want to tell you how sorry I am for everything I've done and the ways I've acted. I was horrible, and I regret it all so much that you wouldn't believe it."

"Just answer me one question." His voice is coated in venom. "Do you love her or not?"

"I do love her."

"Then why? Why did you do the things you did? Say the things you said? Rip her apart like that?"

"I ripped myself apart too."

"I don't give a shit what you did to yourself. I'm talking about her. Get your head out of your ass and tell me the truth."

I straighten my back and try to gather my courage. "Your mom asked me what I would do differently if I could change things."

"And?" he asks as he drums his spoon on the table-cloth.

"I had to think about it, but I decided that it would've been to respect Olivia as a person instead of pitying her as a homeless girl."

His eyes fly open wide. "Well, maybe there's hope for you after all."

"Thank you."

"It wasn't meant as a compliment."

I chuckle. "These days, I'll take what I can get."

"I think that's wise." He takes a sip of his water and sets the glass down before he speaks again. "Are you going to stay in touch with her?"

"I don't think that would be good for her. I'd love to, but I don't think I should. I'm sure she's doing well, and I'd only drag her back into all of my shit."

"So describe your shit to me."

I shrug. "I don't know. My shit."

He sits back and gives me a hard look. "Okay. Let's define your shit. You have a house but no one in it with you."

"Yeah."

"You have a club, but it doesn't really belong to you."

Ouch. "Yeah, that's right."

"You have plenty of sex with women you never wake up with in the morning."

I take a deep breath and let it out in a big sigh. "Yeah. I suppose so."

"You eat alone and you sleep alone. You shop alone. You work alone for the most part."

"All true."

"So, to recap: You're alone with no prospect of being anything but. And you had a woman, a smart, funny, beautiful, capable woman who loved you and wanted to spend the rest of her life with you, and you gave all that up and broke her heart because you couldn't control everything she did."

That truth hits me like a ton of bricks. "Yes. That's exactly right."

"But you have those women at the club, plenty of them, women who'll do exactly as you say when you say it and never question you, and you don't want them."

"Wait . . ."

"So, Dave, what exactly *do* you want? Do you even know?"

When I told her that I was a Dominant looking for a permanent sub, I remember as clear as day what she said to me: *I don't think that's what you really want either.* "Oh, god."

"Uh-huh. Thought so." He waits for a few minutes of excruciating reality to soak in before he says, "You had exactly what you wanted, what you needed. And you pushed her away because you didn't think she was the right person. You've worn labels for so long that you couldn't look past the labels to your heart and see what you were yearning for."

"Oh, god. And now it's too late."

"Yes. It is."

My eyes snap to his. "Have you talked to her at all?"

"Yeah. She's doing very well. They enrolled her in dental hygienist classes, and she thinks she's going to like that field. The dormitories are more like apartments, and she's got her own place. They have a shuttle that goes everywhere, but they're going to help her get her license again so she can drive when she finally gets out on her own."

"How long ago did you talk to her last?"

He shakes his head as he stares at his silverware. "Trish heard from her yesterday via a chat program."

I'm shaking all over, and I can't stop. "Does she ask about me?"

He turns sad eyes up to mine. "She doesn't even mention you. It's like you never existed. I think she's just trying to protect herself, but we all decided that unless she asks, we're not mentioning you either. She doesn't deserve to be dragged back into this, this, this muck."

Now I'm feeling desperate. "Could I call out there and talk to her?"

"No. They don't allow calls in and, even if they did, I don't think it would be a good idea. You need to just leave her alone."

We've had our food for twenty minutes, but I'm having a hard time eating because I can't swallow. Everything seems to stick in my throat. We talk about Trish and the kids, Steffen and Sheila and their kids, and the club. He tells me that Bruce's deal to buy The Catacombs fell through and that they'd all like to come back to Bliss but they're still too mad at me. "You should call him and apologize."

"I will." After a big, deep sigh, I ask him, "And what about you? Can you forgive me? I love you, Clint. Regardless of your DNA, you're my son, and I miss all of you. I was scared and tired and pissed, and I said and did a lot of things I'm ashamed of now. I've never acted that way before, and you know it. This whole thing made me kinda crazy, and I'm really sorry."

"I'm working on it," he says, and then adds, "Dad." Relief hits me instantly, and I know we can fix what happened between us. "You need to talk to Steffen too. He's really disappointed in you."

"I'm really disappointed in myself."

"That's a good place to start."

Something tickles my mind and I remember to ask, "What happened with the court case?"

"Olivia helped the police identify the other men she knew were involved in the murders, rapes, all of that. They rounded them all up. When the detectives started talking to them, they all named each other and even some more officers Olivia had never run across. They're pretty sure they got them all, and without Falco to make them feel bulletproof, they all caved and pleaded guilty. Four for second-degree murder, one for first-degree murder, and the rest on an assortment of charges. And they'll never work in law enforcement again."

"Good. I'm glad they got what they deserve. And Detective Roberts' family?"

"Having a hard time, but damn proud of him. He was a good guy trying to do a good thing. I was honored to have known him even just slightly." He takes another swig of water and then says, "I guess I'd better get back to work." The look he gives me is sad. "By the way, I've missed you. We've always been close, and I felt like I didn't even know you anymore."

"I was a stranger to myself."

"I can see that. I love you and I only want good things for you."

That makes me chuckle. "That sounds like a dad talking to his son."

"Yeah, well, it is what it is." He stands and when I reach to shake his hand, he opens his arms to me. The embrace is like a big, warm sugar cookie to my soul, and it's sweet and just right.

I know right then what I need to do. I have to get some help, get my head on straight, and then try to figure out what to do with the rest of my life. There's not a lot of it left, and I need to make the most of it.

I'm unlocking the car door when I hear footsteps and find him rushing up to me. "I almost forgot. She mailed us a card and sent this in it, asked us to give it to you."

"What is it?"

He shrugs. "I have no idea. See you later."

I look at the little envelope before I toss it on the seat. It taunts me there all the way home, and I can't run fast enough to get inside and read it. It's a beautiful card with her artwork all over it, little birds in flowering trees by a cottage in the woods and I realize: The cabin. Oh god. When I open the card and start to read, I have to sit down because my legs are trembling so badly. As I try to digest the words, I feel like all the air is being sucked out of the world.

Dear Dave,

When you get this, I'm sure I'll be busy doing something or other in my new life. It's been fun and exciting. I'm meeting new people, all kinds of new people. My apartment is cute, and I'm working on getting my driver's license! So many good things are happening to me that I can't believe it.

And I have you to thank. If you hadn't brought me inside that night, I'd probably be dead now. You gave me

hope and a future. And while it wasn't the future I'd orig-
inally wanted, I realize now that it's probably the future
that's best for me. I never wanted to be with someone who
didn't really want me, and I'm glad I had the good sense
not to cling to you like a spoiled child. What you did
opened new doors for me, and I thank you for that. I'll be
a stronger, better person because of your generosity.

I'll never forget being held in your arms. It was the
first time in a long time that I felt safe and loved. I know
you loved me in your own way. I love you still and I al-
ways will – forever. I hope when you think of me, you
remember the good times, the fun things, the cabin and the
quilt and shopping at the mall.

Have a good life, Dave. Find the person you really
love and love her with all your heart. I'm sure someday I'll
find someone I can settle for. But when he kisses me, I'll
always think of you.

Yours forever,
Olivia

I already know I need someone to talk to, a professional, but the thoughts that go through my mind in this
moment scare me more than anything I've ever known,
because the pain is so intense that I imagine what it
would be like to die and escape it. Someone has to help
me or I'm not going to make it through this. I know that
now. I've cut out my own heart and destroyed it. Things
will never be right again, and there's nothing I can do but
stand back and look at the rubble of my demolished life.

Chapter Ten

"How ya doin'?"

"Pretty good, I guess." I wipe down another glass and place it on the shelf.

"Good. Everything else going okay?" Steffen takes another swallow of his beer and waits.

"Yeah. The doctor is really helping me, I think. It's just going to take time. But I'm working on it."

"I'm glad." He sits and stares into his beer. I know he's worried about me; *I'm* worried about me. But I do feel better now, have for the last few days.

Bruce comes through and gives me a bro hug. Gary waves at me from across the room. I look up and Melina is cruising in, so I try to look busy. "Hey, stud, I hear you're single again. Wanna play tonight?"

"Uh, I don't think so, sugar. I'm kinda tired." I keep working, trying to avoid the questions.

"Hey, have I done something to you? You haven't played with me in months! I'm starting to get a complex."

"Not you. All me."

She leans in and whispers conspiratorially, "It's not

that thing, you know, from before, is it?"

"Nah. Just personal stuff, that's all."

She grins. "Whew. I'm glad to hear that! I was beginning to think I was losing my appeal!"

"Nope, darlin'. You're just as hot as ever. It's just that I'm not."

Her eyes narrow and she says, "Okay then. If you change your mind, find me."

"Will do." I watch her ass cheeks jiggle as she walks away.

"You've got to get back in the game sometime, Dave," Steffen lectures me.

"Yeah. Sometime. Just not now."

"Fair enough." He stands and stretches. "I'm going to find that girl of mine. Last time I saw her, she was talking to a new sub trainee over by the St. Andrew's. Catch up with you later." He waves as he trots away, and I wave back.

I watch a brunette across the room and think about Olivia. Wonder what she's doing right now? It's been three months, twenty-two days – wait, let me look at my watch – seven hours and eighteen minutes since the last time I saw her. The classes she's taking are probably in full swing. I can just see her sitting in the living room, wearing those pajamas with the butterflies all over them, working a word search puzzle and eating pretzels. Every morning I wake and think I'll miss her less. Every morning when I think that, I realize I only love her more.

Sure enough, the next morning is exactly that way. I'm putzing around the house, washing some dishes, throwing old stuff away out of the refrigerator, and starting a load of laundry. I plug in the vacuum cleaner and I'm about to turn it on when my phone rings and I look at the screen: three zero three area code. Denver. I dive for the phone, trip over the vacuum cord, and almost fall before I grab the phone and wheeze into it, "Hello?"

"Yes, may I speak to David Adams?"

"This is Dave Adams. Can I help you?"

"Yes, Mr. Adams, this is Amanda Weir at New Beginnings in Denver. I understand you were the one who paid for Olivia Warren's placement here. We were just calling about her. Do you happen to know where she is?"

I'm sure I just heard wrong. "What?"

"Do you know where Miss Warren is?"

"She's in Denver at your training facility."

"No, sir, she's not."

A hammering sensation starts up in my chest. "What do you mean, no, she's not? She's supposed to be there. Where else could she be?"

The young woman's voice is very timid. "Sir, she left a note saying she'd gone to see you."

"When?"

"Two weeks ago. She didn't have anyone listed as a next of kin, so there was no one to call. Then we found your name as her benefactor and hoped we had the right number. So she's not there?"

"No! No, I haven't even talked to her."

"I see. Well, we really don't know what to do. We

were in the process of helping her find another training program for people in her situation."

"What? What are you talking about? What situation?"

"We don't offer residential programs for families."

Now I'm really confused. "I'm sorry, but I don't understand what you're talking about."

"She's welcome here for the rest of her term, but once the baby comes, she'll have to . . ."

The room starts to spin and I'm having trouble breathing. "Baby? What baby?"

"Sir, she's about five months pregnant."

I don't remember much after that. I must've hung up the phone, but in a few minutes I wake up in the floor, so dizzy I can't sit up. My phone is just inches from my fingertips, and I manage to scoot over to it and pick it up. When Clint answers, he says, "Hey! What's up?" When I can't get a sound to come out of my throat, he says, "Dad? You okay?"

I croak out, "No. I'm not okay. Come. Please."

"On my way."

<hr />

"So all they have is a note that says she's coming here? Dad, that's been two weeks. Two weeks. If she were coming here and nothing's happened to her, she should already be here." Clint's pacing. I think he wants me to tell him what to do but, quite honestly, I have no idea.

"Can you call some of the guys at the police department? Some of the detectives who worked on that case?

Maybe see if they have any contacts anywhere who might be able to help us?"

Clint nods. "Yeah. I'll try that."

The front door opens and Trish jets through it. "Oh, god, Dave, what can I do to help?"

I'm just bewildered. I have no idea what to do at this point, what to tell anyone, what to say. I don't know where she is or what's happening to her. She's out there alone somewhere, no money, no car. Oh, god, I hope she's not hitching. That idea makes me sick to my stomach and I know I'm green when Trish says, "You need a trash can?"

"Yeah. Yeah." It's all I can manage before all of my breakfast comes up.

Clint's still pacing. "Look, let's not panic."

"That's easy for you to say!" I practically shout. "There's a woman out there, traveling alone by who knows what means, and she's pregnant with my child. And you tell me to not panic? Have you lost your MIND?"

"I know, I know."

"Son, would you PLEASE sit down? You're making *me* a nervous wreck."

"Sorry." He sits down, then tries to get up again, but I shoot him a look and he settles back on the couch. "I can't think of anything."

"Steffen. Is there anything he could do?"

"I have no idea, but I'll call him." When Clint gets off the phone, he announces, "He'll be here in about thirty minutes."

Sure enough, thirty minutes later he's sitting in my living room and we're brainstorming, trying to think of anything that could help us find her. "Debit card records?"

I shake my head. "Nope. I don't think she had an account. She hadn't gone far enough into the program to be paid."

"Damn." Steffen's eyes stare at the floor, and I can tell he's thinking. "And she doesn't have a cell phone, right?"

"It's in there on the dresser."

Now Clint's thinking out loud. "You're alone, trying to travel. You need money. What do you do?"

Steffen shrugs. "Steal?"

I shake my head. "Not Olivia. She'd never do that. First thing she ever said to me was that she couldn't take a few stale potato chips in a bag because it would be stealing if she didn't pay for them. So no. She would never do that."

"She doesn't have any jewelry to sell, does she?" Clint asks.

"Nope."

We're all silent again for a few minutes. Then Trish says, "So, again, you're alone, traveling, and you need money. What do you do?"

"Get a job?" Steffen offers.

"But you're not going to be around long enough to get a job," Clint reminds us.

Trish's eyes light up. "You get a day job."

Steffen grins. "State employment office. She'd go

there to look for a day job, something temporary."

I'm thinking out loud. "Can the cops check those records, see if she's been in for something like that?"

"I have no idea, but I'll find out." Clint presses a few buttons and I know he's talking to one of the police officers who worked with Olivia. A few of them have gotten to know him very well, and they hang out together from time to time. One's even a Dominant and has started coming to the club on a regular basis. When he hangs up, he looks around at all of us. "He said he's not sure that they can get state records from so many states between here and there, but he said he'll try."

"So who are we talking about here? Idaho, Oregon, Utah, Nevada, and Montana?" Those are the ones I can think of right off the top of my head.

"Don't forget Wyoming," Trish offers.

Steffen frowns. "No, don't. But every town has an employment office. It's a needle-in-a-haystack proposition."

"It's all we've got." I fall back into the sofa. "I don't know anything else to do."

They stay all afternoon and into the evening. Sheila's got all the kids, so Trish leaves to go and pick their three up. Clint and Steffen stay with me a while longer, but eventually they have to go. "Dad, why don't you come home with me so you're not alone? We'd be glad to have you."

"No. What if she shows up here and I'm not at home? No. I can't leave."

"You can't stay here all the time."

"Oh yeah? Check on me occasionally and pick me up some groceries or I'll starve."

He chuckles. "Okay. Fine. And we'll come by and spend some time with you if you want."

All the frustration and hurt I've been holding in finally turns loose and the tears start to fall. I find a big, strong guy on either side of me, arms around me, and I remember what love feels like and how much I've missed it. "I'm okay, I'm okay. Just tired."

"I know." Steffen hugs me again. "It's gonna be okay, I'm sure. Just have faith."

When they're gone, I head off to bed, but there'll be no sleep for me. I think about Olivia, every horrible thing that's happened between us, her smile, her kind, gentle heart, her bravery, and I want to hold her so badly that I can barely breathe.

A baby. She's pregnant with my child. Somewhere out there is a woman, alone and afraid, trying to get back to me. When she gets here, and I have to believe she will, I will never, never hurt or disappoint her again. I'm not sure of a lot of things, but that's the one I do know for a fact.

<hr />

"How many today?"

I'm honest. "Three."

"Taking your medicine?" Clint asks.

"Yes. And that's down from five a day last week."

"Yeah, I guess that's better."

The anxiety attacks aren't quite as frequent, but what

I haven't told Clint is that they're far more severe. When one hits, I'm pretty sure I'm having a heart attack. If I *had* an actual heart attack, I wouldn't realize it until too late. My psychiatrist has been coming to the house because I will not leave. I'm too afraid she'll show up and I won't be here.

The only lead we've even possibly had is a facial recognition hit from a bank in Wyoming where it looks like she was cashing a check. But when the detective asked, the person who'd written the check said she'd worked for them for about a week and then said she had to go.

Two months. It's been two months. Maybe she just left the note to throw us off her trail. Maybe she was never planning to come here at all. I don't know. The only thing I do know is that it doesn't take two months to get from Colorado to Washington State.

But I have a secret I haven't told anyone. I've been ordering things, and it's been very busy around my house. The Salvation Army came and got all of the furniture in Clint's old room and I went to work. I ordered new furniture and wall stick-ons and bedding. The hardware store delivered paint and scrapers and all kinds of stuff I needed, and I hit it hard. It's giving me something to do while I wait. And I will wait. I'm certain she'll be here.

On Sunday, I invite everyone for lunch. I have all kinds of food delivered, and I even invite Marta and Angela. We laugh and talk and eat, but I'm listening constantly, sure every little creak and groan of the house is the door. They're all talking about going home when I finally can't keep the secret anymore. I tap my glass with a butter knife and when everyone looks my way, I tell them, "I have a surprise."

I lead the way down the hall, then open the door and flip on the light. I hear Trish and Sheila gasp, and Clint says, "Wow. This is awesome."

Marta comes straight to me, leans against me, and wraps an arm around my waist. "I'm so proud of you. This is beautiful, Dave, just beautiful."

The walls are a pale yellow and all over them are little sheep, leaping and cavorting. Yellow, green, and blue plaid curtains hang at the windows, and coordinating bedding is on the mattress, the changing table, and the bassinet. I know – bassinets are old fashioned – but I loved this one, and it's beautiful with its floor-length skirt and little fitted sheet.

I stand in this room with my family and I look around at my work. The only thing missing is the woman and the baby. And I've already made my decision.

If something happens to her and she never comes home, I plan to come into this beautiful little room where I've planted the seeds of all my hopes and dreams and put a bullet in my head. Whatever happens to her, good or bad, it's my fault. And if it's anything less than spectacular, I won't be able to live with myself.

Today I've decided that I'm going to cut my hair. I'm not sure how, but it needs it. I won't leave to go to the barber, so it hasn't been cut. Everyone in the family says I look like a shaggy dog, and even Morris said, "Grandpa Dave, you look like a hippie." I think he's been watching reruns of *That '70s Show*. Looking in the mirror, I'm thinking that it would be easiest to just shave it, but Olivia would hate that.

I'm about to run out of coffee and I realize I'll have to remind Clint to get me some. He's been so busy lately, running the club. He brings all the paperwork to me, but he still has to be there, which means he's never home with Trish and the kids. Steffen finally told him to stay home on Mondays and Thursdays, and then Bruce and Gary stepped up and took Tuesdays and Wednesdays, so it's not as bad as it was. But it couldn't be helped; it was either let them run it or close down, and no one wanted that. It's just temporary. As soon as Olivia and the baby are here, I can come back, no problem.

I get the coffee started and follow my morning routine. After I've turned off the TV from watching the weather report, I go out to get the paper. It's a frigid but pretty day. It would be a perfect day to go to the cabin and start a fire in the fireplace, but I can't. On my way back to the house, I unwrap the paper and look at the headlines. All bad news, as usual. I climb the steps and when I get to the porch, I stop dead in my tracks.

There's a backpack on the porch. And it's Olivia's.

I'm hallucinating. I know I am. I turn with my back to it, rub my eyes, and then turn back around. It's still there. When I walk over and touch it, I know beyond any doubt that it's real. But where is she?

"OLIVIA!" I'm screaming and I don't care. I know the neighbors will think I'm nuts, and they'd be right. "OLIVIA! OLIVIA, WHERE ARE YOU? BABY, PLEASE, WHERE ARE YOU?" There are no signs around the outside of the house that anyone's tried to get in a window or the back door, and I'm stumped. She came here and dropped off her backpack? That makes *no* sense. I run back inside and pick up my phone. My hands are shaking so hard that I'm having trouble hitting a simple speed dial contact. When Clint answers the phone, all I can do is scream into the phone, "HER BACKPACK IS ON THE PORCH!"

"What?"

"Her backpack is on the porch! I went out to get the paper and there it was! But I can't find her! What do I do?"

"Keep looking." There's a moment's pause, and then he laughs. "Did you look in the car?"

My phone drops onto the floor with a "clunk" and I take off out the door. I hit the side of the car full speed, peer through the window, and fall to my knees.

There she is.

I wish I had words to describe how I feel in that moment in time, how my heart feels like it will leap right out of my chest, how it sings and flutters and flies about. I wish I had words for the joy and peace and happiness I feel, seeing her there asleep, her head on her jacket and her arm resting across her big belly. I wish I could tell you that I'm eloquent and graceful.

None of that happens.

Instead, I throw the door open, crawl into the floorboard on my knees, and grab the sleeping woman, drawing her up tight against me. All I can do is whisper over and over, "Oh, baby, oh, please be real. Please be real, Olivia, please be real."

She finally pushes me back and stretches, then sits up. "I need to pee." She draws a hand across both eyes, then opens them. "Dave?"

"Yes, baby. I'm right here." I hope she can see the joy in my face, because if she can't, I'll take her to get glasses.

"Dave, can you help me get out of here? This isn't very comfortable."

"Sweetie, I'll carry you into the house if we can get you out of the car."

"Good. I've really got to pee. Bad. Really bad."

"Okay. Let me help you." I take her hands and pull her across the seat until her feet are out the door and on the ground, then help her to standing. "Holy shit, you're huge."

"Wow. Thanks. I'm flattered."

"No, really, you're adorable. Come on. I'll carry you in." I pick her up and damn near give myself a hernia.

"You okay?"

"Yeah, yeah. I'm fine. You're just heavier than I remember."

"Oh, a funny guy, huh?"

"Yeah, that's me. Funny guy." We make it as far as the front porch and I feel something I can't describe.

"Uh-oh." I stare into her face. "I told you I had to

pee." Her face turns red. "I'm sorry. That's gross."

I can't help but grin at her. "Baby, pee on me all day. I don't care. I'm so happy to see you that you could piss in the middle of the living room floor and I'd just clean it up and call it a day. No shit."

"Wait! I need my backpack."

"Got it. Go to the bathroom and I'll grab it."

She waddles off down the hallway and I follow, backpack in my hands. She strips off her wet underwear and maternity dress, and roots around in her backpack. "Damn. No clean underwear."

I disappear for a minute, clean myself up, and then reappear with a pair of my old boxers from back when I wore boxers. Remember, I said they were old. "Here. These'll do." She wets a washcloth, cleans herself up, and slips on the boxers. Now she's in boxers and a bra, and I've never seen anything so cute. "Do you know how adorable you are?"

"Oh, yeah. Adorable. Fat and adorable."

I take a really good look at her as she washes her hands. Her belly is big and round, but the rest of her is emaciated, and there are dark circles under her eyes. The bra she's wearing is two sizes too small, and her shoes are worn out. I want to hold her close and kiss her, but I'm more concerned than anything else. "I'm going in here to make you a sandwich and then we'll talk. But you need to eat, and then I want you to get some sleep."

I find ham, cheese, and bread, hard-boiled eggs, some chips, and a jar of pickles. Pregnant women like pickles, right? Seems like I heard that somewhere. I yell down the hall, "Look in my closet and get anything you think you can wear. I don't care what it is, it's yours if it'll cover you up." While I'm doing all of this, at the same time I text Clint and simply say, *Get in the car and get here now.* Then I add, *And stop at the store and tell Trish to get a maternity dress. Size I don't know but for a skinny pregnant woman.* That should do it.

Yep. They make it there in twenty minutes, Steffen and Sheila right behind them. "Where is she?"

"In the shower. Just go on back there and take her the dress. She doesn't have anything to wear."

"In the car?" Clint asks with a grin.

"Yep. In the car." I'm still happily pulling out anything I can find in the fridge and cabinets. There's a feast of the weirdest conglomeration of stuff you've ever seen on the table, and I'm hoping that, between the baked beans and water chestnuts, she finds something she wants. I put a bowl of prunes on the table and then it happens.

My knees just give way. Steffen catches me before I hit the floor, and between him and Clint, they get me to the sofa. Next thing I know, there's a glass of water in my hands and my head has a cold cloth on it. I gulp down part of the water, then look up at them with a silly grin. "She's home!"

"Yeah. She is. Congratulations." And my son does something very uncharacteristic of him: He kisses my cheek.

I look up to see a very tenuous Olivia waddling back up the hallway, Trish beside her, and she looks like she doesn't really know what to think. When she makes it into the living room, I tell her, "Baby, there's all kinds of food in there. Eat, please."

"Dave, we need to talk."

"I know, but . . ."

"Now. In Clint's room." Boy, is she going to get a surprise when she opens the door. I turn on the light and she looks around. "What have you done?"

"I got the room ready." There's a look on her face that's less than delighted, and I'm really confused. "You don't like it?"

She closes the door, then takes the rocking chair to sit down. It's obvious she's tired. "So we need to talk."

"Yes. We do." I sit cross-legged in the floor in front of her. "You first."

"Okay." She takes a deep breath and blows it out. "Dave, I came back here because I want you to know your child. I have no intention of being a burden to you. I'll pay my own way, do whatever I have to do to be independent, but I don't want to saddle you with something you don't want. I can make my own money, find a place, and . . ."

I look up at her with what I'm sure is a sappy grin. "Would you please shut that up?"

"What?"

"I said, would you please shut that up and listen to me for a minute?"

"Wow. Well, that's rude, but okay. This had better be important."

"It is. It's of the ultimate importance." I crawl to her

on my knees and take her hands. "I made a lot of mistakes, horrible, life-scarring mistakes. I'm not going to make them again. The biggest one was not treating you with the respect that you deserved, and I'm sorry for that." Her mouth opens, but I put a finger to her lips to shush her. "I love you. I loved you the first time I saw you. And you were right. You were right about everything, and you were especially right about me not knowing what I really wanted. And you were right that what I really want isn't a submissive. What I really, really want is a smart, independent, funny, brave, beautiful woman. I treated you like an incompetent child, and I'm sorry." Now her mouth is hanging open. "That won't happen again. I was wrong to try to tell you what you could and couldn't do. I let my fear rule my life, and that won't happen again. I'll trust you to make decisions for yourself, good decisions, and that'll include our child when it's a situation where we can't make a decision together."

The lines in her face have started to soften, and that gives me the courage to go on. "I need you. I don't care how old you are and how old I am. Our love knows no ages or time limits. We're supposed to be together, and anyone who can't understand that can kiss my ass." Now she giggles. "I mean it. I'm done with what other people think. It's us. We belong together."

Her smile is gentle as she rubs her belly. "I believe you. And I love you. I wouldn't have worked so hard to get back here if I hadn't wanted to be with you."

"Why did it take you ten weeks to get here? Why

didn't you call me?"

"The truth?" I nod. "Because I had your numbers in my phone before. And without the phone, I couldn't remember them, and I couldn't remember the name of the club!" And that does it – I start to laugh. I'm laughing so hard that I can't breathe, and she starts laughing too. "Well, it's the truth! Damn cell phones."

I can't stand it anymore. I stand, pull her to standing, then sit in the chair and pull her onto my lap. When she's seated, I look straight into her face. "Please marry me. Today, tomorrow, I don't care, but marry me, Olivia Warren. I love you."

She drops her forehead to mine and sighs. "I love you too, David Nathaniel Adams."

"Hey, what's your middle name?"

She grins. "Danielle."

"Beautiful. I've got another question." When she nods, I ask, "Boy or girl?"

"Sure you want to know?"

"Yes."

She takes my face in her hands and whispers into my lips, "Congratulations, Mr. Adams. It's a girl."

Then she kisses me. That's when it finally hits me: It's real. She's really here, and she's really mine. There's nothing in the world I wouldn't do for this woman, nothing. If *she* were sixty-five and *I* were twenty-nine, I'd still want her. Forever.

<hr />

"For someone who hasn't had good prenatal care, you're

in very good shape." The doctor snaps off her gloves from the vaginal exam and Olivia breathes a sigh of relief. "They'll be in to do the ultrasound in a few minutes. Any questions?"

"I've got one," my voice rings out.

"Yes?"

"We were told she'd never be able to have children."

The doctor smirks. "Well, someone was obviously wrong." She gives Olivia a sad look. "I *am* concerned about your delivery. You've got so much vaginal and cervical scarring that neither will stretch the way they should, and I don't want to see you injured further. I'd like to consider a C-section."

"She'll do whatever . . ."

"Dave?" There's a warning tone in Olivia's voice.

"Sorry. Go ahead, honey."

"Thank you. I'll do whatever you think is best, Dr. Bailey. I just want this baby to be healthy and safe." She looks at me and gives me a gentle smile that makes my heart flutter. "We both do."

"I think that's going to be no problem at all. So let's calculate your due date. When was your last period?"

They talk about it, get out a calendar, and find the likely date so we know when to expect this little bundle of joy. When they decide the date of conception and say it out loud, I get a lump in my throat. The anniversary of the day Marta and I met. I know exactly where Olivia and I were.

We were at the cabin, that place that's always been my refuge. We made a child there that day and didn't know it. I know now that it will forever be the place I love most, as long as she's there with me.

Before we leave, I turn to the doctor and ask, "Wait. Can you tell me: Is it safe for us to have sex?"

"Of course! For about another month. Then you'll have to stop until after her delivery; well, the vaginal part anyway. Anything else will be fine."

I see Olivia blush a deep vermillion, but I just grin. That wasn't the most important question of this trip, but it was certainly my favorite one.

On the way home, I stop at the mall, and she frowns when I park. "What are we doing here?"

"I've got an errand to run. Come on." I help her out of the car and we walk with her hand in mine. We have to go slowly; she can't walk very fast right now, and I try to remember that instead of running up ahead of her or dragging her along. We keep going until we get to center court, and there, on the right, we glide into one of the jewelry stores; well, I glide. She sort of lumbers. I walk up to the counter and say, "Sir, we'd like to look at wedding and engagement rings."

He turns and grins. "Sure, Dave."

Olivia stares at him. "You two know each other?"

"Oh, yeah! I'm a member of the club." Bruce is dragging trays of rings out, and then Olivia's mouth makes an *O* and she smiles.

"I remember you! The day of the shooting. You were there."

"Yes, ma'am, I was, and I'm so happy to see you looking so happy and content. Is he treating you right?

Because if he's not, I'll come over and drag him around the yard by the heels until he mends his ways."

"No, he's being super great! I couldn't ask for better." Olivia looks down and gasps. "That's it right there."

"Sure? We've got a lot more."

"No. I'm positive. When I've always thought of engagement rings, this is what I've always pictured."

I have to admit, I'm a little surprised. The diamonds aren't very big, and it's not a flashy ring, but it has a nice white and yellow gold swirl to it, and it's very tasteful. When she tries it on, it looks perfect on her hand. I make a mental note to give her a gift certificate to a nail salon so she can have her nails done any time she wants. The ring has to be sized, and while Bruce writes up the repair ticket, we pick out a couple of bands. He writes up the repair tickets for those too, I pay for all three rings, and we head back out of the mall. On the way out, I see her eyeing those huge pretzels, so I get us one apiece and a drink, and we sit out in the mall food court and eat them. Neither of us says a thing, and then I look up at her. "Baby, I didn't even think to ask you. You do want to marry me, right?"

She giggles. "Well, of course not! I schlepped across five states just to turn you down, right?"

I chuckle back, "Okay then! I'll cancel the purchase."

"Not a chance, buster! I'm getting that ring." She takes the last bite of her pretzel, then says around it, "Dave, you do realize we can be as happy as we want to be, right?"

"Yes, darlin', I know that."

"And I want to be happy with you."

"I *am* happy with you."

"Good." Then she asks, "Um, do you think I could do a little something with the house? Make it a little less man cave-ish?"

"You do anything you want to, baby. It's all yours."

"Well, it's not *all* mine."

"No, but it's half yours."

"No, it's . . ."

"Half yours. And I don't want to discuss it anymore. What's mine is yours. And I think we should have everyone over to have a talk."

"About?"

"Let's just wait until then. It's something important. Trust me?"

"Yes."

"Good. Want to go home now?"

"Gotta get my maternity vitamins first. Can we?"

"Absolutely."

Maternity vitamins. Stretchy pants. Long naps and weird food and time spent in the mornings rubbing her belly. I never thought I'd be doing this, and I never dreamed I'd be this happy about it.

"Girls, that was delicious." Clint leans back and groans, hands on his mid-section. He's put on about fifteen pounds since he and Trish married, but he needed it. He was too thin before. Now he's not the least bit heavy, plus he looks healthy and happy.

"Thank you!" Sheila grins and leans down to kiss Steffen on her way to the refrigerator. It's quiet; Marta volunteered to watch all five kids, so they're having a blast, I'm sure. When we all finally get together in the living room, I look around at everyone.

"So, I have something I need to talk to all of you about." No one says a word. "First, you know we're getting married, right?"

The room is one huge smile as everyone nods. "Good. Now I have something to say. It's a little sad, but I have to. It's about me and what's going to happen when I'm gone."

"And exactly where do you think *you're* going?" Trish giggles out.

I just grin at her, then sober. "You know exactly what I mean. By the time this baby is eighteen, I'll be eighty-three. My chances of being around that long aren't that great. And I want to know right now that when that happens, you guys will be here for them, my girls." There's a sound beside me, and I turn to find Olivia crying. "Baby, this has to be done. I know you don't want to think about it, but it's important."

"I know, but you're right. I don't want to think about it."

"We have to talk about it." I look around the room. "What would all of you suggest?"

"Well," Steffen begins, "I'd suggest that you name guardians, and then alternate guardians if something happens to both of them." I nod and squeeze Olivia's hand. "And as for you, I'd just make sure your life insurance is paid up. And make sure her name is on *everything*. Once you become terminally ill is too late to do that."

"Right. As soon as we're married, that will all take place."

"And when do you think that will be?" Clint asks.

"We haven't talked about a particular date, but we picked out our rings Tuesday afternoon, so they're being sized and they'll be back soon. After that, it's all up to her." I smile at her and she smiles back. "But if it's agreeable to you, baby, I'd like to get married at the cabin."

A big, fat, silvery tear rolls down her cheek. "I'd love that."

We laugh and talk for a couple of hours, and then Trish says, "Oh, god, look at the time! We've got to go get the kids and get home. Dave, Olivia, love you both." She kisses us both and while she goes to get her bag out of the bedroom, Clint says his goodbyes.

"We've gotta get going too." Steffen stands and extends his hand, but I just stand and wrap my arms around him, and he gives me a good, hard bear hug. "Dave, man, congratulations."

I'm choking up when I croak out, "Thanks. Thanks for being here for me, for us."

"Nowhere else we'd all be. Babe, got the pie?"

"Yup. Night, sweetie." Sheila kisses my cheek and then Olivia's. "See you two soon."

Everyone is seen out the door, and I sit back down, throw my arm around her, and pull her close. "I'm sorry, baby. I know you didn't want to have that conversation, but we had to."

She picks at her skirt and doesn't look up. "I know. But it upsets me so much. I don't want to think like that." When she's quiet again, I put a finger under her chin, turn her face to mine, and kiss her.

It's like time just stops. I love her and I want her so much that I ache. We've fooled around for the last few nights, just a lot of kissing and touching, but I want so much more. I think she feels me tremble, and she says, "Dave? I'll help you. I know you've never done it before, but I'll help you. I want you. Can we go to bed now?"

"Yes, ma'am. We most certainly can." I kiss her again, but this one is different. All of the longing and passion and lust that we feel for each other is there in that kiss, and I can't wait to get down the hallway with her. "I'm going to brush my teeth and get ready for bed. You?"

She tries to stand but just plops right back down. "Right behind you."

"No, you're not. I'm always behind you. I'll always have your back, baby, always."

"You'd better. Pretty soon there'll be two girls in this house. And don't think for a minute that we won't gang up on you, Mr. Adams!" We're both laughing when I help pull her up off the sofa, and we walk down the hall with an arm around each other's waist.

When she finally comes out of the bathroom, I stop and stare. She's got on the cutest little sheer babydoll pajama set I've ever seen. "Where in the world did you get that?"

"Trish took me to the adult store the other day. Like it?"

"Like it? What's not to like?"

"Well, it's supposed to have this slit down the front, but my belly just sticks right through it."

"No, no, I think it's supposed to look that way. I think it's maternity lingerie," I smirk.

"Oh, yeah, sexy maternity lingerie. Because whales want to look good too." She starts to laugh.

"Get over here, big girl. I want something I haven't had in a while."

"And what would that be?"

I pull her as tightly to me as I can and whisper, "Every delight your body can afford." My hands wander all over her, and when I get to her nipples, I pinch hard and she shrieks. "Sensitive?"

"Yes. Very." I bring my fingers to my mouth and suck off the moisture there from her breast's leakage. I think about the fact that those breasts will be engorged soon with milk for our child, and my cock hardens to stone. "God, baby, you're perfect, just perfect."

"I just hope I'm perfect for you." She smiles into my mouth as she kisses me, and I want her so much I can barely breathe. "Take me, Dave. I just want you inside me. I want to know we're back together for good."

"You don't want to come first?"

"No, god no. I'm so horny I can't think."

"Well, okay then!" As we lie there on our sides, I slide into her and listen to her moan. "Oh, shit, baby, that's so good. And you're so damn tight."

"That's her taking up too much room."

I can feel the baby moving around, kicking and squirming. "I think she doesn't like this very much!"

"Probably not." When I slip out and thrust back into her, she moans, "Can you please fuck me harder? I won't break."

"No, but I will if I hurt you. This is one time that I'm going to insist on doing things my way, okay? I'm just looking out for your safety."

"Okay, okay. Hey, make me come and watch." She points to her crotch. "Stroke it and watch."

I grin. "Stroke what?"

"My clit. And watch my belly."

I'm wondering what's supposed to happen, and I work the little nub over. When she lets out a huge groan and comes, I'm shocked.

Her abdominal muscles all contract and there, under her skin, I can see the perfectly-formed baby, the ridge that's got to be one arm and one leg, and something that I think must be a head. It's amazing, not to mention that it seems very, very angry. *I've got to quit thinking "it" and start thinking "her,"* my mind barks. I finally let her stop, then pump into her gently but fast, and she's panting and groaning. After not nearly long enough, we both come, and I'm as exhausted and happy as she is.

I smile down at her. "Did you ever think we'd be here again, doing this?"

"I don't know if I thought we would, but I hoped."

"I hope you're happy," I whisper to her as I kiss her again.

"I'm happier than I've ever been." She kisses me back and then says, "I've got to have some sleep. I'm exhausted."

"Go to sleep." I lie there and listen to her breathe, and then I think of something. "Hey! What are we going to name her?"

"Actually, I had a name picked out when I thought I was going to have a baby without you."

"Yeah?"

She grins and her cheeks turn pink. "Nadine Michele."

I'm guessing she thinks I'll argue with her, but all I say is, "Oh, that's beautiful!"

"You really like it?"

"Yes! Why wouldn't I?"

"I don't know. I guess I thought you wouldn't like it because you hadn't helped pick it out."

"Not a problem. But there is something I want to say." Her eyes question. "I'll give you as many children as you want, but I really think that, at my age, one is enough."

"I agree." Now that surprises me. I thought I'd get a big argument, but she just says, "You have Clint. And there's Kathy who, by the way, I've never gotten to meet. When might that happen?"

"Wedding."

"Ah. Good. Night, baby," she whispers with a peck on my cheek.

Yes. It's a good night. It's the best night I've had in a long time, and there's been no alcohol involved. I must be on a roll.

Chapter Eleven

"You ready?"

"As ready as I'll ever be." I'm looking in the tiny little mirror and straightening. It's not like I'm dressed up or anything – white shirt with the collar open and my leathers. I didn't want to wear them, but I was wearing them the first time she ever saw me, and that's what she wants, so that's what she's getting.

The camping trailer Tim loaned us is kind of cramped, but it's okay. It's out in the field where we park the cars because we can walk. Olivia and the girls are already at the cabin.

I'm ready – at least I think I'm ready. But when I turn that curve in the path and see her standing there, I almost come unglued, not because of how she looks, and she looks amazing, by the way, but because of how close I came to not being here today. She could've been shot. I could've never seen her again. I could've killed myself. So many things that could've happened, but here we are, and when she turns and sees me, the smile across her face, the twinkle in those hazel eyes, they're all I need to know that this is the right thing for us.

I reach her side, then take her hand, and she smiles up at me, so much love and trust in those eyes. If I ever let her down again, I won't be able to forgive myself. Sure, I'll probably forget to stop at the store, or I'll remember a special day at five that evening, but I'll be there for all the important things, the things that matter.

And I'll be there for first steps and learning to ride a bike and losing that first baby tooth. I missed all of that with Clint. I was never married to Kathy's mother, so I missed a lot of that with her too. Hell, I was just a kid when she was born. This will be new territory for me, and I can barely wait. I remember a lot of things from when Hailee and McKenna were little, but I was Grandpa; this is mine, all mine. Well, mine and Olivia's. I'll share with her, I suppose.

"Everyone ready?" Austin calls out. He's officiating. I had no idea he has one of those mail-order ordinations, and he can perform marriages, so when he volunteered, I took him up on it. He's a good guy and I'm glad to have him here. I wanted to invite everyone, but it just wasn't possible, so it's just family. Well, and Steffen and Sheila, of course. He might as well be my son; I certainly treat him like one. Everyone nods at Austin, and he gets started.

Just looking at the woman standing beside me is something that's more awe-inspiring every day. Thinking about everything she's been through and how she's come out the other side makes me want to be a better man, a better person, a better father. Yes, a better husband. I never thought this would happen to me again, and if I'd been told it would, I most certainly would've laughed, especially if I'd been told I'd marry her. I've been going to therapy and I realize that, while what Marta did was wrong, I had a role in that too. I wasn't attentive, I wasn't present, and I wasn't as loving as I should've been. I also didn't have a pussy. Everything else I could've done something about – that, not so much – but everything else, yes. But the things Olivia's gone through need to be honored and revered. She's made it. She's here.

She's going to be an excellent mom, I can tell. There's been a flurry of activity in our house, and all of my stark leather furniture is gone, replaced by brown upholstery, brightly-striped pillows, matching curtains and area rugs, and lots of clean wood instead of metal and glass. The kitchen décor's been redone too, and it's bright and cheerful instead of the gray and red I had in there before. So far she's done nothing with our bedroom, but I figure that's next. I like it the way it is, but if she wants to change it, hell, she can do whatever she wants. But maybe she'll get busy with the baby and forget about it. Fingers crossed.

Listening to Austin, I think about the hardships and joys of a marriage as he speaks, and then it's time for our vows. She promises me that she'll always consult me and always respect me, and she'll always be there for me. I promise her that I'll never, ever hold her down or hold her back, that I'll always cherish her, I'll always protect her and care for her, and that she'll never be alone again. Guess I've kinda sealed that with a child, but I really mean this family I've managed to put together, these unlikely individuals I love who love me back.

On her finger is something blue, the ring I gave Kathy for her sixteenth birthday, a big sapphire that she wanted Olivia to have. The borrowed is Steffen's mother's locket with her and his father's photos inside it; he thought that would be good luck, because their marriage had been long and happy before they both passed. The old thing is my great-grandmother's embroidered handkerchief, which she's stuffed down inside her bra. The new thing is the diamond earrings she's wearing, beautiful hoops I bought as a wedding gift for her. She's got everything she needs.

And then I realize that she really does. She's got a home, a family, a man who loves her, and a baby on the way. She's got food and clothes and a warm place to sleep. Somewhere to take a shower. Every electronic gadget known to man – yep, I fixed her up with a laptop, a tablet, her smartphone, a Bluetooth device so she can talk while she drives, and even a heart rate monitor. Hey, I want to know if anything's about to happen to her. No, she doesn't wear it very often, although I have begged her to as long as she's pregnant. Oh, and she's getting a car as soon as the baby's born and we can get her driver's license reinstated. Something with at least four doors so it's easy to get a car seat in and out. She told me to get a new one and give her mine to drive, but I want her to have the newest one in the family. I want her to be safe.

Family. I have a family. Yeah, I had one before, but now I have one to come home to. And I want to come home to her every day for the rest of my life.

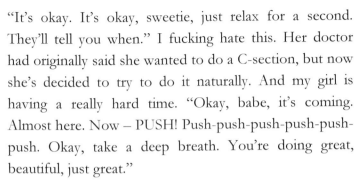

"It's okay. It's okay, sweetie, just relax for a second. They'll tell you when." I fucking hate this. Her doctor had originally said she wanted to do a C-section, but now she's decided to try to do it naturally. And my girl is having a really hard time. "Okay, babe, it's coming. Almost here. Now – PUSH! Push-push-push-push-push-push. Okay, take a deep breath. You're doing great, beautiful, just great."

"You ever touch me again, David Nathaniel Adams, and so help me god, I'll rip your balls off."

"Okie-dokie. I'll remember that. Here – have some ice chips."

"ICE CHIPS? What the hell? I want this to be OVER! Oh my god, how in the world did I manage to get myself into this?" she's muttering as I wipe sweat from her face and the back of her neck.

"Well, there was this day when we drove out to the cabin and . . ."

"I KNOW THAT! Oh my god, get out of here!" she yells at me.

"No way. I'm staying right here. You can't run me off," I just grin at her.

"Great, great." She smiles at me. "I know. I'm sorry. I don't want you to leave. I'm just, oh, god, here it comes again . . ." she trails off. "OHHHHHH! MY GOD!" she starts to scream.

"Just squeeze my hand, baby."

"Mr. Adams, come here! Look!"

And there it is – the crown of her head. She's coming. This is real. It's really happening. And that's what escapes my mouth: "This is really happening."

That's followed by a really, really loud, "OH, MOTHERFUCKER! SHIT, SHIT, SHIT!"

"Breathe, baby, please, just breathe." I can't look up her kootch anymore. I've got to help her get this baby out into the world.

Ten minutes later, it's over. I kiss my beautiful wife, tell her how much I love her, and hear my baby girl scream from across the room as they wipe her down and do whatever it is they do. Then she's with us, wrapped in a pink and blue striped blanket, just her head sticking out, and they lay her on Olivia's chest. Even with the sweat still rolling down her face, I can see her tears as she touches this tiny child's cheek for the first time and looks up at me.

She doesn't have to look; she already knows I'm crying too.

<hr>

"Your turn." I try to roll over and go back to sleep.

"Every turn is my turn." Olivia gets up out of the bed and in a minute or two, she's back with Nadine in her arms. I feel her lie back down on the bed and roll to watch as she opens the slit on her gown, draws out a huge, swollen breast, and stuffs her nipple into that tiny mouth. It takes Nadine all of ten nanoseconds to figure out what's going on, and she's sucking away.

"Wish that were me," I moan.

"One more week, baby," she whispers and blows me a kiss.

"One more week. Might as well be a year." I roll to my back and sigh.

I doze a little, and then wake again, but it's to something else. When I get my wits about me, Olivia's kneeling between my legs, my pajama pants and boxer briefs in her hand, and her gown is gone. Those two enormous, full breasts are right there for me to ogle, and my hands go to them automatically. But when I squeeze them, I get a shot right in the eye.

She lets out a peal of laughter. "Yeah. You should know better by now."

"I wish I could get that sucking thing down. You'd think as many nipples as I've sucked, I'd know how it's done."

"It's all in the back of the tongue and the soft palette. But that doesn't matter. Just lie back and enjoy the ride." Before I make another sound, she bends down over me and takes my cock in her hot, tight little lips.

Holy shit. Yeah. That's good, super good. As she works, I feel drips of warmth running down the insides of my thighs and realize her breasts are leaking. My god, it's like some kind of fantasy come to life, some kind of perverse, weird, fucked-up fantasy, and I love it. Then I realize: I'm not the only guy in the whole world who's had a nursing wife. And I've seen lactation porn, but I never paid much attention to it. Guess I should've watched more of it and maybe I would've picked up some tips. In a minute or two, that little fantasy is replaced with the growing need to empty my balls into her throat. Oh, holy damn. And I do.

More than satisfied, I hug her tight when she slides back up beside me with a sneer. "One more week, Mr. Adams. Think you can handle that?"

"If you plan to do that over and over, yeah, no problem."

"Over and over, huh? What are we talking about here?" she laughs.

"I'm thinking, oh, three times a day?"

That's when she raises up on one elbow, grabs a tit, and shoots a stream into my eye. And that's what I get for being a smart ass.

But she still didn't answer my question. I'm wiping breast milk out of my eye when she asks, "Dave? Do you still want the lifestyle? Do you miss that? Is that going to cause us problems down the road?" Her smirk has turned to fear, and I know what she's thinking. I'm going to put that fear to rest right now.

"Cuddle up here." When she's all snuggled into my arms, I kiss the top of her head. "Angel, everything I want in this whole world I have right here in this house. There's not one thing I've wanted that you haven't supplied, and if it's that important to me, I'm sure we can work out something that's not too disagreeable to you and takes care of me." I feel her shudder. "And I won't ever, ever do anything to you that you don't want, do you understand? It'll never happen. So if you're afraid of that, don't worry about it."

"I just know that before, in the club, you . . ."

"Stop, Olivia. That part of my life is done with."

"But you still work there."

"I know that. And I guess I always will. I'll enjoy watching the members scene, and I'll be there to offer my expertise." She shudders again until I finish with, "Hands-off expertise. No hands-on. I belong to you. End of discussion. Ask Melina."

"Melina?"

"Porn queen."

Her head snaps up and she stares at me. "The one I met?"

"Yeah. Ask her. Even while you were gone, I turned her down over and over. I don't want anyone but you, babe. Nobody but you."

"Nobody but me?" As her head drops back onto my shoulder, she sighs and her fingers play across my chest.

"Nobody but you, forever and ever."

"Well, then, Mr. Adams," she whispers, "three a day just may be in your future. Of course, that's depending on how much sleep I get."

Okay. Next time it's my turn.

"Can I hold the baby?" Hailee asks. "I'll be careful, I promise."

"Sure! Sit down here on the sofa so you don't have to worry about dropping her." When she gets all snuggled into the corner of the sofa, Olivia places Nadine gently in Hailee's arms. "Just rest your arms on your lap and you'll be fine."

"But she's asleep. I wanted to play with her."

"Don't worry," I scowl. "She'll be awake soon." I hear Trish laugh from the kitchen where she's helping with the food.

"Wait." Hailee looks up at me. "You're my grandpa."

"Last time I checked," I chuckle.

"She's your baby. That makes her my aunt?"

My eyebrows go up as I grin. "Yeah, I think that's right."

"But aunts are supposed to be older than me."

"Not necessarily."

"Leave it to you to mess it up, Grandpa," Clint laughs as he comes in and takes a seat by Hailee. "She's so little, bug! You used to be that little. You were my first little baby, and I was so excited."

"What about me?" McKenna whines. "I was your little baby too. I was your last little baby."

"Yes you were. And Morris was my invisible little baby." Now Clint's fighting laughter, and I'm losing the battle.

"That doesn't even make sense, Dad," Morris frowns.

"If I'd known about you, you would've been my little baby too."

"Right. Okay. Can I have another cookie?"

Together, Clint and I both snap out, "NO!"

"Fine, fine. I'll just sit here hungry." He pouts from the chair across the room like he's famished and cookies are the only food available.

"Guys, ready to eat?" Trish calls out from the kitchen.

"Finally." Morris stands and heads that way. "I'm starving to death and no one will give me food."

"You're not starving," Sheila reminds him. "Hunger and starvation are not the same thing."

"And I should know," Olivia tells him. "I remember what starvation feels like."

McKenna looks at Olivia out the corner of her eyes. "Is it true that Grandpa found you in the dumpster?"

I almost laugh and Olivia turns to her and smiles. "Yes. He was quite the dumpster-diver." Then she winks at me.

"You were looking for girls in the garbage? What?" Now McKenna's completely confused, and we all start chuckling.

"No, pumpkin. When I met your grandma here," I say and enjoy the shocked look everyone in the room shoots my way, "she was just outside the back door of the place where I work. Some people had taken away everything she had, and she had nowhere to go and nothing to eat. And I had more than enough, so I decided to share."

Out of the blue, Morris offers, "And then you had sex and decided to get married."

"Morris!" Clint blurts out.

"No, no, the boy's naturally curious. That's good, I suppose." I don't know which is funnier, me calling Olivia grandma, Clint's discomfort, or Morris's question. It's really a toss-up. "It wasn't exactly that way, but we did fall in love."

"And then you didn't."

"Well, not exactly on that either. It's more complicated than that. But those days are over. We're together forever now so you don't have to worry about that."

"Wait." I can see Hailee's gears turning. "Aren't grandmas supposed to be older than dads?"

Oh lord. I just smirk at Olivia as she wheels to face me, eager to hear my answer, and I say, "Okay, baby, why don't *you* take this question?" Yeah, that look in her eyes is not a "thank you," I can tell you that.

I hear Nadine gurgle and look down to see her spit up something on the front of her little onesie. Nice, really nice. Right here at the table. I grab a burp cloth and wipe her face up, then watch as she tries to grin. She's almost got that down. The arm-waving thing, well, she's a pro at that. And pretty soon she'll be sitting up, then crawling, and then walking.

Oh god help me. I wonder if they still make Geritol?

Chapter Twelve

"No. You cannot have another piece of cake." Trish and Morris are in a standoff. He wants it, and she says he can't have it. "Clint, back me up here, please?"

"Morris, two pieces of cake are enough. No more."

"But Dad . . ."

"There's plenty of broccoli left. Have some." Oh, my son is wicked.

"Ick! No!" I'm trying hard not to laugh as Morris stomps off.

Clint just shakes his head. "That kid would weigh a ton if we didn't watch him. Talk about a sweet tooth."

"Must've come from Adele's side, because you were never like that," I offer. About that time, I hear a squall. "I'll get her!" I call out as I head toward the nursery.

Nadine's in full-blown hurricane mode when I get there. Yep – poopy diaper. That's gotta go. I get her all cleaned up and she's still snuffling and snarling, so I head out toward the den with her, but Olivia intercepts me and takes her right out of my arms. "Time for some real food, little doll," she coos to the baby, and Nadine grins and blows bubbles. I know there's about to be carrots and peas all over the place, and I'm really glad I'm getting to bypass that celebration this time.

"Hey, step out here with me, guys." When Clint, Steffen, and I are standing on the concrete pad right outside the sliding door from the den, I sweep my arm out. "Well, what do you think it's going to take to get this yard ready for a toddler."

"That broken-down wheelbarrow's got to go," Steffen points out.

"Well, yeah, I know, but I was . . ."

"What the hell is that?" Clint asks and points at my feeble attempt at a trellis.

"It was supposed to be . . ."

"Would you consider hiring a professional?" Steffen asks pointedly. "Because I know someone who would do this for not a lot of money."

"I was kind of hoping you guys would help me." I wait. Crickets. "Well?" Still nothing. "I take that as a no?"

Clint starts to laugh, and then Steffen joins in and slaps me on the back. "Yeah, we'll help you. Steffen's the real authority here though."

"Yeah, I've seen your back yard. Very impressive," I tell the tall, blond mastermind of the familyscaping scene.

"Thanks. I worked hard on that – well, in fairness, *we* worked hard on that. Sheila and the kids were out there working too. We're all very proud of it."

"Olivia will help, I'm sure," I throw in.

"Trish and Sheila and the kids will too," Clint assures me. "We'll all help. You'll need it. You're, how old are you now? Eighty?"

"Smart ass. Sixty-six is hardly eighty."

"Close enough," Steffen snickers. "I need a beer. Anybody else?"

We both follow him in and I almost start to laugh when I look up and see Marta and Angela fighting over Nadine and playing with her. That's a sight I never thought I'd see. Before I can get into the kitchen, I hear Olivia yell out, "Okay, everybody, gift time!" God bless her, she shows up at my side with an open beer and steers me into the living room with a hand on my lower back.

I open all the gifts. "Thanks, bitch," I growl at Angela and she laughs.

"I found it at the store and thought it was fitting." Everyone else is shrieking with laughter at her joke.

It's my bottle of Geritol. Apparently they *do* still make it. Who knew?

But when everything else is opened, there's one left. It's big and flat and I think I may know what it is. I open it and everyone gasps.

There, on a piece of high-quality drawing paper, in colored pencil no less, is a drawing that almost breathes in its realism. I recognize the picture instantly. We were at the park down the street, and a lady with a little boy snapped the shot on – what else? – Olivia's phone. It's me, Olivia, and Nadine. Nadine's little face is all scrunched up in the sunlight, and we're both squinting a little, partly from the sunlight and partly because we're grinning so big. We look happy.

We look like a family. That's what I'm thinking; what I manage to say is, "That's just amazing. It's incredible, angel."

"*We're* incredible. Against all odds, we're here."

In that tiny little moment, with everyone I love around me except for Kathy and her husband, I feel like the luckiest man in the world. I look at my beautiful wife and find her glowing. But when I sweep her into my arms and whisper, "I'm so glad *you're* here," into her ear, she whispers back the one thing that makes my heart sing.

"I'm so glad I'm home." Before I can say anything she whispers again, "And I want you to know that I trust you completely."

That's a weird statement. "Gee, I hope so. You married me!"

"No, David Nathaniel Adams – I trust you completely." There's a look in her eyes that I'm not really sure about. I'll have to ask what she means when everyone's gone.

Three hours later, the goodbyes are said and the house is finally quiet. Nadine is down for at least a little while. I've locked up everything and headed down the hall, and I find Olivia sitting on the bed with a very, very elaborately-wrapped gift. "Well, what's this?"

I know that smile, the one she shares with me as she gazes up at me, and it makes everything in my body start to burn. "Oh, gee, I don't know. Just a little something for you from me. Open it."

Wrapping paper be damned, I just tear into the package. Opening the top of the box, I find another package, and when it's ripped open, it's something beautiful and sexy: A lacy bra, thong, and garter belt, including some fishnet stockings. I'm laughing as I tell her, "I don't know, honey. I think these things might be a little too small for me."

"Well, maybe the other package will suit you better. And by the way, I trust you completely." There's that weird statement again, but I notice that she's watching intently as I open the second package inside the box. And I nearly have a coronary.

Fur-lined leather cuffs. My eyes dart up and I manage to sputter out, "Are these for what I *think* these are for?"

She just takes the lingerie from beside me on the bed and heads slowly for the bathroom. I watch her beautiful ass meander across the room and, when she's finally in the bathroom doorway, she turns and smiles. "I'll only be a minute. While I'm gone, maybe you can figure out some uses for the rest of your gift."

Yeah. Maybe so. There are dozens of things I can think of to do with them, but only one woman I want to do them with. If you'd told me a year ago that the dungeon master would be a one-woman man in the near future, I would've laughed you right out of your leathers. And I'm not sad about it. A beautiful wife. A beautiful baby. A real home.

And a disaster of a back yard. I've seen an awful lot of miracles in the last year. If I can muster up one more miracle, maybe there'll be hope for that little jungle. There'd better be because if we lose that baby out there in the weeds, my wife will kill me.

⚬⚬⚬

This is the end of the Me, You, and Us series. If you've enjoyed the journey with Trish, Clint, Steffen, Sheila, Dave, and Olivia, as well as their extended family and friends, please consider leaving a review. I'm sure they'd all appreciate it, and I *know* I would!

About the author

Deanndra Hall is a working author living in far western Kentucky with her partner of over 30 years and their three crazy little dogs. She enjoys hiking, kayaking, working out at the gym, and cooking healthy food. Oh, and chocolate – lots of chocolate. Some of her favorite things are Victoria's Secret, frankincense and myrrh perfume, happy hour shakes at Sonic, not-very-healthy Italian food, and driving her Mustang convertible, Ruby. Water is pretty much her drink of choice, but an Angry Orchard, Fat Tire, or cosmo is always welcome. Look her up and make friends with her – there's nothing she loves more than to laugh and have fun. And it won't be a problem; she's easy to find.

Email:
DeanndraHall@gmail.com

Website/blog:
www.deanndrahall.com

Facebook:
www.facebook.com/deanndra.hall

Twitter:
@DeanndraHall

Pinterest:
pinterest.com/deanndrahall

tsü:
tsu.co/DeanndraHall

Mailing address:
P.O. Box 3722, Paducah, KY 42002-3722

Connect with Deanndra on Substance B

Substance B is a new platform for independent authors to directly connect with their readers. Please visit Deanndra's Substance B page (substance-b.com/DeanndraHall.html) where you can:

- Sign up for Deanndra's newsletter
- Send a message to Deanndra
- See all platforms where Deanndra's books are sold
- Request autographed eBooks from Deanndra

Visit substance-b.com today to learn more about your favorite independent authors.

39834435R00158

Made in the USA
Middletown, DE
26 January 2017